T0162052

Also By Diane Lefer

Radiant Hunger
Very Much Like Desire
The Circles I Move In

California Transit

Diane Lefer

Winner of the 2005
Mary McCarthy Prize in Short Fiction
Selected by Carole Maso

Sarabande Books LOUISVILLE, KENTUCKY

FIRST EDITION

Managing Editor
Sarabande Books, Inc.
2234 Dundee Road, Suite 200
Louisville, KY 40205

LIBRARY OF CONGRESS CATALOGING-IN-PUBLICATION DATA

Lefer, Diane.
California transit : stories / by Diane Lefer. — 1st ed.
p. cm.
Winner of the 2005 Mary McCarthy Prize in Short Fiction, selected by Carole Maso.
ISBN-13: 978-1-932511-47-5 (pbk. : acid-free paper)
ISBN-10: 1-932511-47-4 (pbk. : acid-free paper)
I. Title.
PS3562.E37385C35 2007
813'.54—dc22 2006015982

Cover photo by Judith McKernan
Cover and text design by Charles Casey Martin

Manufactured in Canada
This book is printed on acid-free paper.

Sarabande Books is a nonprofit literary organization.

The Kentucky Arts Council, a state agency in the Commerce Cabinet, provides operational support funding for Sarabande Books with state tax dollars and federal funding from the National Endowment for the Arts, which believes that a great nation deserves great art.

For Lisa Alvarez, Andrew Tonkovich, and Louis
— with gratitude and love

Table of Contents

Acknowledgments

The author is glad to have this chance to acknowledge the *Santa Monica Review* for years of encouragement and support and for publishing so many of my stories including "Angle and Grip," "At the Site Where Vision Is Most Perfect," "Naked Chinese People," and "The Prosperity of Cities and Desert Places."

David L. Ulin included "Naked Chinese People" in *Another City: Writing from Los Angeles,* the anthology he edited for City Lights. Thanks!

My appreciation to *Faultline* for publishing "Alas, Falada," to *Saranac Review* for "How Much an Ant Can Carry," and *Witness* for including "The Atlas Mountains" in the special issue *Exile in America.*

The living creatures—human and otherwise—at the Los Angeles Zoo and Botanical Gardens and at the Marine Mammal Care Center in San Pedro are in no way responsible for my fictional portrayals. But a special nod to Anne LaRose and Ruthie Yakushiji.

A big thank you to Carole Maso. (Reader: this book wouldn't be in your hands if she hadn't picked it.) And to Sarah Gorham, Kristina McGrath, Nickole Brown, Kirby Gann, Jen Woods, and Jeannette Pascoe at Sarabande. Without them, nothing.

Foreword

From the world that could not be saved, the storyteller salvages small, strange stuff and assembles it into a narrative of alarming beauty and mystery and sadness. And in the longing these particular moments strung together in this particular way have created in us, we follow her anywhere.

"We were always finding naked Chinese people in the shower," the storyteller begins.

> We called them Chinese, though one was Korean and one was half-Korean with a father who was an American GI. She was the first. She'd wandered away from a rave in the desert and came upon our cabin where she walked right in and stood under the shower until the water ran out. We found her slumped in the stall, incoherent and already almost dry. The other Korean had been invited to a friend's, took a wrong turn, ended up at our place, and unwittingly made himself at home.

So begins this engrossing dream-journey filled with wish and dread, at once desperate, hilarious, bewildering, hope-filled. We're ready to go. Have been ready for quite some time.

> We didn't really mind leaving town. Our city had changed. Those of us who lived in a house found ourselves living two families to a house, and then three, and then four. And then they said we couldn't because of zoning. The people who clean the houses and tend the gardens live ten or a dozen in an unventilated garage, but since they don't have papers, zoning doesn't count.

In transit, the narrative ground subtly shifting under us, our storyteller transports the head of a dead eland whom she calls Falada in a plastic bag from its eland autopsy. Recalling another Falada, the one from the Brothers Grimm, she tells us:

> In the story, Falada, the horse, spoke intelligible German even before he (or she) was killed, but it must have been the lingering effect of that story that made me feel, now as an adult, when I no longer expect to share a spoken language with the zebras and the seals, that Falada's head in the passenger seat, mute in life, had something to say and I would surely hear it if I could only divine the right way to listen.
>
> Surely there was a message. I pulled over and put her head in the trunk.

Surely the animals, our storyteller's charmed totem, might reveal the message, or the right way to go, no? Perhaps the consolation of cats?

> And when I took Dinah in my arms, I could feel our hearts beating at different rates and that had to be why she didn't like to be held close. It troubled me

> too, the different rhythms, her pulse versus mine, proof I could not be her mother.

It haunts our storyteller, what it means to have a human life. What it means to be alive.

> There were parked cars that talked when you got too close, like savage tropical flowers responding to touch. There was a bedspring mounted in a chain-link fence and used as a gate. There were thunderstorms but no lightning. I sat high up in the swivel chair, drank screwdrivers, and read the newspaper to him aloud.
>
> The Elephant Alliance needs land for the growing numbers of abused and unwanted elephants in California.
>
> Classified ads for boa constrictors and pit bulls, kittens that were "spaded and natured." Cemetery plots—a companion crypt, lot 149, $1500 obo.
>
> "Who's your government bombing this week?" he asked.
>
> "No more mine than yours," I said.
>
> "Is anything left of Afghanistan? Sudan?" he said. "Not that I care."
>
> I had stopped caring and it bothered me. It would be inaccurate to say it hurt.

Our storyteller tells us:

> I was trying to understand something, or trying to be something.
>
> I was looking for a feeling in the air, something that said change.

Foreword

The storyteller, while seemingly telling stories in a casual way, telling jokes and singing, distracting us a little, gathers an unlikely amount of power and emotion without our quite realizing it—so much force of emotion in fact that more than once we are taken aback, marveling at her sly and perfect gift.

She still believes in the magic of the sentence. And in the pleasure of thought, the rush of it, its intensity, still, now:

> "In this country, you trample on human rights to protect an imaginary past. You crush and kill and punish brown people for presuming to want freedom. Capitalism requires the spectacle of demonized millions trying to get across the border. The only way to measure value is not by quality," he said, "but by artificially induced desire."

And questions, not to forget the questions—their melancholy import:

> The sound of the incoming mail used to make my heart beat. The postman's whistle as he climbed the stairs in San Andrés, the lobby door opening, the clunk of the mail in the box in New York.
>
> What on earth was I expecting?

Meanwhile:

> Walking home from first grade, the man pulled up beside me in his car. Down came his window. In the opening he held up a bride doll.
>
> "Come with me," he said. "You can have her."

> I ran away like the wind. How dare he! I don't play with dolls. I read!

Our storyteller tells us a next to last story:

> I bend, because I recognize that in myself I'm lacking, compared even to the musk ox. If I were going to draw the Great Chain of Being, that's who'd be on top. They were around in prehistoric days and they're still here. Every other species had to adapt or die. But the musk ox—driven out of California, driven from the South of France, it was equally suited to the arctic North. Ready for anything, perfect, the musk ox didn't have to change.
>
> See what happens through a simple shift of perspective? Here's a simultaneous and contradictory truth: Our caravan grew larger. Our caravan grew smaller. Hundreds of immigrants from the Middle East joined us, afraid to stay home, seeking safety in numbers, but we also divided pretty neatly in three, some of us still anxious to find the Nazis—one group to bash them, one to join them because my enemy's enemy is my friend. Others set off in the opposite direction to trash a mosque.

And then a last one before she leaves us again to our own devices, but now we are remarkably a little different than we were before, a little more resourceful, a little less alone—how we've enjoyed the menagerie! Her parting is filled with the kinds of questions we have come to expect, to rely on. For it's turned out to be a rigorous and passionate inquiry of the highest order.

As she prepares to go she wonders:

> "Is the spontaneous response the most natural? Or does its very spontaneity prove the training is so deeply ingrained we no longer realize we have forcibly learned it? Is the imperative to strike back born into us or is it the artifact of that great early rupture from a greedy, devouring, selfish, oceanic yet essentially and profoundly peaceful self?"

We had wanted to live on this earth in peace—whatever that would mean. On every page of the storyteller's extraordinary book, we are made keenly aware of that fact and of what is day to day, always at stake—and as painful as it is, we are enormously grateful for it.

—*Carole Maso*

California Transit

Naked Chinese People

We were always finding naked Chinese people in the shower. We called them Chinese, though one was Korean and one was half-Korean with a father who was an American GI. She was the first. She'd wandered away from a rave in the desert and came upon our cabin where she walked right in and stood under the shower until the water ran out. We found her slumped in the stall, incoherent and already almost dry. The other Korean had been invited to a friend's, took a wrong turn, ended up at our place, and unwittingly made himself at home. The third, who may or may not have been Korean or Chinese, was shouting in what may or may not have been his mother tongue. He spoke no English and could not give any account of himself. The police arrived accompanied by two white men who claimed to be doctors, but something about them seemed undoctorlike, including the fact that one of them spoke to the man fluently in his own language.

Things come in threes, and so we could have gone on as we were, expecting no further intrusions, but after the third Chinese man was carried off by the so-called doctors, Richard and I decided it was time to put a lock on the door.

California Transit

It's in and around our weekend cabin in the desert, now equipped with a lock, that the events I'm about to narrate took place. The lock on the door is irrelevant, as are the naked Chinese.

We call it a cabin though it's actually a trailer which the high winds might at any time overturn. Up until the dirt turnoff, there's only one road and yet we often feel we've gone wrong. In one direction, the way is flat and without interest. In the other, it's a marvel of rock formations and distant peaks, cacti and even lush stands of leafy trees. Even after years of making the trip, I often panic part way there to ask, Where are we?

The land seems so flat, I can't explain how hidden our place turns out to be from view, how you don't see it until you come right on it. There are other trailers scattered about the land, none within sight of ours, but all so similar and surrounded by Joshua trees that vary only in the slightest, you can understand how people might confuse them. So it wasn't all that strange that Chinese strangers came to our door by mistake, or that my ex-husband, who would be alive if he had only found us, lost his way.

When I was a child, whenever I saw a Chinese person, I used my index fingers at the corners of my eyes to pull the skin aslant. Happily, I chanted *Chinky chinky Chinaman.* I loved the Chinese and did this to greet them, to say *Hello! I see you! Welcome to America!* Ah, to see through the eyes of a child! It never occurred to me these Chinese people might be in fact Americans. It never occurred to me they would interpret my greeting as anything other than a friendly gesture.

But I was telling you about the cabin.

Naked Chinese People

All of a sudden, it seemed people kept giving me things I couldn't hang on the walls. For example, a poster for a French-Canadian film, *Comment faire l'amour avec un négre sans se fatiguer.* I'm more comfortable saying the title in French, although the poster displays it prominently in English: HOW TO MAKE LOVE TO A NEGRO WITHOUT GETTING TIRED. There's a white woman and a black man reclining, but not together. She lies in the foreground reading a book, dressed in socks and underwear. He is stretched out on the bed, draped in a sheet. What appears to be the Washington Monument rises from his midsection. His face is covered.

We tacked the poster up in the cabin. It was a private joke, just to emphasize how private the cabin was supposed to be. A place to get away, a place where no one would ever be invited, especially not Richard's grown children. A place so far from others, I imagined Richard and I would have very noisy sex.

One of the police officers was black and I wondered what he thought of the poster.

Did he wonder why Richard let me hang it? Did he think we chose it together? Or was it Richard's choice? Was it some pointed reference to me?

Which part embarrassed me the most? The word *Negro*?

Sometimes I wonder how did I become a white woman married to a white man? When you have an unhappy childhood, surely the Other always looks better. White woman/white man. I imagine that's what the black cop saw. I felt defined, confined, less than who or what I am. I wanted to say: *but that's not me.*

California Transit

When Skee and I were still married, I never stopped to wonder who I was, though eventually I had to wonder who he was. A brain tumor will do that to a person.

I had never wanted to be "taken care of" by a man, a phrase I always heard as threat. But when I lay my head on Skee's chest and he held me, I felt safe and cared for in a way I'd never before known. It was not that I felt he would protect me, but that I didn't have to protect myself against him. I suppose what I'm describing is trust.

Early on, Skee warned me: "A black man isn't used to being loved. There's times I'm going to push you away. Please wait it out when it happens. Please let me go and let me come back. Remember that I wouldn't panic if I didn't love you."

So when things started to go wrong, I attributed it to blackness.

I may be a white girl, but my life hasn't been without pain. When I was twelve, I was raped by a man dressed up as a priest. We were Jewish, but I had been raised to respect priests and nuns, partly out of pity. They hadn't chosen such a life, I was told. Their parents had given them to the Church. It sounded so much like human sacrifice, like throwing young girls into volcanos, I was not surprised that what the man did to me was so painful. I arrived home dazed and bleeding and told my mother. "Did you come?" she asked. I had no idea what this meant. The priest had said "Come with me," and afterwards, I'd come straight home. Yes, I said, and she hit me.

Neither my mother nor the police seemed to think it strange that a priest would rape a child. They only knew he was a fake because he'd drawn a knife across my thigh and left a wound. "A priest wouldn't do that," said the cop and I said, "He said he wouldn't hurt me."

Naked Chinese People

* * *

In *The Turner Diaries*, women like me get hanged from lampposts.

"Let me in!" he kept saying, while I kept saying, "Where are you?"

What if I'd said, "You're not acting like yourself." What if I'd said, slyly, "Hey, shouldn't we have an annual physical?" What if I'd seen a man changing every day before my eyes, instead of seeing a black man?

What if they'd diagnosed and caught it earlier? They saved his life, but could they have saved his mind, saved *him*, the man who had been my life-partner until he was suddenly, irrevocably, gone?

After we divorced, there were nights I slept with his science journals piled around me, or clutching one of his notebooks written in his almost microscopic hand. During the good days, there had been times when we just looked at each other and burst out laughing at the sheer unlikely joyful luck of having met. Once he was gone, I spent hours at his computer, trying to guess passwords, half-believing that the answer to this misery was there to read in one of his locked files.

I didn't know where he had gone. I didn't know he'd lost his job. I didn't know he'd been arrested. And at the university where he'd taught (and then grabbed his crotch in front of students and grabbed at women's breasts) and in the courtroom where he was arraigned (after a wild scene in a 99¢ Store), no one saw a man who'd lived for years an honorable, exemplary life. No one saw that what was happening wasn't normal.

"Let me in!" Skee was just trying to find me in the cabin where I'd gone for the weekend with Richard.

* * *

The night Skee and Richard first met: Skee showed up at my apartment. Richard and I were half-undressed on my bed. It was the third time we'd had sex. We were new enough I was still keeping count. I would have ignored anyone else at the door but it was Skee and I leapt immediately from the bed, covered up and let him in. It was clear something terrible had happened. He wouldn't tell me. He kept saying *If I couldn't have come here, if I couldn't have come here, but of course I could, I knew I could.* Do you know there were mornings I walked out the door to go to work and found him sitting on the sidewalk, banging his head against concrete and then all I'd have to do was say his name or touch his shoulder and he'd stop? Do you know what it is to feel so much power over someone, the power that you alone can make him stop hurting? I made up the couch for him and went back to bed with Richard and though we had to do so quietly, we made love. His fingers were electric on my body and it wasn't that I felt I was making love to them both or that I was jubilant to be with a man who was so vigorous and healthy when Skee, much as I loved him, was so ruined and it was not the *frisson* of having sex with my new lover while my ex-husband lay only several yards away. It was that Richard had not known who Skee was or why I was so quick to care for him, he merely saw that Skee mattered to me, and he had treated him in a gracious and welcoming way and then left the room to leave us alone. And I knew then I wanted Richard because I knew he would never try to come between us. In bed, though we muffled our sounds, I looked up at him and said, "I'm falling in love with you. You know that, don't you?" and in retrospect, I think that was the closest I ever came to loving Richard.

I loved our cat. Though she was an indoor cat, Richard and I never had her declawed, thinking that someday we might move to the country and she'd enjoy the outdoors. The first time we took her to the cabin, she was afraid to go outside–inconvenient as we hadn't brought the litter box. The second time, she ventured out and something ate her.

Don't say I loved seeing Skee reduced to *this*, a black man like a pet or a helpless child.

What's true is marriage is indeed a contract in which each of two adults has responsibilities. It was only after Skee's brain was mutilated that my anger against him disappeared. I could no longer hold him responsible and so could regard him again with that original and so emotionally satisfying unconditional love. There was nothing to resent, no reciprocity to expect. It was the passionate attachment one might feel for a Down's syndrome child or for God.

When he died, I stopped feeling. I could no longer bear to have Richard touch me. There was a kind of overload which seems strange because I felt so little. What I felt was not sensation itself, but the feeling of always being pestered. Richard talked too much. It may not have been very much at all, but whenever he spoke I wished he would be still. His words meant nothing. They were pebbles thrown against my head. His hands were like dead things up against me; perhaps they disgusted me because they proved to me my own unresponsive flesh was dead.

I wanted to roll myself up in a ball and cover my head with my arms. All I wanted was to be left alone.

The cat would have understood. She was dependent on us, she formed attachments, but we knew not to touch her when she didn't want to be touched. After she was eaten, there was no one left to understand me. Sometimes I thought about being eaten by a tiger. I wanted to be eaten alive though I know the way it works is first a swipe of the paw to break your neck.

And I thought of what it had been like to lie in Skee's arms so many years ago and no matter how our senses merged, it was always possible, except in the most profound darkness, to see where he began and I left off.

"Let me in!" he said.

When people lose their way, you try to help.

We drove the naked Chinese woman to the nearest emergency room, a good half-hour away. The Korean man laughed, dressed, apologized, and drove off in his car, a Volvo. With the third man, the police and the men who called themselves doctors appeared at our door as if they'd been tracking him.

I remember the beautiful delicacy of Skee's ears. How pleased I was he never pierced them. They were perfect.

And I remember lying with Richard, him inside me, and how I jumped up at the sound of Skee's voice on the answering machine. "Here I am, Skee. It's all right. I'm here." And I felt a moment's guilt toward Richard, but he showed no sign and never said a word and so I told myself I hadn't hurt him.

It's a misconception that people die because something inside goes wrong. I think we die from the outside in. A bullet, for example, penetrating a body, or in my case, it started with my skin. If I turned on the fan, and stood in front of a mirror, I could see the breeze move my hair, but there was no tingle in my scalp. The circulation of my blood had retreated deep into the interior leaving no sensation where my body met the world.

Early in our marriage, when Richard first let me down, I remember how hurt and anger tied my stomach up in knots. Then, in time, it seemed

I no longer had a stomach. My mind could register the disappointment, but to my surprise, there was no more physical response. My husband didn't make me happy, but at least he no longer made me sick.

I was driving to the cabin alone one night when I heard a siren and saw a motorcycle cop in the rearview. I had no idea what I had done. I pulled over. He stopped yards behind me and as I watched him walk toward me, I felt something I had forgotten beating hard inside me.

How do I remember my best-loved best? When he held me close, or when he hit his head against concrete till I said no?

He wandered the streets and sometimes slept there. I gave him a cell phone and paid the bills. "So you can reach me whenever you need me."

Maybe the doctors who came for the third Chinese were real and there was a mental hospital in the area after all. I wished I knew where because I understood it might not be a bad idea for me to go there.

He took a bus, he hitchhiked, he walked, who the hell knows how he got to the desert.

The phone rang. He said, "Let me in. Please let me in."

He had been here before. We had brought him.

I opened the door. Skee wasn't there.

"Please," he said. "Please."

"Are you in L.A.?" I asked him. I said, "We're at the cabin."

"I'm at the cabin," he said. "I'm in the desert. At the cabin. At the trailer. Please," he said. "Please."

"I don't see you," I said. "The door is open."

"Why have you locked me out?" he said.

I said, "The door is open." I said, "I'm right here. Where are you, Skee?"

"Let me in!"

He was at someone else's trailer. A black man trying to get in.

"Where are you?" I said. "You're lost. Don't do anything. Where are you?"

I heard shouting, and then I heard gunfire.

They said the suspect turned with something in his hand. The cell phone that I gave him.

People deal with grief in different ways. I went to a rave just like our first naked person. Paid ten dollars for a map and drove out into the barren flats.

At the rave they dance as in a trance. In the firelight, everyone's skin glows. You can't tell color. And these days everyone wears dreadlocks. Not everyone, of course, what I mean is anyone who wants to. The locks bob and tremble and flail, like a headdress, in the firelight, and I think of the Spanish padres watching the Indians dance, how they saw not men but devils.

Everyone was uninhibited. I felt very old. I was sure they were using drugs I'd never even heard of. At my age, everything *me fatigue*. No one cared what I did. No one watched me. I squatted in the dirt and cried for my sweet darling cat who got eaten.

I wasn't stoned. But these days, I don't like driving because I find myself forgetting to look or staring without seeing or seeing without registering or looking in the wrong direction and so I drive very slowly because I can no longer remember to be careful.

Naked Chinese People

The Highway Patrol pulled me over for going too slow.

It was the black cop, and so I thought, *He's not the one,* and I wondered if he remembered the poster.

They say sometimes it starts with a peculiar smell. Sometimes with an auditory hallucination. Do you think it can start with thoughts of race? Thoughts of race as a symptom of psychopathology, the first manifestation of psychotic break.

We went back to Los Angeles and a terrible man stormed in firing in the Jewish Community Center and then he killed Mr. Joseph Ileto who was delivering mail.

Richard said, "Where do you think you're going?"

I was going out into the street. I imagined wearing a sign that said *Race Traitor*. I imagined shouting, *I'm a Jew! I loved a black man!*, shouting, *Kill me! Here's my heart! Shoot me now!*

I hardly leave the apartment. Richard goes with me when I need Advil, as if a pill made in a factory can ease the pain.

The girl behind the counter looked Filipina.

"My condolences," I said. "For your Mr. Ileto."

Just because she's Filipina, or looks it, does that make his murder important to her, does that entitle her to condolences from strangers?

"Do you think," I asked, "that when one becomes acutely aware of race, it's advisable to put oneself under a doctor's care?"

I said, "I'm not going to hurt you," which is what the rapist says to the woman or the child, so it's no wonder the Filipina girl seemed frightened.

I said, "They shot him."

By the register, they were selling guardian angels in the form of pins you pin to your lapel. I took one from its cardboard backing and, before Richard could stop me, stabbed it into my hand, just to see.

I remember slanting my eyes and calling the naked people Chinese even after we knew that they weren't and the watercolor set I got for my birthday as a child with a color called French Green. Later, when I summered in Maine, there were houses painted in just that color and the people who lived in those houses were invariably of French-Canadian descent. French Green, the Yankees said, and French was not descriptive but pejorative. And I remember when they called black people "colored." If they'd been called brown, it would have been fine, but they were "colored" which meant someone had done something to them, they had been painted. If I got close, the color would rub off. If it came off on my skin, I wouldn't mind, but if I came home with brown stains on my clothes, my mom would hit me.

After I brought Skee to meet my parents, no one mentioned race.

And I think about the scar on my thigh that Skee kissed and Richard pretended not to see. And I think that Skee is dead and that They killed him.

We stay in L.A. I don't want to go back to the cabin. We've left the door unlocked in case anyone needs to get in and every day I wonder if I had made Skee go to the doctor if they could have saved all of him. Or if he had been diagnosed before our marriage crumbled, would we have stayed together? Would I have devoted my life to caring for him? I would have been willing. It's not so easy to say whether he would have let himself be cared for.

. . .

Naked Chinese People

In the poster, the man lies draped in a sheet, his face covered. His prick stiff with—it could be rigor mortis. He could be dead.

Driving down Highland I went through a red light on purpose, hoping a cop would stop me. I wanted to see if my heart would pound.

He asked for my license.

I asked, "Were you there? I want to know what happened in the desert. I want to know what happened to my husband."

"Stay in the car," said the white cop, but I opened the door and stepped out, daring him to hit me.

"Are you the one?" I asked. "Are you the one who killed him?"

I could see he wanted to shoot me, but he didn't.

"Racist pig!" I said. "If I were a black man, you would kill me. If I were a Latino male, you'd cuff me and shoot me in the head." I had the sudden thought that I could pull up my dress and show my thigh and say, *Look! Look at this! Do you see what that white man did to me?* I could say, *Hang me from the lamppost!* Instead I said, "Reverse discrimination! What are you going to do? Ticket me? Send me to Traffic School?" I said, "Just because I'm a white woman. Kill me. Why don't you kill me? It's skin privilege, dammit. Kill me."

When Skee acted crazy, that was normal for a black man. When I acted crazy, it was decided that what I needed was Richard's care and the latest meds.

Richard takes care of me, at least for now, and at least for now I let him.

This is normal life. He goes to work. Like a woman, I stay home. Most nights, we stay in and watch TV.

On Fridays, we go out to eat.

We go to the Korean barbecue. I'm learning not to stare at the Korean people, but discreetly, very discreetly, I watch to see what they do. Use the lettuce leaves like a tortilla, wrap up meat and kim chee, and eat it like a taco.

My heart is hard. I'm going to get better.

All around us, Asian people are eating. They are fully clothed, and so are we.

Alas, Falada!

Humans get cremated. Animals just get burned. With a person, you do an autopsy to determine the cause of death. With an animal, we call it a "necropsy," and in the eland's case, the distinction did make sense as we knew damn well what she died of. We had euthanized her ourselves. But she'd been sick a long time. If there was a microorganism spreading through the herd, we needed to know it, and so Ralphie drove her body out to the lab in San Bernardino. Then they sent me to bring back her head.

They told me to take one of the zoo trucks, but I'm not comfortable driving those things so I went in my car. I assumed they would have the head packed on dry ice. They assumed I was bringing a container. They said they'd find a bag.

"Something opaque, please," I said, "and big." An eland is a *large* antelope.

A thirty-three-gallon garbage bag was the best they could do and I put it on the front seat next to me, her two-foot-long horns sticking out. Not those massive heavy spirals, at least; she was a female.

It wasn't easy getting her to the car. An eland's horns go straight back, so I couldn't carry her facing away from me. Sideways would have worked but I wasn't thinking all that clearly. As I carried her head in my arms, the plastic slipped and I saw her face. Her eyes, gone flat and dry now, looked right at me.

Once I had her on the seat, I touched her—a nose that was no longer soft, but icy, a charcoal black smudge at the bridge. They must have burned the rest of her body. No one said.

The head was frozen solid, and unless I hit traffic, was intended to stay that way the sixty-five miles to the Natural History Museum.

This is a good example of civic partnership and cooperation—cooperation being something I believe humans are genetically programmed for. Followers of Robert Ardrey (*African Genesis*, 1961)—not that we have anyone like that working here—would argue that no, our hardwiring is for aggression. A cynic might point out that we cooperate most selflessly and enthusiastically when the purpose *is* aggression and I can't say I disagree. In any event, the museum was getting the head for their domestic beetle colony.

We are now in the midst of the Sixth Great Extinction and while too many species are on the verge of disappearing altogether, it seems a new beetle is discovered almost every day. I understand if you're a major enough donor, the museum may name a new beetle species after you. I don't know how much you have to pay to put your name on a bug. I do know that it will cost you $2,000 in "trophy fees" (plus travel, accommodations, meals, guides, and gratuities) if you kill or wound an eland in South Africa in order to bring the head home. A bargain compared to a white rhino head which will run you about 30,000.

Once the beetles eat away the hair and flesh, we get the skull back for the education hall. I've never understood why we show children animal skulls so that they can no longer look on living creatures without thinking of death. All the same, and even though there's someone at the museum I really don't want to see, at first I thought our arrangement was a very good idea. The eland's end would come about much as though she'd died a natural death on the African plains where she would have been returned to the soil as bacteria worked their decay and beetles, hyenas, and scavenger birds purified her right down to bone.

Ralphie, the vet tech, set me straight: "What? You think it's like a natural habitat where these bugs swarm over her head and pick it clean?" He told me the museum's beetles live half a dozen together in file drawers.

"Her head isn't going to fit in a file drawer," I said.

"Of course not. It has to be flensed."

Flense turns out to mean the hair and skin disposed of, though Ralphie declined to say how, and the flesh sliced up and dried. Then a slice is left in each drawer. The beetles eat very slowly, inefficiently, Ralphie said, and it seems to me if someone is going to devour you, you would hope at the very least it would be with gusto, with a very great hunger.

Even before I got in my car to go to San Bernardino, when I thought about it—hundreds of file drawers with tiny little beetles working their way without interest through her dried flesh—I had decided. No way could I be a party to this.

Sometimes we do the necropsies on-site. I don't know what the determining factor is when we send them out. Much of what happens at the zoo is on a need-to-know basis and we seem to be moving toward greater and greater secrecy.

The matter of names, for example. I used to know every animal by name and not just from the ID number in the stud book. But people talk and word starts getting out and you have members of the public waving their arms and crying out "Caesar!" or "Inti!," confusing these creatures who've learned to come when the keeper calls. Actually, we're not even sure which species and which individuals recognize the human speech sounds we've assigned them, but better to err on the side of caution.

The "someone" I don't want to run into at the museum, by the way, is named Jamal. He is—or was—a juvenile chimpanzee. When he hanged himself—by accident, it is presumed, since though we do share almost 100% of our DNA, no one I know of has detected in the chimpanzee any tendency toward suicide—his body was so young and healthy and unmarred that rather than feed him to the beetles, it was decided to have him preserved and placed in an exhibit hall where he now delights schoolchildren by swinging on a vine just above their heads. They say he's very lifelike, but I knew *him,* his vitality, playfulness, and how just plain stubborn he could be. The thought of walking in and seeing Jamal stuffed? I couldn't bear it.

I don't believe he committed suicide, but I do know animals get sad. Many of us believe they—at least some of them—have consciousness, a range of emotions equal to humans, and a capacity for rational thought while to others—the Ardrey-types I too often find married to my friends—this is heresy.

My office is decorated with paw prints on textured paper, handsomely framed. (Sometimes when an animal—lion or bear—is unconscious in the O.R., we take liberties.) More to the point are the abstract paintings done by JimBob the elephant and an orangutan named Colette. The compositions are so pleasing and the colors so harmonious to the eye, you cannot convince me the artists were not taking pleasure in what they were creating, that they were not operating out of a true aesthetic sense. When

Colette's mate-to-be was here in quarantine, he liked to look through magazines. It was clear some pictures pleased him more than others and, while his taste and mine don't necessarily coincide, his show of preference surely proves he had his own criteria for passing judgment.

If an orangutan can think in aesthetic terms, a human should be able to, so you'll have to agree that the eland's still beautiful head deserved better than to be flensed. If you argue, instead, that Beauty earns its bearer no special dispensation, I—who am not myself beautiful—will argue back that *aesthetic* is the opposite of *anaesthetic*. It's the awakening of feeling, a welcome stimulus these days to heart and mind.

No story bores me more than one that begins "When I was a child..." This is true even when I'm talking to myself, which I am in fact doing right now. The preceding argument about aesthetics has been raging—albeit in quiet and civilized fashion—inside my own head. Scientists say—though I'm not convinced—only humans can do this: project a mental image of ourselves and regard it. Use our imagination to explore choices without immediately suffering the consequence.

There is a frozen head slowly but surely beginning to defrost in front of my television set, large enough to block the screen, huge enough in import to block most other thoughts. I should have used my imagination before I brought this thing home. Now I have to decide what the hell I'm going to do with it. It is not offering me a solution although I somehow absurdly thought it would. The dread words sneak up on me: *When I was a child...*

When I was a child, like most children, I suspect, I believed animals could talk. I saw no separation between them and me. I wanted a pet zebra I could ride bareback and a monkey smart enough to beat me at gin rummy and when asked what I wanted to be when I grew up, I thought the choice was open enough that I always answered "a sea otter." Other children wanted to be tigers, eagles. I had no dreams of power or imperial might.

"You wanted to be cute," Ralphie has said to me, but I was never thinking *cute*. Sea otters looked happy.

My favorite Grimm fairy tale was the Goose Girl, in which the severed head of the betrayed princess's slaughtered horse is nailed on the dark gateway to the city. Whenever she passes it while tending the geese, she cries "Alas, Falada, hanging there!" and the head answers her. As I drove back from San Bernardino, I spoke to the eland's head in the trash bag beside me and I called her "Falada."

In the story, Falada, the horse, spoke intelligible German even before he (or she) was killed, but it must have been the lingering effect of that story that made me feel, now as an adult, when I no longer expect to share a spoken language with the zebras and the seals, that Falada's head in the passenger seat, mute in life, had something to say and I would surely hear it if I could only divine the right way to listen.

Surely there was a message. I pulled over and put her head in the trunk.

I was there when Falada died. My job title is administrative assistant, but we're shorthanded—budget cuts—and sometimes I get called to the waiting room, to keep a frightened animal company until the vet is free. Sometimes I get to watch surgery through the window, and sometimes I'm even called to the O.R. to stroke an animal in distress. My favorite vet is Ginger. They're all great. They come in on their days off, forego their vacations, come in early and stay late—they have to because we only have two plus one part-time—and they do it willingly, because they love the animals. But it was Ginger who, when we had the tiger in quarantine, said, "I never wanted to have babies, but if I could give birth to a tiger cub, I'd do it in a minute."

"So would I," I said, "if you could guarantee it would only take a minute." I made it a joke even though I was profoundly moved.

Falada was so old and weak, she could hardly walk anymore or hold herself up on her feet. They'd already knocked her down with tranqs before they loaded her into the truck and brought her to us from the barn. She'd lost so much weight, her skin was loose on her shrunken frame, and Ginger, Ralphie, and I were able to get her to the O.R. by ourselves. We have a hydraulic lift to get animals onto the gurney, but when you're talking about something big—a camel, say—it still takes several men pushing to get the gurney to roll. Or women, if you had women strong enough, which none of us working here now happens to be.

Ginger set up the I.V. The three of us gathered around to say goodbye.

You have to understand that veterinary medicine, especially for zoo animals, is a very inexact science. In the old days, not so long ago, Ginger says if an animal got sick, you just called the nearest horse doctor for advice. Sometimes animals are still taken to specialists in human disease. There's a lot more research done on dogs and cats than on elands, so a lot of what happens at the zoo is based on trial and error, experience, seat-of-the-pants, which is maybe not so different from medical care for humans except with humans you don't like to admit it.

Falada's hold on life was already so tenuous, it seemed it would take little to snuff it out, but drugs can have unpredictable effects. When muscles twitched beneath her coat, we assumed this was approaching death. But then, as though someone had turned on the switch for an animatronic figure, all at once, everything started up: lungs wheezing, white lips flapping, her thin legs drumming against the table, eyes flaring open, rolling, her whole body jerking like Frankenstein's monster, galvanized. Her head shook, dangerous with those horns, and we swarmed her body. We fastened straps and we held her down, with the rat-a-tat-tat of her drumming jolting, vibrating up my arms. It would have been more humane, I thought, to fire a bullet right into that light-colored chevron patch between her eyes. I could feel her heart racing and I could feel the impulse to run beating against her skin as Ginger prepared another syringe and Falada's dewlap trembled and slapped against me as she strained and my fingers twisted through the coarse fringe of hair. My cheek against her chestnut flank, I stroked along each white stripe and over the raw places where her coat was mangy and scabbed.

The eland was not an animal I knew well, but I lay against her body, selflessly, I like to think, with no concern for ticks or fleas as Ginger administered still another injection until the jerking and quivering and straining stopped.

When indigenous people kill an animal, they honor or propitiate it in some way, or so I've read, because only this will ensure that the animals will continue to thrive and allow man to kill them. When we euthanized Falada, we did it sadly, solemnly, without pleasure, to the best of our ability, with horror and with great regret, but we failed in the ritual that would ensure the multiplication and swarm of life.

When it was finally over, Ginger put her arms around me, which was a little scary because while I swear I'm not a lesbian, the truth is, if I were going to love someone—a human, that is—again, I really do think it would be Ginger.

. . .

In the story, the true status of the princess is revealed and she marries the prince. Nothing more is said about the head of the ever-faithful horse–no mention of decent burial, or a magical restoration, or its reduction to bone. An oversight? I consider it injustice.

All of which may help explain, though not excuse, why instead of going to the museum, when I left the lab, I drove back to the zoo.

"The museum must have sent someone," I said. "The head was already gone."

Then I finished my regular shift, hoping she hadn't yet thawed in my trunk.

The museum had Jamal. That was enough. I wasn't going to let them have Falada.

Once I got her head home, I knew that sooner or later I'd be caught. Like any criminal—or most—I wasn't thinking about how I was going to get away with it. It didn't seem to matter. It was obvious I hadn't thought any of this through. She wouldn't fit in my freezer. You may be thinking, so what? Go out and buy a full-size, but a person who commits a crime on impulse is not thinking coolly and logically. I certainly wasn't. The only reality that got through to me was this:

I was in danger of losing the best job I ever had. Once, I did two years of social work, but having reached the conclusion that altogether too many humans are greedy, mean-spirited, and just plain stupid, I could no longer bring myself to make any efforts on their behalf. Now it's a privilege to be working alongside such good people who are doing so much good.

As I said the other day to Ginger, "When you save the life of a bear cub, you don't have to worry he'll go out and vote Republican."

. . .

Ginger had tears in her eyes when Falada died.

I'm probably more of a pedophile than a lesbian since I'm only attracted to women, like her, who look like young boys. Slimhipped, flat on top, smooth hairless skin. I tell myself it's not sexual desire for a child, but nostalgia for puppy love. They remind me of the first little boys I had crushes on, the little boys I wanted to kiss and marry and live with forever after. It's a desire for that innocence, those attachments that were fierce and fiercely ignorant of the world. The attachment I feel for the animals.

Which side are you on? Theirs, I think, *theirs*.

Do I bury her furtively at night? Leave her head in the open air beneath the great oak in Stough Park where a woman once told me she'd been very satisfied so far with the Druid lifestyle? Will I end up tossing her from my speeding car on a stretch of the Angeles Crest Highway reputed to be a landfill for victims?

Tell me, I say. *Tell me what you want.*

I have comforted a frightened tamarin. Baboons have masturbated in my direction with zestful glee. An anxious white-cheeked gibbon once grasped my hand while her mate was being treated by Ginger. I held Falada throughout her last struggle. Even now, I can't say if in those throes that didn't want to end she was struggling harder to live or to die. If I could shed my humanness, I would. But such transformation happens only in myths and fairy tales.

There were many variant stories collected by the Brothers Grimm. Mostly we know the child-friendly sanitized versions. Is there another tale in which Falada is acknowledged? In which the princess meets her death and the horse is restored to life? I have never found it. *Alas, Falada, hanging there!* You were the most vivid part of the story, the part I remember, and when it ends, with right triumphing over wrong, you are not only dead, but forgotten, still forsaken.

She has tipped over onto my floor and a puddle begins to spread past the plastic. In all her years of being looked at, I wonder how many people ever saw her as anything more than one of the herd. I think how she strained so hard and rhythmically against the bonds that held her, her whole body like one big heart, beating, beating.

My own fight ends so quickly. What can I do but deliver you into those human hands? A private transaction. No exhibition hall, no public door. I knew this all along: There's a service entrance with a long slow ramp winding down into the dark. That's where we'll tread, you in my arms. I won't have to see Jamal. I won't have to look into your eyes, Falada.

How Much an Ant Can Carry

Yesterday a letter came in the mail along with a book—187 photocopied pages folded and stapled inside soft covers, written in a language I don't understand. A gift from Lorenza.

"It would break your heart to see her." That's what Aurora said about Lorenza during my last visit to Oaxaca. "Barefoot, stooped under a load of firewood. She looks like an old woman. An old Indian woman."

"Didn't she become a teacher?"

"Yes, and from what I hear, she's a wonderful teacher," Aurora said. "She went back to the sierra and she's doing a wonderful job. But the man she got involved with! It's all his fault. He doesn't work, he just drinks. He probably beats her."

"Is she afraid to leave him?"

"Well, who knows? She has five children by him," Aurora said. "It must be love."

In many ways, Oaxaca had become so modern. Little bus stations making reservations on video display terminals and machines spitting out computer-generated tickets. Acupuncture clinics and health clubs. Twelve-

Step meetings and gender-specific disposable diapers. Chocolate cake imported from Germany in the grocery store, and Aurora clapping her hands in anticipation of NAFTA, "Oh, any day now we're going to have *everything!"*—an enthusiasm that wouldn't last once she saw what free trade did to the local economy.

New Age thinking comes naturally in Oaxaca, as people automatically resist labels: "I'm not an epileptic; I take anti-convulsive medication so I *won't* be one." "I don't have a heart condition. I take nitroglycerin so I won't." But Aurora, who even twenty years earlier had talked comfortably about Freud and complexes, had never heard of the dynamics of abuse and as we talked more about Lorenza, I could see that to her it made no sense.

It didn't make sense to me either that Lorenza would let a man push her around. The Lorenza I knew was someone who stood up for herself. She was still a child in her village when she witnessed the male teacher—the only literate adult for miles around—rape a twelve-year-old. She was afraid to tell or go back to school, but she already loved reading more than anything. She stole some tortillas and started walking. She walked for days until she arrived in the state capital, presented herself at the first school she found and announced, "I want to learn."

Aurora's family had taken her in. And years later, as a student-teacher, when she had to hitchhike back and forth to her assignment at a rural school, a driver who stopped for her "made improper advances." I was the only one Lorenza told; if anyone else knew, she was afraid her reputation would be ruined. "I told him I was married and had children," she said. "Why?" I asked. Her brown face flushed and she answered me earnestly: "They say men don't like it so much when you've had children." Then she added—it was safe to let a foreigner know she had this knowledge—"It's not good and tight." The man persisted until she hit him over the head with one of the empty bottles she was carrying to teach the little children how to measure. Then she jumped out of the car and ran. So at least once as a student, once as a teacher, Lorenza had known when—and how—to get the hell out.

If she was carrying firewood on her back, if she looked "like an old Indian woman," it had to be politics: Lorenza as radical, leader of the indigenous movement. If she was poor, it had to be by choice.

"Have you seen her recently?" I asked Aurora.

"Not at all."

"Then how do you know?"

"Bad news travels."

I decided to head for the sierra to see her.

"You shouldn't go," said Aurora. "It will break your heart."

The first time I met Lorenza, she was still called by her nickname, Hormiga, which means Ant. She was about eight years old and came dashing up to show off that she knew Jorge Washington had been the first president of the United States.

"I'm from the Sierra Juárez," she said, "same as our great president Benito Juárez. That means if I want to, I'm going to be president someday." Not the words of someone you push around, though years later, a teenager self-conscious about her breasts, she blushed and hugged her books closer when I reminded her. She hung her head and muttered—but with force—"I never said that."

It was probably Doña Josi who explained "good and tight." I couldn't imagine anyone else in the household who would have. For a while Lorenza shared a room with Doña Josi and her two daughters who'd taken shelter with the family after Doña Josi lost her job for going out on strike.

Doña Josi was tall and beautiful and illiterate. Her black hair fell to below her waist and instead of braiding it, she left it loose and flowing. She was from the coast where women were said to be lascivious. She behaved discreetly in the household until her downfall which came about with a protest trip to Mexico City.

"Oh, what happened to her!" Aurora said. "You should have seen her, her condition when we got her back!"

Many of the union leaders had been arrested, tortured. I'd seen a young man after his release from prison, bent over and bowlegged, letting himself wince but not cry with pain at each step.

"Her hair!" said Aurora. "Cut off and curled. And her hemlines way above the knees. She still can't read or write but some things, let me tell you, they learn very fast."

So when Aurora spoke about Lorenza, I tried not to worry. What was horrific to Aurora was not necessarily so tragic for Lorenza or for me.

In the Oaxaca I knew, people went away, but no one was ever lost for good. We all had faith in this and from it took great consolation. Of course there were also people whose return no one looked forward to and, sure enough, they came back too.

No one stayed put. People traveled: to Veracruz, Chiapas, Mexico City, Tijuana, across the border to California and to Texas and New York and Chicago and anywhere else you could think of. In a dusty rural village I met a man who'd been to Alexandria, Egypt. Oh, wow! I said. What was it like? "A lot like Juchitán," he said.

Many can't read or write, so don't expect letters. And often there's no address to write to. But mothers who gave up their children and disappeared would be back twenty-five years later to raise the grandchildren. Girls rode out of town on the back of some man's motorcycle and rumors spread—she's been murdered, she's working in a brothel, some people took her in and she's a maid—and one day she'd be back without warning, showing up with a husband and baby or maybe a degree in architecture. Husbands would cross the border and five years later return with enough money to build a little house on a little piece of land. The dead, of course, came back too: when my friends were sad they would sit in corners and ask the departed for advice; the dead, being from Oaxaca, were too courteous to withhold a reply.

I, myself, had returned from L.A. again and again. If I managed to find Lorenza in the mountains, she'd be surprised—but not all that surprised—to see me.

The bus to the sierra was as always: seats with stuffing coming out; aisles filling up with cartons, baskets, sacks of scallions, tomatoes, dried fish. But something new: some of the cartons contained computers, and on the divider behind the driver's seat, a red light and a notice that it would signal excess speed.

I took a seat. Two little boys helped an Indian woman load her sacks and baskets into the aisle. Then she came clambering over. She was dressed in white with a red wool sash, the traditional costume Lorenza used to wear when her school asked students to demonstrate folkloric dances. The woman seated herself on top of her cargo and I saw her feet. The soles of her feet, because she was barefoot. Skin hardened and cracked like old leather that's been through water and dried, hardly recognizable as skin. If they'd been shoes, I thought, she would have thrown them out long ago. Did Lorenza have feet like these? Feet that could ignore sharp bits of rock, even deflect cactus spines. These feet could walk through fire.

They were not meant to hold a woman back. With feet like these—if Lorenza had feet like these—I wanted to think she could walk anywhere.

The horizon turned white while clouds stood out black and gray like dirty smoke. We pulled out of the station, down streets where the adobe walls were painted with political slogans and exhortations about drugs and unwanted pregnancy: JOVEN! DI NO A LAS DROGAS! ADOLESCENTE! EVITE LA ANGUSTIA DEL EMBARAZO. PROTEJETE!

The dome of the sky deepened to blue and the red light began to flash till the driver slowed. The sun rose higher, and as we approached Tlacolula there was a magnificent fire opal resting on the tableland between two mountains.

We stopped for breakfast in a town of log cabins and sod houses, where corn husks were spread out on roofs to dry. In a small dark room, light filtered in through oilpaper squares in the roof and glowed from the cooking fire where two women in black stirred the contents of several cauldrons. Everyone sat around a few long tables and wolfed down chicken stew, beef, and beans with fingers or tortillas or big metal enameled spoons and bought bottled drinks from a little girl who people, for some reason, called *Papá*.

We stopped again so the driver could piss by the side of the highway, three times when he had to snatch some tools from the wooden storage box beside his seat and tinker under the hood, and finally at a town where the road was blocked by parked cars and men with rifles.

"Passengers," our driver announced. "Pasajeros. We have come across a political protest. No one is being permitted to travel the highway. Much as I sympathize with the revolutionary ends of our comrades, I made a commitment to get you to the sierra and I will accomplish that, one way or another, you have my word. Anyone who desires may get off the bus now and stay here awaiting further developments. But if you wish to reach the sierra tonight, stay aboard, and I will take you there."

"Politics," said a man. "Politics," people echoed, pronouncing the word carefully, a label rather than an opinion.

Everyone stayed on the bus and so did I. If Lorenza had become a revolutionary, I hoped she would forgive me for evading the roadblock.

Our driver left us and when he returned, well maybe, yes, he'd had a drink or two, but he also had a local man in tow, a campesino in stained white field clothes.

"Pasajeros. It is my great pleasure to inform you that we have found a friend who will guide us away from the highway and by a little known and highly circuitous route to our destination. ¡A la sierra!" he cried.

And we shouted back "¡A la sierra!"

We pretended to retreat. Once out of sight of the roadblock, we turned off the paved highway and onto a narrow dirt road that wound its way up a cliffside through a region of scrubby bushes and small-leafed trees. The bus kept climbing. At higher altitudes we began to see spruce and pine, dry moss hanging from branches, dried up ferns, an occasional trickling waterfall. Far below in a valley, there was a fiesta. The music carried through the mountain air and there were moving spots of color, people dancing.

We hit some bad spots and men materialized from nowhere and laid down rocks to help pave a way. A belt snapped and the driver tinkered. He was our hero.

We passed fields where peasants stopped work to laugh and to stare. What was a bus doing here? Our driver waved out the window: "I'm going to get these people to the mountains!" and everyone laughed and shouted "¡A la sierra!"

Our driver explained, "Have to hurry. We don't have headlights," before setting off the warning light as he sped mercilessly around the mountain curves.

It was easy passage for a while across the flat landscape of a ruined hacienda until we got stuck at a narrow stone arch. Again, men appeared as though we'd been expected, and with grunts and laughter began to dismantle the entryway stone by stone.

"¡A la sierra!"

This journey—Lorenza had done this alone and on foot when she was six years old, as determined as she was scared. Presenting herself to strangers: "I want to learn."

And if I found her, then what? If Aurora was right, what could I possibly do?

The sun went down.

"Pasajeros." Pasajero, *passenger* or an adjective for *fleeting, brief*. The song Aurora used to sing: *La soledad es pasajera*. Loneliness is fleeting. Or should you translate it as solitude? Your solitude will never last.

"Pasajeros," said the driver.

He could take the bus no further in the dark. We were within minutes of the town of San Juan del Monte where he intended to park for the night. He invited those who had reached their destination or wished to continue on foot to take their leave. The rest of us were welcome to stay on board and catch what we could of sleep. He brought the bus to a stop. When he opened the door and stood, we all stood, too, with applause and cheers: a standing ovation.

In the morning, the sun came up on a town that looked like a poorly wrapped package tied together with new power lines. The Indian woman with the feet climbed down and a few men helped her unload the sacks and baskets on which she'd slept. Vendors came to the windows selling tortillas, beans, and coffee and then the bus lurched on.

Passengers banged with fists and hollered to signal a stop. People got off in villages. They got off by footpaths. They got off in the middle of nowhere with no landmark or distinguishing feature recognizable to my North American eye. There was some controversy over whether the wrong sack of dried fish had been unloaded in Betaaza.

The road grew narrower. We entered pine forest and then emerged into clearings with wildflowers six feet high. Towering black-eyed Susans, purple flowers blooming atop hallucinatory stalks. I hoped Lorenza lived in a landscape like this, that her life included beauty and a heart that could enjoy it. Cows grazed in meadows so thick and deep they seemed to be drowning in green.

At the end of the line, I named Lorenza's village. Several fellow passengers pointed to a trail marked with crushed lime. I didn't ask how far. The answer was bound to be *Oh, a ways*, which could mean anything.

I walked through clouds of butterflies and, glad to have plastic sandals, forded streams. Willows grew by the water, and cactus on the rocky hills. When I began to cross paths with people, I asked for Lorenza, the teacher, and—good sign—people knew her and smiled and pointed me to continue on my way.

Then, that had to be it: a small building made of cinder block, children running out the door. I could feel myself smiling even before I turned the corner of the schoolhouse and saw her in the doorway, a little stooped, her hair in a single long braid, her toes splayed wide in sandals. Still a toss-up whether Aurora was right.

There was a little girl pegged to her skirt and holding, almost dangling, a baby. Students, or Lorenza's own?

We ran to each other's arms. "It was you! It was you!" she said. "They told me my boss was climbing the hill to check on me. My boss from Mexico City."

"Oh, is this a bad time for me to—?"

"No," she said. "They meant you. A white woman up here in the sierra. They figured it had to be my boss."

"Do you have children now?" she asked. "These are two of mine. Elpidia, and the baby, Miguelito."

She led me inside. I opened my backpack and covered her desk with what I'd brought: some of that cheese they make only in Chiapas, and one of the German chocolate cakes so good it made Aurora clap her hands, and a bag of the sweet bread Lorenza used to love.

"Hormiga." I used her nickname.

"Oh," she said, "no one's called me that in years."

Elpidia was quiet, eyes fixed on the pan dulce. Lorenza nodded and Elpidia grinned and reached. Before she ate, she let the baby suck some sugar from her finger.

"You have beautiful children," I said.

There were bottles of different sizes on the windowsill. "Measurement?" I pointed. "Or self-defense?"

"What do you mean?" She didn't remember, or else pretended not to.

"Lorenza," I said, "do things go well?"

"Some children learn," she said. "Some don't."

I said, "I mean for *you*."

She didn't answer right away, and when she did, though she spoke in Spanish, it wasn't her college-educated Spanish. She spoke the way she had when I first knew her, her eyes lowered and her words coming out in the Zapotec way, by which I don't mean she had an accent so much as that she breathed her sounds out rather than spoke them.

"When I was little, I wanted to learn. Not so I could be more prosperous." Her words rode in hushed bursts on soft puffs of breath. "I had never seen the way people lived in the city. I didn't know about it. I didn't know enough to want it. But when I first learned to read, *that* was what I wanted. More and more of *that*. And you see where it got me."

"Is your life here very hard?"

"Oh, at first," she said. "I never wanted to be a rural teacher. But you know how it is. That was the only education they would offer an Indian girl like me."

"Remember when you said you'd be president?"

"Oh, who would want that?" she said. "I'm happy as I am. Now that I've learned to be selfish."

She didn't look selfish.

"Look," she said. From her desk, she took a softbound notebook, and then another. "I write stories. Years ago, I tried to write in Spanish, but I couldn't."

I opened the top notebook. I couldn't make out a single word.

She said, "I know Spanish, of course. That's what I teach in the classroom, but I couldn't use it to write words from the heart. The only books I ever saw in Zapotec, in idioma, are the dictionaries and Bible lessons from the evangelists. And grammars: *I eat tortilla. He eats tortilla.* Who wants to read nothing but Jesus and tortillas?"

"Translate one of these for me?"

"I can't," she said. "The words don't sound right. But here, this one is about roasting mangoes in the fire until they burst with juice, and about hunting giant mushrooms. And this one tells about my brother who headed for the north and we never heard from him again. I like this one," she said. "It's about a woman in the city who pretends she's not an Indian at all, but when they hand her a bowl of atole, she jiggles it without thinking, just the way we all do in the sierra.

"Now I don't mind teaching the children to read," she said. "A few stay after class and we learn to read and write in idioma. It's the only way anyone will ever be able to read my stories. When I keep my selfish goal in my mind, teaching makes me happy."

I was glad I'd seen her with my own eyes. I decided I would tell Aurora that Lorenza's life was good.

"Stories will keep your language alive," I said.

"Maybe."

She hugged me and thanked me for coming to see her. "Sometimes I feel so forgotten." Then she told me she would love to invite me to her home but it would not be a good idea. She said I should head back to the bus. It usually left for the return trip at 2:00.

I could have told her it was doubtful the bus was keeping to the schedule, not today. Instead I said, "But I just arrived. We haven't had time to talk, or anything. It took me two days to get here."

"Yes, thank you," she said. "That's how I know you still think of me and it makes me glad." She hugged me again. "You should leave before dark." She would love to introduce me to her husband, she said, but it was not a good idea. He might be drinking.

In her letter, Lorenza said she'd given her book to more than twenty people who could now read Zapotec. "Not everyone likes the stories," she said. Of her own children, only Elpidia, she said, had read them. "Some people like some and not others, but it gives me a lot of pleasure anyway." She wrote, "I don't expect you to learn idioma, but please keep this book and remember the distant one who does not forget you." She closed with greetings and hugs from all her children. She listed six by name. She didn't mention her husband.

At the Site Where Vision is Most Perfect

·1·

"They tell us to dress ugly and then they let the TV cameras in," Courtney says. "Call your mother to come get us. Now."

Matt and Courtney are in a shed like an airplane hangar all the way out in Azusa where it's flat and smoggy and, even the day before Christmas, too hot. They're here because Courtney thought decorating Rose Parade floats would be fun. Matt thinks it is.

Courtney says, "I can't take much more of this."

Matt's wearing paint-spattered clothes from the Habitat for Humanity project his mother supervised. His jeans are torn at the knee, the rip narrowing as it moves up his thigh, and he thinks about what it would be like for Courtney to slip her hand inside there and touch him.

At this moment, his mother is being handcuffed.

Matt tries to block out Courtney and concentrate instead on pasting tiny oval leaves onto the dragon's claw. Most of the leaves are a pale ivory, almost transparent, but some have lingering traces of color—gold, brown, green, even purple, and you can get some interesting gradations as you overlap them.

His mother is thinking it's a terrible mistake but her main worry is her family, because when she doesn't come home, they won't know what's happened.

Matt's father is walking across campus with Minfong en route to Medical Plaza where Dr. Singh is going to show off virtual surgery.

"Can you believe Matt only got a B on that paper?" David says.

"His paper was good," says Minfong.

"Points off the grade because he reported on the research and didn't ask why we do it. Be damned if I know why," David says.

Minfong says, "We're curious."

"We're funded," he says. "And you get a work permit."

It's a marvel, Matt thinks, hundreds of people doing this precise, detailed, labor-intensive work that no one along the parade route or watching on TV will be able to appreciate. There's something ancient in this notion, so even though he knows each float costs a quarter of a million and has a corporate sponsor, there's something in it positively un-American.

Up above him, Courtney's complaining and little Asian children are slathering paste and poppy seeds on the structure in swirling black lines.

In the lab, his father tells Minfong that his wife is becoming a citizen. "Cliff finally got around to it," he says. "What about you?"

"Oh, no," Minfong says quickly. "Two years permit only," quickly, as though she thinks someone is listening.

"Why do I see seeds on the floor?" One of the yellow jackets who supervises the volunteers hollers up at the children.

Courtney says, "They're dropping them on my head. All over my hair."

"I thought I told you," says the woman. "No dropping seeds on the floor!" Then she turns and looks at Courtney's work. "*His* look scaly, like they're supposed to. Yours look furry." The yellow jacket walks away.

"Jeez," Courtney says. "Instead of criticizing, you'd think they'd say thanks."

Matt doesn't answer.

"First they tell you start from the bottom. Then they say the top. She says to me, *Look how your fingernails grow, don't you get it?* As though my fingernails have anything to do with a dragon's toes!"

Minfong gets to wear the headset. A needle substitutes for scalpel, mounted in a thimble. Matt's father watches her do a virtual dissection of a human eyeball. Slice, rotate. It's just a simulation, but as she moves the robotic arm, her knuckles are white.

"You can feel," she says. "Resistance, yielding."

"That's force-feedback," Dr. Singh says.

"The haptic interface." David hasn't seen this before but he knows his stuff. "Cliff would love this."

Cliff would, but right now, she's in trouble.

In real reality, David and Minfong work in the lab with *Drosophila*, cloning in full-length human DNA sequences and mapping the QTL's that control variation in the architecture of the eye. It's complicated stuff, he thinks, and his son wrote a damn good paper.

Minfong cuts through the sclerotic coat. The tunic of protection protects no more. Incision, excision. She gasps as the membrane over the cornea curls up by itself like a fallen leaf in time-lapse photography.

Slice, rotate, back to the back of the retina and she reveals the yellow oval at the place where vision is most perfect.

"Use more glue," Courtney mimics. *"I don't want to spend New Year's Eve sticking your leaves back on. Too much glue. Not enough.* Why don't they make up their minds?" Matt sifts through the leaves gently, looking

for ones that are flat, not curled. "You get to stand on the ground," Courtney says. "That's easy. Look at me, balanced up here. My legs are shaking."

Matt focuses on handling the dead dry leaves one at a time carefully carefully so that they don't crumble. Courtney gets ahold of a yellow jacket who leads her outside.

A medical student needs to use the computer, so David and Minfong have to step aside.

"What do Americans do for New Year's?" Minfong asks.

"I don't know about Americans," David says. "I think this American will just stay home."

A research scientist isn't home much. That's why, to David, spending time with Matt on that paper really mattered. "Didn't ask the right questions!" he says. "How does the *frizzled* gene initiate signaling pathways with downstream targets to ensure DV polarity? And will Berkeley get there first? That's what I ask."

"Oh, Dr. David," Minfong says, "not true. You ask many questions."

A yellow jacket puts a hand on Matt's shoulder. "Why don't you take a lunch break," she says, and "I hope you can make it again tomorrow. You're good."

Matt mumbles something noncommittal.

David's expecting a rare and quiet New Year's Eve with Cliff. Matt will be out with Courtney. But he realizes Minfong has no plans. "You're welcome to join us."

"Oh, thank you!" she says.

"You're welcome."

"You're welcome," she repeats. "In China, that's not how they teach us. They teach us to say, *Not at all.*"

"It gets pretty exciting down the home stretch," the yellow jacket tells Matt. "Last year, at the airport, Customs wouldn't let the Costa Rican flowers through. Right up to the last minute, we didn't know if we could finish the float. Can you believe the government's that mean?"

Downtown, his mother is saying, "I have to pick up my son. You have to let me call someone. I have to find someone to get him."

Matt finds Courtney sitting on the pavement pasting rice on metal curlicues.

"You could feed all of China with what's going to waste," she says. "I'm starving."

Matt's mother won't get anything to eat.

Minfong tells David she's grown used to American food, but it's not the sort of thing you want to eat every day.

Outside the shed, the catering truck has hot dogs, hamburgers, pastrami. Nothing Courtney can eat—she's a junk food vegetarian who lives (and somehow looks great) on a diet of cheese doodles, devil's food SnackWells, and Red Vines.

"Please," she says, "let's get out of here."

"And get a room." He wonders if he needs to add he's joking.

"Lunch first," Courtney says, poking him with an elbow.

"What year is it in China?" Matt's father asks.

"Same," says Minfong. "We use Western calendar. Chinese calendar will be Year of the Dragon."

"But what year? What number year?"

"We don't pay so much attention," says Minfong. "Someone could tell you. Not me."

"Is the dragon a good year?"

"Oh, yes. Very very good."

Matt and Courtney leave without signing out and walk a few blocks to the nearest convenience store where they linger a moment outside, Courtney hoping an adult will come by who'll be willing to buy them beer.

"Did you see that place?" Matt says—the place that from the freeway looked like a nuclear power plant and turned out to be a brewery. "Would you drink anything that came out of there?"

There are surveillance cameras inside the store, maybe some, Matt thinks, posted outside, too, that could record an illegal transaction.

"Who cares?" says Courtney.

Sometimes, often, Courtney scares him. He says, "I'll phone my mom." Cliff wasn't going to work today. She had her interview, so maybe she's done and can come for them early. No answer.

Downtown, his mother is saying, "My son." She says, "My husband." She says, "My job. My car." She says, "You have to let me call someone."

Matt and Courtney go to a nearby park and sit, Matt with his back against a tree while Courtney leans against him drinking the Diet Coke she had to settle for while he runs his hands all over her and wonders if anyone will see them if they lie down together on the grass. He breathes in her hair and puts his hands under her T-shirt and inside her bra and she runs a finger inside the hole in his jeans.

When he tries the pay phone again, his mom still doesn't answer.

"Doesn't she have a cell phone?" Courtney asks.

"That's what I'm calling," Matt says.

"That's weird."

He says, "What about your mom?"

Courtney says, "She dropped us off. Your mother *promised*."

"She's probably in traffic." She never answers when she's driving. People in L.A. do it all the time, but Cliff is careful. He says, "She's on her way. She'll be here." Right now she's in shackles and handcuffs, but days will go by before Matt knows it.

Weeks will go by before she makes a phone call, before she has a piece of paper and can start to write her letter. In the meantime, she writes it in her head and repeats it over and over again to remember. In the meantime, in the holding cell, the guard tells her his name is Tycho Brown.

"I was named after an astronomer," he says. There are at least fifty people crammed into the cell and she thinks, *Why am I here? And why does he have to talk to* me? "It takes the earth three hundred and sixty-five days. And the moon twenty-eight." Only two nights ago, or was it years, she and Matt and David lay moonbathing by the pool, beneath the solstice moon, the brightest full moon in more than a hundred years. *Me toca la luna*. The moon touches me, you say in Spanish, my time of the moon, my period. She thinks, I sure hope I'm out of here by then. "Where does the sun rise?" asks Tycho Brown. "If the sun rises in the east, where does the moon rise? Where would it rise if the earth stood still? Come on, you don't look stupid. Use your head."

Her head is filled with the letter she's writing, with words that fill the space and leave less room for fear.

"Where *is* she?" Courtney says.

For David, there's usually no such thing as a weekend or holiday, but even he leaves work early Friday, Christmas Eve, a good thing, too, as Cliff, strangely, isn't home and so he has to go to Azusa to get Matt and Courtney.

"Come on, girl." He lets Ruby bound into the car.

It used to be a family joke: Daddy's American, Matt is American,

Ruby's American—even though she's a *border* collie, and Mom—now Mom will be American too. As for Desirée—all cats are French.

It's late, already dark, when he picks up the kids. Traffic is heavy with last-minute shoppers, and they're just past Glendale on the 134 when everything comes to a halt. They see police cars. An accident? No one moves. David turns on the radio, but they can't hear the traffic report with the din of the news helicopters overhead.

David phones home, to tell Cliff they'll be late. No answer, and Courtney's allergies kick in because of Ruby. She begins to wheeze so Matt says, "I'll walk her," and to his father, "I'll be careful."

He leashes the dog and opens the door. Nothing to worry about. Traffic is at a standstill. They lope to the shoulder. A cop on motorcycle pulls up.

"Get back in your vehicle."

Matt tries to ask what's going on, how long they'll be, but the cop has on his game face and doesn't answer.

David is leaning on the horn. A different cop comes over.

"She's having an allergy attack," he says. "Can you escort us to an exit ramp?"

"You can't go ahead," says the cop. "There's a suspicious vehicle. We're waiting for the police robot to check for bombs."

The police robert, thinks Matt. It's his mother's joke, she always refers to David's dour assistant as Robot, making Minfong ask at last, "It is American custom to name baby like machine?"

"We can't take you backwards," says the cop.

"Get her an ambulance."

"We'd have to call a helicopter. I understand you're uncomfortable, young lady, but it doesn't look like a bona fide emergency."

"How long is this going to take?"

The cop says, "It's for your own protection." But he's a nice guy. "Is it the dog?"

Courtney bobs her head, and the cop relents. "You're welcome to sit in the squad car for now."

"Handcuffed?" she asks.

Matt feels a jealous twinge as Courtney goes happily off with the cop.

They make it home at last at a quarter of ten. No Cliff. No message. Just a calendar slipped inside the door.

"It's from the exterminator," says Matt. The page for each month features words from the Bible.

David calls the police to report Cliff missing, but for them it's too early for it to matter. The doorbell rings, startling them as though it promises bad news but it's just the next-door neighbor. "I notice you don't put up lights," she says, "but I do hope you'll join our effort"—a petition against white Christmas lights and in favor of bringing back traditional colors. "For next year," she says. "To preserve the neighborhood's character."

They get to laugh a moment when she's gone. The neighborhood's character: a Valley suburb on the way down, for people on the way up. A place the Pearlsteins can afford and convenient via the 405 to their jobs at UCLA. The local schools? Matt's the kind of kid who'll always do well in school and be dissatisfied with any.

David tries calling INS but of course the office is closed.

The house in Van Nuys looks so modest on its modest little street. Nothing to attract a break-in, but Clifford had her way with the backyard and the inside. Skylights and terraces and a glass atrium with cacti and indoor trees. (No Christmas tree, a small consolation to David's mother, who doesn't know Matt gets presents, Mexican-style, on January 6.) In the back, the obligatory pool, and lemon trees and guava. This is where Cliff got to be an architect. She gave up private clients, too much money and too little taste, she always said, and instead she chose to work at the Virtual Cities Project. To Cliff, architecture is as much a way of thinking as of building. ("CONstruct," she used to say to Matt, "conSTRUCT"—as if the words were visual, flipping back and forth between figure and ground.) Cliff spends her days with a parallel L.A., in cyberspace, created out of satellite images and constant input from street-level videocams, a city that can be constructed and reconstructed and deconstructed, experimented with to see what if?—fire, riot, earthquake, slum clearance, freeway widening, what if? Click: two men husking coconuts with machetes at the corner of Beverly and Alvarado. Click: Pico and Hill where a dozen naked mannequins show their buttocks in the window and two Latino men squat on their heels in front of the store, looking out into the street. Click: A woman studies a battered mailbox at 8th and Olive and finally decides to walk on without depositing her letter. Click: A traffic jam in front of Cedars Sinai where a little girl loses her knot of helium balloons to a gust of wind and the camera picks up the get well message on the ribbon.

And with all those videocams and all that data, with the city under constant surveillance, Cliff Pearlstein has disappeared when no one was watching.

Monday morning, a live human being answers the phone at INS, but key employees have called in sick—David did too, he's not going to work until he finds his wife—and no one can help him. Clifford Pearlstein? They don't believe Clifford is a woman, surely not a Mexican woman.

(Her parents, headed for the U.S. when she was born, gave her a good English name, not knowing it was a boy's name.) "Is this a marriage," says the bureaucrat, "or a domestic partnership?"

It's not till Tuesday that David and Matt know for sure the Immigration and Naturalization Service has her.

It's not till Thursday that Cliff's office calls. When she didn't come in, they thought at first she was working from home and David's been too confused to call them.

The cameras, of course, are rolling. A gray minivan emerges from an alley. Click. The videocams record the TV cameras filming a front yard in Downey with prize-winning Christmas decorations: animated reindeer, a neon Santa plunging down a chimney, and thousands of white lights, an electric bill that could put a kid through college. Click. The flash of a welder's torch on the 3500 block of 7th.

Cliff's car is located, it's been towed, and David goes to get it. At the sound of the familiar motor, Desirée bounds to the door, then backs away slowly, fur fluffed out, when she sees that it's just David.

Now David's holding the phone, on hold. Matt sits at the kitchen table, his left leg jiggling, while he flips through the exterminator's calendar. January shows a snowcapped mountain and a quote from Psalms: *Thou hast seen, for Thou dost take note of trouble and grief.* The words jog David's memory. He replies, *Be gracious to me, O Lord, see what I suffer from those who hate me,* and Matt feels all his muscles clench. He's always worried a lot about whether people like him, but this is new to him: he's never felt hated.

Someone answers at the other end. David says, "My wife."

You can't see her, they tell him. She's not yet officially in any place. We can't talk to you until you have her A#. Until they have her processed, no phone calls, no letters, no lawyers, they sort of have her but she sort of isn't really there.

·2·

In her head she writes: *I don't seem to be in the place where I find myself. The woman I am does not—cannot—spend her nights on a plastic boat underneath a cafeteria table. She is not brought here each midnight in a bus, with forty or fifty others, made to wait, stripsearched and put to bed at 2:00 or 3:00 a.m. only to be awakened at 5:00 for the trip back to the holding cell downtown with its cold air and overflowing toilets and Mr. Tycho Brown. (Hour after hour he harangues me about the difference between fact and theory. I want to tell him the difference between justice and law.)*

They've rounded up so many of us, there's simply no room.

Can you imagine, we look longingly at the prison, envious of the prisoners who live there. In less than a week, freedom already seems impossible, my own home a distant memory. All I want is to be spared this nightly transit, to have a prison I can call my home.

She tries to memorize her story, the way poets have done in one gulag after another, starting again and again from the beginning. *They stripped me and took away the clothes I was wearing. They issued me a plastic ID bracelet and a red jumpsuit. Red signifying that I am an aggravated felon. Aggravated, sí! felon, no! No toothbrush, they've run out, and we're not allowed to bring our own. No underwear, there's not enough to go around. In the Sixties, didn't women go braless? I tried to see it as an opportunity: enter a time machine and live an era I missed out on. But no one ever tells you about the fabric burn of cloth against nipples. Today, a guard handed me a bra and a pair of torn panties. It had never before occurred to me to question: a bra, with two cups, is singular, but panties are a pair. I have indeed become an alien, everything once familiar, all I have taken for granted, is strange.*

"Why are they doing this to us?" Matt asks.

At first they leave her things untouched, her bathrobe still hanging on the bathroom door. Then David packs it along with other essentials in the carry-on bag he'll bring her.

Ruby paws at the bag, barking, even howling. The bag goes into the closet. Ruby scratches at the door and whines. And when David is informed he will not be permitted to give anything to his wife, he unpacks. Ruby, usually so well-behaved, snatches out the robe, shakes it and rolls about until she's half on, half in it.

"What did she do?" Matt asks. "How could she do this?"

Fifteen years ago, Cliff remembers, *I stood in a bathroom trying to find the light switch and I experienced a sudden psychic illumination along with a terrible vertigo. My hand against the wallpaper, seeking a protuberance, a panel, something to press. Feeling the pressure of its resistance against my hand. Why hide a light switch in a bathroom? Why hide what must be found, what has no need to hide? I felt myself slipping in the dark into some secret and disorienting recess, and then they battered down the door and found me. How could I guess then what it would lead to?*

Matt's never heard the story and there are parts David thinks he should not know. That Cliff was pregnant with him, and unmarried, that day in the dark bathroom. That David's mother had said, "You marry that Mexican, I'll die." Her threat delayed the wedding and when David finally announced nothing would stop him, Matt's Grandma Ida had a heart attack on the spot. At the hospital they said she'd been clinically dead, and Matt doesn't need to know any of this as Ida turned out to be a nice person after resurrection.

What Matt's heard over and over again from his mother are her mocking stories: having to cater to the rich with their hideous homes in the Hills and the Palisades, tear down and build a bigger one, bedrooms as large as bowling alleys, second stories cantilevered over first, but most of all it was the bathrooms that killed her: they wanted 500-square-foot bathrooms with twin matching marble tubs, showers big enough to be equipped with breakfast nooks—in this water-starved region to run the shower just for the sound of it!, Jacuzzis, toilets with heated seats, a bidet for the Continental touch, and glass!, not even frosted or one-way glass or glass brick, but crystal-clear transparency so they could look out on the sky and mountains while taking a shit, and all this in the good old days, fifteen years ago, before the current age of excess. How they loved glass walls. Those men standing naked in their windows, surveying the city, imagining that no one sees them.

"Come with me to the lawyer," David says.

The lawyer is someone he's found in the Yellow Pages because none of the lawyers recommended by friends do immigration law.

It's a shabby office, but David's been told prosperous lawyers don't do this kind of thing.

He tells his wife's story: Cliff was a young architect, still paying off student loans and supporting her mother. Her firm sent her to do a walkthrough for a record producer up in the Hills. The guy had money, but a bad reputation as a client: demanding, erratic, his check always in the mail. The firm didn't really want the job, but he had too much money to just blow him off. So they sent Cliff. She walks in, and the client's in the sunken living room cutting up cocaine with a couple of other guys. It's all too much for her, and (David doesn't say this) she's pregnant and needs to pee. She rushes off to the bathroom and next thing she knows, the police are taking down the door.

The lawyer says, "She was convicted?"

"No," says David. "She couldn't afford a lawyer but she wasn't indigent and couldn't get a free one. I would have helped her," he's quick to add, "but she didn't call me. They offered her a deal. She pled guilty and they let her off with a suspended sentence: no fine, no jail time, nothing. She went right home."

"That's a conviction," says the lawyer. "A drug conviction. The sentence that counts is the one they didn't impose. Under the '96 immigration law, it means they can deport her."

"That's crazy," says David.

The lawyer shrugs. "It's the law."

"No, they can't," Matt says. "I studied this in school. If she was convicted back then, and the law wasn't passed till '96, it doesn't count. It's unconstitutional."

The lawyer shrugs. "The Constitution doesn't apply to people who aren't citizens."

"My mother's a *good* citizen," Matt says, except a citizen is exactly what she isn't.

David says, "OK, once she's gone, she's my wife. I can file papers for her, can't I? So she can come back."

The lawyer says, "She comes back, she's facing twenty years in federal prison." He lets that sink in. "Sometimes there's an adjustment that can be made." He says, "Call me as soon as you have her A Number."

David writes out a check for $3,000 and a few days later he'll phone with the A number and he'll never hear from the lawyer again. But for now, he's both stunned and, with faith in the lawyer, hopeful.

The videocamera picks up a gray car with a side panel perforated with bullet holes. At Roy and Figueroa, a man is shaking the security gate at Tita's Pupusería which is locked though the sign in the window reads ABIERTO/OPEN.

Cameras see inside the holding cell downtown, but don't hear the women crying. Someone says, "A dictator, he'd give general amnesty. A president hasn't got the courage to let us go. Fuck the millennium," she says. "Fuck democracy."

On Matt's desk in his dark bedroom, a blue science folder glares accusingly, marked with that B and the words: *Lots of facts, but you never tell us WHY the study is being done. What is its purpose?* The cover can't be reused now. Hasn't Mr. Ortega ever heard of recycling? There's a question for you.

He hated to be a grade-grubber, but he's a straight-A student, Science is *his* subject, and he hadn't thought this fair. How little he knew about unfairness back then! He'd gone to Mr. Ortega after class to complain. "Facts *always* imply a question," he said. "How do you organize them, give them context, make sense of them? Information is a perplex"—which Mr. Ortega, being of the pre-computer generation didn't understand—"facts without structure, you can arrange or combine them in a multitude of valid ways. *That's* what's important," Matt said, "not the *Why?*"

"You must be a fortunate young man," said Mr. Ortega. "People who've suffered *always* ask *Why?*"

"But what does that have to do with Science?"

Mr. Ortega said, "Your life must be very good if you never have to question it."

It was true that Courtney always asked, "Why is my father such an asshole? And why on earth did my mom marry him?"

I get it now, he thinks, I get it. Mr. Ortega was right. He was too complacent. Even a B was too good for him.

You have to question *everything*, he thinks. *Everything.*

Matt has questions now.

Q: What about my mom's Constitutional rights?

A: She's not a citizen and therefore has none.

Q: What about my dad's rights? What about mine? If she were property, you couldn't just take her away.

A: But she's not property.

Q: Are you blaming feminism?

A: No, the fault is your mother's. Why didn't she become a citizen?

Q: Hey, I'm asking the questions. She tried to.

Clifford Pearlstein put in her papers and waited more than five years. At last, they called her for the citizenship interview. She took the day off from work. She went downtown. She entered the office. Next thing she knew, there were handcuffs on her wrists, her legs were shackled. She was not to be a citizen, but a prisoner.

Matt walks Ruby, slamming the door, as he leaves the house, behind him. Ruby twists and whines and whimpers, not like herself at all. Does she smell a skunk or a coyote or just that something is very wrong? For a moment hers is a very suspect breed, though there's only one border we need to think about now. With reference to COLLIES, "borders" refers to the counties between England and Scotland, OK, not American, but clearly Anglo and white. And they're descended from reindeer-herding dogs brought by the Vikings. Cliff missed Christmas and now she'll miss the New Year too. Matt uses a plastic bag to pick up Ruby's shit and the desire surges through him to throw the mess on someone's lawn. But whose lawn? Not the Van Horns' who have cameras posted for just such an eventuality. Anyway, the enemy isn't here.

He doesn't get it. His mother speaks *English,* she's had a green card *forever,* his grandparents had a McDonald's franchise outside of Bangor, Maine; you can't get more American than that—and yet he almost envies Clifford her adventure. To be falsely accused, forced to endure, to prove yourself, ultimately to triumph. To learn ultimate things you'll never learn in school.

(What Cliff has already learned:

1. Women are better off with male guards. When you have your period, the men get embarrassed, and give you a napkin right away, even extras, so you won't have to ask again. The women pretend not to hear you, they ignore you, then humiliate you and call you dirty when you bleed.
2. They don't launder the jumpsuits very well. She is itching and scratching.
3. What she has, Mirta tells her, is *sarna*.
4. It's a new Spanish word for her: *sarna* means scabies.)

Aside from taking Ruby out, Matt doesn't leave the house until the morning he opens the door and can't believe his eyes: it's Courtney. The other day was such a disaster, he was afraid he wouldn't see her again.

She hands him a Christmas present which he doesn't open as he hasn't bought anything for her. They stand awkwardly in the doorway. He doesn't ask her in.

"So what's happening with your mother?"

He doesn't answer though he's hopeful this means she isn't prejudiced.

She says, "I told a friend, I hope that's OK, and it's kind of weird, but maybe she can help."

They ride their bikes, Courtney out front where he can see the way the seat rides beneath her. As if she feels him looking and doesn't like it, she slows till he catches up and then they pedal side by side.

Courtney says, "My mom says she and my father used to have New Year's parties with everybody naked. But she says people reveal more about their true selves when they keep their clothes on."

Matt makes a noncommittal sound. He still has hopes for New Year's.

A postal worker with a cart stops them and demands to know why they're not in school.

"It's a holiday, asshole," says Courtney, "Or haven't you heard?"

"Not very attractive language, young lady. And where's your helmet?"

"It takes a village," says Matt.

"Sir! Sir!" Now the guy's bugging a grownup who's smoking a cigarette in front of Tony's Burgers. "What are you doing here? Don't you work? Where are you supposed to be?"

Courtney's friend calls herself Windsong which she says is English for her Hebrew name. Matt's father says Jewish law forbids tattoos, but Windsong's sweater is low off the shoulder to show off the ankh and rose gracing her arm. Her bedroom is red: red drapes, red wallpaper, red comforter on the bed, the windows done in what she herself calls "genital pink" with a little black framing for depth.

"It sounds like there could be a diabolical negativity," Windsong says.

"But going against the government—that's a biggie. We're going to have to call up Beelzebub."

Matt asks if you can believe in the Devil if you don't believe in God.

"You must believe in God," Courtney says. "How can anyone not believe in God?"

"I don't," he says.

"Your arrogance is misplaced," Windsong says. "You mustn't harbor resentment against Her."

Courtney says, "We don't know for sure that God is a woman."

"What we do know," says Windsong, "the Supreme Deity definitely prefers the female pronoun."

"So God's a drag queen," Matt says.

"You're pretty sure of yourself," Windsong says. "You could end up in trouble."

She boots up her computer. Access to Beelzebub is through the Demonology Chat Room.

"That's it," Matt says. "My mother's locked up and you thinks it's a game."

"We're trying to help," says Courtney.

"You're enjoying it a tad too much," he says.

"She should have become a citizen," says Windsong, and even though Courtney touches his arm, he storms out, alone.

Why didn't she become a citizen? She didn't apply till Grandma Rose died, and now they're fucked.

Perhaps it's an evil thing to become a citizen. It reveals something disloyal and opportunistic about you. No matter how much you love the United States, how do you stand there and say you renounce the land where you were born? Maybe you came here waiting for a change in the government, or because you were starving, but that doesn't mean you don't love your homeland. Matt thinks you can't ask this of a person with a heart. It's like a widow who remarries. Her first husband is dead, but you don't ask her to stand before the altar and repudiate him and deny him before she's allowed to remarry. (Matt never knew either grandfather. Neither grandmother remarried. He remembers, as a child, asking his father, "Why do only men die?") Will his father remarry?

My mother has a heart, he thinks.

He thinks about her all the time, which isn't fair. A fifteen-year-old boy shouldn't be thinking about his mother. He should be thinking about Courtney which is what he used to do. Trying to figure her out, trying to figure out how to get into her pants, especially the fake snakeskin tight ones.

He should be thinking about New Year's Eve.

He can't quite believe it. A week ago, all he had to concern him was an unfair grade and whether he was going to lose his virginity.

Matt's not quite a geek, but he never expected girls to be calling him up, certainly not Courtney. (He sees himself as shy and clumsy, but girls—at least some—see him as a young animal whose awkwardness is endearing.) When Courtney phoned in September and asked him to the movies, he was overwhelmed. Of course he realized from the start that they were very different. "I only go to action flicks," she'd told him then, "the crappier, the better," and when he said his favorite film ever was *Shakespeare in Love*, she dismissed it as a dumb love story tricked out with significance. "*Titanic*," she sneered, "without the boat." They went to see *The 13th Warrior* which would have been impossible to sit through if she hadn't been beside him, and afterwards they went back to her house where her mother wasn't home. She wasn't really into kissing, but she took off her bra and her bare breast was a miracle, how good it was to touch skin and warm flesh, how good it would be to feel his own bare flesh pressed against hers, skin to skin. How could people know this and yet bear to spend most of their days, even whole lives, not touching? How did people keep from falling all over each other all the time? (He *does* ask questions!) Her bra fastened in the front, and when she put it on again she started from the straps in back, like a cop, he thought, getting into a shoulder holster. He still hasn't figured out if he's in awe of her or terrified.

After that night, she didn't call again and when he called her she was always busy.

"What did I do wrong? he finally dared ask.

"Nothing," she said. "You go out with someone to get to know them. You're so quiet in school. I gave you a call.... I just wanted to give you a try."

"And when you got to know me... what did I do wrong?"

"Nothing," she said. "What's the big deal?"

He tried to forget about her, and couldn't, and then all of a sudden, she called about the Rose Bowl floats. "I don't want to go alone, and it seemed like something you would do."

Not exactly flattering, but she also mentioned she had vowed to lose her virginity to celebrate the millennium. She didn't say to *him,* but she did say *to someone trustworthy* and he had hopes.

Sometimes he came just imagining what it would be like inside her. When he remembers how much he used to feel, he has to struggle not to cry, because now all of that is ruined, because of his mother.

Instead of making love with Courtney, he spends New Year's Eve at home with his father and Minfong. (*Min,* he thinks. She's so lovely, and Minfong sounds harsh and male.)

"She has nowhere else to go," his father says. "I didn't want to cancel."

Matt says, "It's just a date on the calendar."

"We can use the distraction," says David.

"Maybe I don't want to be distracted."

But he accompanies his father through the supermarket and then the Asian grocery preparing for their American version of a Chinese feast, a teenager and parent shopping together, a retro vision of family togetherness in the face of Cliff's absence.

"I think cold sesame noodles to start," David says, "and dumplings from Trader Joe's." How can he think about a menu? Shrimp and tofu in oyster sauce, mixed vegetables, sliced beef in black bean sauce. Fortune cookies, oranges. But they can't find the American bamboo Minfong says she's partial to, only cans from Thailand, China, and the Philippines. David keeps looking.

He must be fucking her, Matt thinks.

Minfong arrives late, and shaken. She was on the bus, she tells them, when two men boarded through the rear door. The driver shut off the engine and radioed the police. The men walked up to the fare box and argued that the news said it was free today, but they were willing to pay. The driver wouldn't accept their money and wouldn't budge.

Was America always like this, Matt wonders, and I just never noticed?

"Two police cars come," Minfong tells them. "Four cops. And at same time, next bus."

When the driver opened the doors for the police, everyone but

Minfong fled out the back. She watched the other passengers board the new bus and go on their way. The police laughed at her for waiting and wished her a Happy New Year. They were still listening to the angry bus driver twenty minutes later when the next bus came and she got on it.

"It's all lies," says Matt. "This country."

"Matt—" says his father.

"Not all," says Minfong.

They eat dinner in front of the TV, watching the crowds around the world. Matt broods, but eats plenty, in spite of everything, he's always hungry. Min praises the food. It turns out "American bamboo" is just the direct translation of "asparagus."

"Oh, sorry. We could have found that easy," David says.

She's made leek cakes—something they've never come across in any Chinese restaurant. Matt pretends to like them, and eats three so that David won't have to.

"Cliff?" Min asks.

"We haven't been able to see her. Your husband?" David asks.

She brightens. "I speak to him today by phone," she says. "In Beijing."

She hasn't seen him since May, she tells them. Matt bristles. Is she suggesting their separation from Cliff is easy?

May, he thinks. Unless she's fucking my dad, she probably hasn't had sex since May. No, she can't be fucking my dad, he thinks. She works for him. That would be sexual harassment. Maybe then tonight, he, Matt, will get to fuck her, a thought so exciting that he hates himself.

"Of course I'll drive you home," David offers. "Though I'd prefer if you spent the night." Of course, thinks Matt. "So I can have some champagne and not worry about driving."

Matt makes up the bed for Min in his grandmother's old room. And later that night, when he can't fall asleep, he opens her door and sees her sleeping there alone and stands on the threshold, just watching.

And what is Cliff doing, as the new century begins without her? She's on the bus again, in transit, seeing firsthand how quiet L.A. is this night. Sitting beside her, Mirta cries quietly and repeats again, "I want to go home." She lives (or, before this, used to) in East L.A. She names the street, one that Cliff has studied and knows well. They close their eyes and each sees a geranium in a second-floor window.

And Cliff, crying too, begins to think she's always been homeless.

In Bangor, Maine I sought my homeland. The lost birthplace I never knew. I haunted The Canteener, that dreary lunch spot with its sterile vending machines, thinking Cantina, cantina, and each time I walked through the door, such disappointment!, as though I truly expected to be transported to Mexico. My dates, few though they were, had to take me to the Oronoko, named not for the river, but for Orono, the college town, where we ate steamed clams and I imagined myself in South America, imagined parrots and music and a sudden awakening in my blood. It was almost as if I sought it, that calculated disequilibrium, one place superimposed faultily upon another, the peculiar excitement or contamination engendered by a name. I never learned from disappointment, each time the door, the threshold, hypnotized me with its power. There was always a moment on the brink as I stood poised for the invasion of nostalgia, my longing for things unremembered and therefore stolen.

"Let's move the bodies," says a guard.

They enter the prison.

She thinks, I am buried alive.

•3•

"Remember when Grandma drank those rum and Cokes and Desirée sniffed her breath and wouldn't sleep in her bed?" Matt asks.

"Remember when Mom forgot to pit the cherries before she baked that pie?"

Night after night, they reminisce about both women, fondly, as if Cliff, too, is dead.

Matt remembers asking his mother, "Was it hard being Mexican in Bangor?"

"No one really thought of me that way," Cliff answered, then shrugged: "Up there, they have French-Canadians to hate." She didn't tell him the Yankees figured *she* was French-Canadian, dark with Indian blood.

No one at school thinks of Matt as Mexican. He's fair-skinned except for freckles (though he does know Mexicans who are blue-eyed and blond), and he's taking French in school instead of Spanish. "So I can study in Paris like you did," he said. (Cliff was disappointed and he had to say something. But what if he wasn't good at Spanish? Wouldn't that disappoint her more? When he thought himself Mexican, he always felt he was pretending.)

When she heard bad news, his grandmother used to cross herself and blow into her fist. ("Just a habit," she said. "I'm not a believer.") Now Matt brings his thumb and forefinger together and tries it, with a prayer, but his mother doesn't appear. It's as though his mother doesn't exist. Until they give her a bed in San Pedro, Cliff might as well be a ghost.

He asked his grandmother once if she believed in ghosts. He'd been told all Mexicans talked to the dead. "You can't talk to the dead in America," she told him. "They don't live here."

At the Site Where Vision Is Most Perfect

Matt knows he isn't Mexican the way other Mexicans are Mexican, though maybe they aren't either? There must be parts of him he doesn't even know about like the way he assumed till he was twelve that "chanclas" was an ordinary English word. ("Where are my chanclas?"—Grandma Rose searching for the old shoes she wore as house slippers. "Don't let that dog eat my chanclas!"—as though well-behaved Ruby ever would!, the shoes that made a *chank chank chank* sound—not Spanish at all—as she walked.)

His grandmother spoke English, though in public she sometimes pretended not to. She didn't make tamales. ("I couldn't get the ingredients in Maine, and here, why bother when you can get perfectly good ones at the corner?")

She taught him to respect the rule of law and never to look down on Mexico. "We left because of your grandfather's enemies," she said. "Nochixtlán was so beautiful. But a little town, isolated. No law," she told him. "No police. Remarkable, Matt, that there was so little crime. It was peaceful there because the people of Nochixtlán are peaceful and honest. But without the rule of law, for a person like your grandfather, sometimes a little town like that can be unsafe."

His grandfather had been a bracero in the U.S. during WW II; he'd done a great favor for the American who eventually helped him settle in, of all places, Maine.

Matt had never asked: His grandfather, a scarcely literate Indian from Nochixtlán—what had he done to make such enemies, and how had he made such a powerful friend?

He never asked the right questions, and neither did Cliff. Roselia told her, "Your papa swore to me he never killed no one," and Cliff had never asked, "Did you believe him?" All she knew was that when she was twelve, her father made an urgent trip to Nochixtlán and what returned was his body in a coffin. The little girl stayed haunted by the fear: something in Mexico was going to get her.

In Maine, *Gutiérrez* had become *Guterson*. *Roselia* became *Rose*. To be American, or to be hidden?

And Desirée was proof of his grandmother's assimilation. She used to make fun of Americans—so silly, how they loved their cats!, until dying, she expressed the sudden wish for a kitten and she treated the little gray cat like a miracle child.

These are the simple facts of his family.

That his mother did her graduate work in Paris and went to conferences in Montreal.

That his father has spoken at conferences in Italy and Argentina and Japan.

That he has been to Mexico once, on a (boring) family vacation in Mazatlán.

That when Roselia passed, Desirée wriggled under the comforter on the bed and stayed there trembling and eventually accepted Cliff but never took to David or to Matt.

That both grandmothers had accents and a horror of drafts, though Grandma Ida was more likely to say, *Put a sweater on, wear a scarf*, while Grandma Rose went around shutting windows.

Sometimes Grandma Ida and David joked in Yiddish.

Sometimes Grandma Rose spoke to Cliff in Spanish. His mother seemed to understand, but always answered in English. Now Matt thinks one of the weirdest things is that the first time they hear from her, the only thing inside the envelope is a poem that he reads without understanding:

At the Site Where Vision Is Most Perfect

Mariposa negra
en las alas te han puesto cadena
y mi condena
es acordarme siempre de tí.

First Visit:

January 15. Cliff has been detained for twenty-three days. She now has a bed! And for the first time will be permitted visitors. (Though no one will be permitted inside the pod. Families are not allowed in, or the press or TV. Amnesty International has been turned away.)

Visiting hours begin at 8:00 a.m. David and Matt arrive and find almost fifty people already lined up at the gate. They take their places and wait. The line moves slowly and Matt is worried. His father has a driver's license, but he has nothing and the woman in front of them says without a birth certificate or passport he won't be allowed in. At 10:50, the guard comes out of his booth and says, "That's it. The rest of you, line up earlier next time."

Second Visit:

They get in line at 6:30 and are the first to be admitted, first past the booth, then inside the building where they have to show ID and leave their jackets, wallets, watches in a locker. Then wait again for Cliff to be brought down.

"You have five minutes," says the guard.

The visiting room—the size of a phone booth—is too small for both David and Matt to fit at the same time. "You go first," says David. "Dad, she'll want to see you," and they continue this Alphonse and Gaston act till the guard reminds them "Four minutes left."

David goes in, and comes out again and calls the guard. "The phone doesn't work. I can't hear her."

The guard shrugs. The door closes.

When it's Matt's turn, he can't believe what he sees through the window, his mother's haggard face and unwashed hair, her chapped lips opening and closing, and time runs out in an instant so that it might not even have been his mother but an image projected oh so briefly on some sinister fearful screen.

She writes:

Dear Matt,

During the weeks I rode the bus, I looked forward to being imprisoned with all the nostalgic anticipation of a return home. To have a constant roof over my head! A bed of my own!

I have a bed!

And a constant roof. One hour a day, we're let out into a crowded yard. Aside from that, no sky, no air, no sun. And since we're never allowed out at night, since I've stopped riding the bus, there's been no moon.

I live in a shadow world. I fought it at first, it seemed a border-crossing that might be irrevocable. Then I gave in and then I had no choice. Think of rape fantasies. That's what I want you to understand. Think that in fantasy, a rape is not rape but stands for something: being swept away, of emotional flood (that oceanic feeling!), of the grateful relinquishing of responsibility and control, in short, the ideal sexual moment we are taught to crave and rarely if ever experience with the silly clumsy men we have consensual sex with. (I'm not talking from personal experience. I love your father. The "we" is social, the socialized female American self, it has nothing to do with me, it is not I, who loves my husband and has never been raped even in fantasy.) I admit I have at times in my life fantasized being suddenly and unjustly arrested. I've imagined being alcoholic, or addicted, or imprisoned, being someone whose circumstances made it inevitable that she should let people down. Matt, don't be like me. I never knew how to say no to anyone, which is why I put off becoming a citizen, for your grandmother's sake. I never wanted to disappoint. Now I can't help it.

It could be this is the best thing that ever happened to me. The song the band played when I married your father.

(Your father, she writes. Not *David.* She can't even let herself think his name. Those first three weeks when she couldn't reach him and he could not reach her, she panicked—abandonment—and her heart squeezed with pain: *David, David.* She knows better now, but *David, David* still sends her reeling.*)*

I'm happy here, she writes her son. *Don't worry about me. This experience is doing me good.*

But you're too smart and sane to believe me. It is a horror. It is an unending horror. Sorry, I don't mean to upset you. It's not a rape that at least comes to an end and leaves you with the overwhelming task—but still a task, a concrete defined task, and I've always been good at tasks—the task of reconstructing a self and a life. There is no indication when this will end. No one can say—there's no sentence, no one tells me when I'll see the judge. No books no magazines. Nothing to do. Eighty women crowded in a little room. Screaming guards. They're rent-a-cops, not INS or Corrections, untrained and probably minimum wage. They let me see the nurse to get a prescription for the scabies, but wouldn't let Mirta. "No English; no medicine." I said I'd translate and they said, "Mind your own business." I asked one of them, "Why do you hate us?" She said, "They don't pay us to like you."

I would feel sorry for them, their frozen hearts, if they didn't have me in their power.

The TV blaring night and day. Guards shutting off the hot water without notice while you're in the shower. Ha ha ha. Guards frisking you each time you enter the cafeteria and each time you leave, tearing your bed apart every day looking for contraband clothing, although where on earth would we obtain it? I can't tell you how I fantasize about clean underwear. Maybe the worst of it is being locked up with all these hysterical women. Doesn't anyone wonder what goes on behind these walls? At a certain point I slipped into this foggy place where the days run together in a dream and I can tell myself I'm free for the first time and happy. The pills they gave me for my nerves helped of course. They didn't help me, the real me, they helped drop me into this state of consciousness in which I can make sense of nothing which makes sense since all of this is senseless.

The worst thing is, people are afraid of me. It hurts so much, Matt. The undocumented women, decent simple women from the countryside of Mexico and Guatemala, women from simple places like Nochixtlán—they've been warned about the Girls in Red, the violent criminals like your mother. In here, you forget what it's like to be treated as human. I would listen to them, touch an arm, hold a crying woman's hand, but Matt, they are afraid of me.

It's OK. Guess what we eat? Lunchables! The crackers are stale and the cheese snaps apart. Mirta shows me the expiration date on the package. The date means nothing to me. Time means nothing. They say there's going to be a full lunar eclipse tonight. Poor Tycho Brown. If he's on-duty, he'll miss it.

I treasure each trip to the cafeteria because I've come up with a way to stay sane. I must build. I've been collecting the building blocks, very carefully, one piece at a time, bits of paper napkin dyed brown with coffee. I mold them into adobe bricks, into logs and tiles and slip them inside my bra, now that I have a bra, where they dry and when I have enough, I'll start to build.

And when they deport me to the homeland I never knew—It's all like a dream. As a child, I longed for that place that was mine, of which I was a part, I was a daughter of that always unknown soil. Can an act be both injustice and restitution?

I LOVE YOU.

Is this a letter you want from your mother? Matt thinks his father has a right to read it, and yet what he really wants to do is hide it somewhere where it won't be found.

P.S. Please don't come back, she writes. *I don't want you to see me this way.*

She writes, *Just get me a lawyer.*

The first lawyer never gets in touch with Cliff and doesn't return calls, so David calls someone he heard about from someone in line. This lawyer says she'll find a sympathetic D.A. to reopen the old drug case but it will cost and there's no guarantee and she can't represent him till he fires the first one. He does, and files a new appointment form, and pays her, up front, $5,000. Eventually, he'll fire her, too, and hire still a third who asks for $10,000, most of it, he says, to pay a necessary bribe. David can't believe Americans take bribes, but he never would have believed any of this could happen, and so, after sleeping on it for a night, he'll write the check and never again hear from that lawyer either.

"I wish there was someone we could bribe," Mirta tells Cliff. "It's a better system. It's personal. Someone pays attention to your case and listens to you. Sometimes, you just smile and they let you go. In this country," she says, "once they get you, you're forgotten."

Matt, she writes. *They say there are a thousand of us being held in Southern California. Why aren't there a thousand yellow ribbons?*

There are women here who've been transferred after serving prison terms in full. What about double jeopardy, they ask? If you ask about your right to a speedy trial, the guards laugh at you for imagining such notions apply.

Why aren't you tying ribbons on the trees?

David is doing everything he can but apparently Cliff thinks he's let her down. How else explain—it leaves him feeling unsettled, disoriented, resentful—that she never writes to him, but only Matthew?

· 4 ·

David and Cliff love each other, they do things together, share things, they have Matthew, yet David suspects she's always wanted more from him. (He's right.) What if she sees this—what he sees as their tragedy—as a chance to leave him behind guiltlessly and start over?

He sleeps on the living room floor. He can't sleep in the bed where she isn't.

At the lab, David catches Robert crouched beside the jars, speaking softly (through the glass, no less) to fruit flies. Less a robot, then, but no less weird. But who could be more weird than David? Trained as a doctor, and when's the last time he looked at a human eye? Or even at the compound eye of one of these winged creatures? The lab techs mix up the agar, tegosept, dextrose, and something real—cornmeal? yeast?—to feed them. Robert uses the feather tool and CO^2. When has David touched a living creature at work—even one of the third instar larvae he's spent the last two years on? He does computer analysis, he reads everyone else's report and takes a look through a microscope now and then at the thickened polytene chromosomes, recognizable as bar codes. He sees those bands and reads them as if they're something real and now he thinks of the jokes going around about Larry Shimkoff who is said to jerk off looking at PET scans that show sexual arousal though at least no one has ever suggested these are brain scans of subjects other than human.

Robert rises slowly and says, "Have you got a moment? We need to talk."

The "we" includes Minfong.

David is surprised to see this mismatched pair in obvious complicity. They urge him down corridors, past students and post-docs, looking for an empty conference room, somewhere private, where they tell him kindly, but in no uncertain terms, that he ought to stay home.

He's not doing the project any good but, as Robert reminds him, staff retention is a major factor in grant renewal. "We'll cover for you," Robert says. "If we have to stay all night analyzing data, we'll do it."

David says something about not wanting to ask so much of them.

"Not for your sake," Robert says. "If it's known we need a new director..." If it's known the current director wanders about befuddled... "The project goes down..."

They all go down. Minfong blushes. She'll lose her work permit and be sent back to China. Where she belongs, David thinks, with her husband.

"No," David says, though in truth he's not entirely sure what he's most reacting to. He's a man whose eyes hurt and who's losing his hair and whose wife is inexplicably imprisoned and he's neglected his family devoting years to the genetics of fruit flies when he could have been a surgeon, doing cataracts and lasers, no emergencies, regular hours you set yourself and more money than you know what to do with. (Deprived of Cliff's salary, he's gone through their savings and has begun to do what he swore he wouldn't—plunder Matt's college fund. "Why not?" asked Matt, "I'm not going anyway.") "No," he says. "I have work to do here," but his heart tells him he can't be in this place anymore, the floral prints on the walls, the soothing pinks and mauves you find in hospitals and time-share resorts, the conference room that consists of a long scarred table and shag rug and a VCR, his cubicle with its desk and inboxes and always on-line computer, the shared printer down the hall spitting out reports that overflow the tray so there's always a spill of paper on the floor, the lab with microscope workplace and the vials and bottles, the flies you can't hear buzz which are fertile within the day and lay the eggs to keep the whole show going, the hundreds of larvae eating and moulting and eating and eating and eating, first instar, second, the crucial third, the point of all this (what *is* the point?), the pupa, the CO^2 knockout gun, the Petri dishes and tray-packed vials, boxes of cheesecloth and foam plugs, the autoclave in the corner and, through the door, the food prep room he's never even entered. How could this all have been so important—and he so indispensable—when today it seems he can walk out for good without a backwards glance?

"No," he says, but the very next morning, the familiar drive to work defeats him. He exits the 405 on Sunset instead of continuing to Wilshire as he usually does. The route isn't determined by him, but by a replica of him, that is, his wife Cliff: this is her route.

They never commuted together. He always worked late. *Good at tech* was the rap on him. No teaching faculty berth for him, with normal hours. No private practice income. *Good at tech*—and he was damn good and it trapped him. A life sentence in the lab that's maybe been commuted on humanitarian grounds. Let him out, his wife is fucked.

Now he finds himself approaching the northeast end of campus, her end, exactly where he doesn't want to be, not the south end which is his.

And he realizes he doesn't want to be there, in his own lab, either. *My wife,* he thinks, and it's the strangest word, it has no resonance for him now, my whistle, my stick, my window, my what. He can't concentrate, he doesn't want to. He'd hoped that concentrating would block out thinking, and without thinking of her, no fear, no feeling, it would all work out, but it's not working.

He comes around Dead Man's Curve, expecting to feel a certain magnetism left here from her daily passage. He feels nothing.

He's written letters, Senators Boxer and Feinstein, Janet Reno, the President. He's hired lawyers. He's seen her in that terrible phone booth. He's worked and voted, paid his taxes. And now his double driving the car continues taking the curves on Sunset. The campus is left behind. He ends up in West Hollywood, the McDonald's at Crescent Heights. *Cliff,* he thinks, *Bangor,* clutching the steering wheel, trembling.

Matt ditches school and rides his bike to Sepulveda Dam. Why should he go to school? He thinks of Mr. Ortega saying, "Why don't you kids challenge anything? *Anything*? I can understand that for some people, it's counterproductive to question the status quo, but you don't live in Beverly Hills. Look around you! This is Van Nuys!"

And Danny Khan said, "But if I want to end up in Beverly Hills, won't listening to you hurt my chances?"

If Matt were in school right now, he'd go up to Mr. Ortega and say, "You're right, but you're wrong about *me*. You have no idea what's happening to me," but it's no one's—certainly not his science teacher's—business.

The traffic gets a bit scary as you approach the freeway ramps and head up the slope, though he would never admit it gets him nervous. It's not all that scenic, but there's good flat areas where you can ride fast. He wishes Courtney were riding here with him, and he thinks about the pumping of her legs, the wind tickling her scalp through her cropped blond hair. That day as they biked over to Windsong's, she'd turned to him and said, "Don't you think Jesus had a beautiful smell?" What she really said was *smile, beautiful smile.* "Smile," he repeated, "I thought you said—" and that was the last time they laughed together. Now there's the cricket field where you need a permit and he's never seen anyone playing. The picnic area where people let their dogs run, and if he were old enough to drive, he'd bring Ruby. That will never happen now. Before he's old enough to get a license, he'll be gone. A sign says *Patrolled by Plainclothes Officers—Avoid Lewd Behavior* and he looks up to watch the flight of a goose overhead and then another. Two solitary birds, when he always thought a flock flew in a V. They're not migrating, just hanging out, he thinks. No one's forcing *them* across the border. He thinks Mr. Ortega is not being fair. What about all the kids who do volunteer work, those Asian girls in their club with the red T-shirts: SERVICE BEFORE SELF. He acts like no one cares. "Which of you went to Seattle?" Why the hell should they go to Seattle? It's hard enough to get a ride out to Azusa. The sun is beating down, Matt's leaking sweat, but there's a carpet of fallen golden leaves. He thinks sometimes L.A. does have four seasons, but all at the same time: other trees are shimmering with the soft new green the past night's drizzle tricked into an early spring, and over on the island, there's what looks like a hundred cormorants with a couple of dozen scattered about on the bare wintry branches of the trees. He tries to take it in, because it's part of what he's losing. Click.

Click. 9:00 a.m. At 97th and Wilmington, a black man on a ladder is painting over the SOUL in SOUL FOOD.

Noon: He's replacing SOUL with GOOD. GOOD FOOD and he adds in script, red letters on a whitewashed wall, BUNEA COMIDA! Click.

At Clifton and LaPeer in Beverly Hills, a woman in a red leather coat makes a kissy face at a Malamute in the window of a parked car. Click.

At Grant High, Latino and Armenian kids are signing a peace treaty, and Mr. Ortega begins class with an announcement. "It's official. At a time of unparalleled prosperity, the gap between rich and poor is growing greater, nowhere more so than here in Southern California."

"Let them work," Courtney says. "My parents work."

"Tell that to your gardener. Tell it to the home health-care workers getting minimum wage if they're lucky and no health insurance. Tell that to the men and women in the sweatshops."

Courtney says, "This has nothing to do with Science."

At Third and Muirfield, an orange sports car pulls into the circular drive at Cliff's favorite house: the white one with the filigreed fence and twenty statues of David—Michelangelo's, not hers—on the roof and lawn. There's no contradiction here: after growing up with the cold and crampedness of personality in Maine, Cliff loves the shamefree way L.A. people express their private fantasies, outsider art by people with money. She'll applaud any individual vision as long as no architect is implicated.

Click click click. With every click she sees her home, what she'll be losing. She doesn't dare think about her husband and her son. If she's sent off into a foreign land, will they—does she dare to think of it?—will they go with her?

She writes:

They are always screaming at the little Chinese women. These are some very tiny women. They are probably no more fragile than the rest of us, but the guards take special pleasure in abusing them.

There's a Canadian woman they're always confusing me with as her last name is Clifford. I promised, remember, that I would tell you about my companions. She says, "You know who they let in? They wanted to hang a man in Washington State, and no one knew how to do it. They found a Turkish executioner. He *got a work permit. That's the kind of immigrant they want in America." You know what else Jean Clifford says? In America, on the night when someone is executed, the guards show pornographic films to the other inmates, using sex to take their minds off death, or else—I wonder—to move their minds to that subterranean realm where they'll never be able to separate the two.*

Matt asks, Why does my mother write me these things? He thinks, It's not fair. I just want to be normal.

She writes, *A Cambodian man threw himself beneath the wheels of the bus the other day—I can't say which day, I've lost track of the divisions of time. When we heard that someone had escaped from this hell, a man from El Salvador hanged himself in the bath. We can't have any more hangings. They have confiscated our sheets. We can't have books. You could poke out someone's eye with the hard edge. Or magazines—rolled up, ditto.*

This is how my mind works now, in fragments, but not jumpy, the fragments run together, as fluid as a tiger's leap, my mind racing racing leaping flying only every now and then it just stops. Like a computer screen freezing. God bless CAD, though I haven't given up the pencil. I was always good at the quick sketch on a paper napkin. But I'm not meticulous, Matt. My mind going faster than the hand could follow—what a mess I made of presentations with Letraset. I was born for the computer. When it starts up again, sometimes something is lost, sometimes it all comes back. It's the stress. It's the meds. It's not having paper to write it down. It's like a prisoner in the gulag, or some South African prison, it's like everything you've read about that they do in Those Countries, not here, and those prisoners who wrote poems in their heads and memorized them, I think of them, however did they do it? Their brains so much better organized than mine. You'd call mine a perplex. Your favorite word—sometimes I chant it over and over, perplex, perplex, because I miss you.

Otilia just got word that the bank foreclosed on her home. She's been in here six months, waiting for a hearing. Her five-year-old is with her sister. First she lost her job, then her car, now the house. She says her papers are in order. Eventually, they'll have to let her go, but she's lost so much. After years and years of work. How will she ever be made whole?

Nho married her GI at age sixteen. He brought her here, her lord and master, her father and mother. He got her hooked on heroin, beat her, left her. Her criminal record: multiple convictions for prostitution and drugs. You ask me, she's a casualty of the war, they ought to pin a medal on her. Instead they want to send her back to Vietnam and Vietnam won't take her. She seems remarkably sane for someone who's been locked up here three years. Sometimes she grows silent and distant. I don't know if she's using some ancient Asian meditation technique or if she goes to the same place I assume that I go, a place like cyberspace, where you exist in some nonphysical form, your life and suffering turned to retrievable data though for a sweet blessed space of unfelt time the machine is down.

In the mail, David gets a ticket for going through a red light in Beverly Hills. He's sure it never happened, but a surveillance camera caught it. He could not have gone through a light without noticing, though he admits these days his attention wanders.

The TV drones on about the police corruption scandal.

"Corruption," says David. "That used to mean a cop taking a free meal. Now they frame a guy and shoot him in the back of the head and call it corruption."

"Is this a police state?" asks Matt, and David suddenly feels guilty at the cynicism he's imparting to his son.

This is early in the second month of Cliff's detention, when her two men are still eating meals together, still trying to make the household work.

"Cynicism is *good,*" Matt says. "How can you be sane and not cynical?"

David thinks they've reached the place where a thing becomes its opposite. When democracy betrays itself, the treachery must be hidden. Government brutality in America isn't aimed at intimidating the populace. It's even more brutal because it happens in secret, in the dark, but its hiddenness betrays its own deep shame. How can this happen in America? The very question proves he still believes America different, and better.

"I'm cynical," Matt says. "But I hate the people who run things when *they* are."

"Who do you think runs things?" David asks.

"*All* of them," Matt says. "The people who produce movies, and video games, who publish books." Mr. Ortega wanted them to protest: the Disney video game in which to move up a level you have to kill a Mexican. "I don't even mean that," says Matt. "Everyone complains about sex and racism and violence. It's not just that. It's that they don't even pretend, they don't even hide it that all they care about is money. They don't care if you're hungry for something to think about or something to believe in, or something that keeps you going, something that tells you the truth. All they want is your money and they want you to be stupid so that you're empty. Isn't that what they want? They want you to stay empty and stupid so that you buy things. And they know it and they do it anyway and I hate them."

In detention, the TV is blaring, the detainees arguing over which channel—Spanish or English. On the English language news, an earnest reporter says, "Not *everyone* achieves the American Dream." On the Spanish news, "Not *every* American Dream is betrayed."

Everything is falling apart. Grandma Rose used to prepare the meals, American meals, pot roast, chicken. After she died, Cliff did most of the cooking though David enjoyed producing the occasional extravaganza, e.g., the New Year's Eve dinner, and for the first weeks of Cliff's captivity, Matt and David cooked together, a time when they could talk while chopping or else feel connected even if they didn't talk. Now, no one cooks, or cleans.

Matt and David don't consult, so each brings home boxes of frozen pizza, hot dogs, salami, salad-in-a-bag, garlicky take-out chicken, lamahjun and spinach borek from the Armenian bakery (Matt) and sardines, noodle ramen, and yes, Lunchables from the 99¢ Store (David). Never McDonald's. Sacks of dog food, cat food, and cat litter pile up in the hallways, along with dirty clothes. (David dumps laundry and detergent in the washing machine, then takes the clothes out an hour later having forgotten to turn the washer on.)

Matt eats in front of his computer, obsessively checking the latest news on Elián González. He's convinced their fates are intertwined: if Elián goes home to his father in Cuba, Matt will stay in the U.S. If Elián stays with his relatives in Florida, the U.S. will owe Mexico Matt. His father says Nature generates symmetries. A sacrifice, a simple trade.

David eats on his feet, wandering aimlessly around the house, dropping food that Ruby gobbles down.

Minfong shows up one night with groceries. She prepares three steaks, French fries, salad, and asparagus. The men squirm in their seats and Matt wipes his mouth on his shirtsleeve. David offers her a ride home before the table's even cleared, not—Matt is sure—to get her alone, but to get rid of her.

When Matt gets a letter from his mother, he leaves it open on the kitchen table, but doesn't know if David bothers looking through the unread newspapers and the mail. (David does find every one of Cliff's letters, though until DWP shows up in March to shut off their water, he neglects to open bills.)

This slow disintegration moves rather quickly.

At night, they move around without the lights on to avoid seeing the mess or each other and the less able they are to cope, the more they start to suspect they deserve it.

David sends money to her account so Cliff can buy a phone card. She usually manages to call them in the evening, but she's not very communicative on the phone. And for three nights she doesn't call at all. They have no way of knowing: she was taken to Jeanne Clifford's hearing before the judge, protesting the mistake, she was Clifford Pearlstein. No one bothered to check her ID, and for this insubordination, the hearing was postponed and she was given seventy-two hours lock-up in solitary.

She never tells them this. Instead:

Isn't it interesting how foreigners bring a new perspective? There's an Englishwoman here, got picked up at the airport when she came to see her grandchild. They waved her into another room. Secondary inspection. They didn't search her. She sat for two hours while a silent guard stood watch. Then they handcuffed her and shackled her feet.

"What is it about America," she asks, "that nothing seems to work? But of all the U.S. cities, I do like L.A. best. It's most like London."

Most like London! Can you imagine! She says we, too, have a financial center and the rest of the city is all spread out, each neighborhood with its own special character, its own shops and restaurants and—get this—"not at all like Atlanta, where one needs a car."

And one night on the phone, she says, "I can always be an architect in Mexico," slurring the words, is he imagining it? David thinks she said *a narchitect*. "They need houses, too. Specialized facilities." Does she mean Mexicans? Or narcotraficantes? Is he imagining this, that she'll build bunkers and labs and subterranean mansions underneath the landing strips? Matt was listening on the other phone, but David doesn't ask him if he heard it, too. Matt heard something. David sees the letters drawn on his son's hand, tattoo-style: ANARCHY TECH.

Matt ranges about with Ruby, letting her shit where she will. Sometimes he buries his face in her fur or stares minute after minute into her sweet brown eyes. He carries a marker concealed in his overgrown hand, scrawls swastikas (what could be worse than that?) on walls, several at Valley College where once upon a time his mother set up a program to teach computer graphics to teenage prostitutes—his bleeding-heart mother, always "giving back to the community," making her civic contribution. Lately he's begun to get used to her absence, taking her imprisonment for granted. He fights the slippage into numbness. With each scrawl, he feels the kind of crazed confused arousal it seems to him he ought to feel. Another swastika and his heart misses a beat, not from the fear of being seen, it's enough that he has seen himself and the venom sweating in him. If they catch him, he wants to tell them: *No, I don't listen to death rock. No, I don't play violent video games. I am not an innocent victim or a symptom,* defiant, bewildered. *I am I!*, he thinks, doing the impossible, the unthinkable, in harmony with the fucked up world around him.

On the 5800 block of Tobias, where he knows not a soul, he lobs a rock through a random window. The window breaks, but he doesn't, the experience enters him in slow-motion, deafening, calm, and cold.

He reads, *The Turkish hangman is not a legend! I have met his wife! She came to visit him and they got her. Their little girl died in the earthquake. She wanted to be with her husband, and, frankly, wanted to get pregnant again. They got her. She was on a tourist visa and INS says she lied and intended to stay. Emina says Turkish prisons aren't this crowded. She says Turkish guards aren't so cruel. She says Turkish prisoners get good fresh food, not date-expired Lunchables.*

Matt has secrets now, and David keeps secrets, too.

He knows that people care about him though, of course, they don't know what to say. (The messages left on the answering machine at home: *Hello, this is Robert,* his former assistant checking in, leaving only his name, presumably to indicate his good will.) No one refers to the fact he no longer goes to the lab, and he hasn't told Matt or Cliff. Every morning, he goes instead to Medical Center and Yusef Singh greets him casually, as though they both think he works there. David gets a cup of coffee and takes his place at the computer. If the computer is in use, he lingers by the coffee machine or hides in the men's room. Sometimes Singh gives him a donut. ("Krispy Kreme," he always says, as if to be encouraging.)

David works the way he's never done before. He puts on the headset and directs the stylus into a human eye that's merely a body made up of voxels, polygonal maps constructed of thousands of photographed slices. He goes through, feels and hears the pop. He doesn't work here, there is no eye here, and yet who can deny it? He removes the HMD and turns on the animations. In the transverse section through the head, the image of the eyes in the skull looks like an empty crab shell. Is he still a doctor? The coronal section is an African mask. He's becoming a poet, not a scientist and thinks of Matt, who seemed to understand the science but was most of all enchanted by the words: tunic of protection, lachrymal canals. In the sagittal plane, he runs the animation and as it moves from right to left and back again, the head and brain entirely disappear. Apparently it's possible for something that isn't really there to be doubly not there, an image rotating itself into the unseen.

At the lab, the work goes on as if he never existed, was never needed.

He returns home and must confront the report that Matthew hasn't been in class all week.

"Why should I? We're not going to live here anyway."

"Who said anything about our leaving?" David says.

"They're going to deport Mom, and I'm not staying here without her."

"They're not going to deport her," David says. "And even if they do, the law's going to be changed. It's a terrible mistake."

"And if they change it, there will be another law. Don't you see? Don't you get it?"

"Matthew," David says.

"It's nothing but lies, Dad. They say, *We made a mistake and we're sorry.*"

"Mom's going to be OK," David says.

"We're sorry we experimented with syphilis on black men. We're sorry we put Japanese Americans into camps. We're sorry we exposed our citizens to plutonium. We're sorry—"

"Matthew," David says.

"We slaughtered the Indians. We locked up your mother. I hate this country."

His father's hand draws back as if to strike him. And then David stands there, staring at his own hand in disbelief. When he says, "I'm sorry," they both have to laugh. "This family wouldn't be alive if it weren't for this country."

"Grandma's parents were just lucky. What about all the Jews they wouldn't let in?"

"This country has been good to the Jews."

He can't believe his father doesn't see it. "Tell that to the millions who died." Then he says, "Maybe there's a reason Mom writes to *me*."

Her letters are chatty. She tells Matt about Birgitta who had a fight with her husband. The police came and charged both with the domestic disturbance. Her husband, an American, got sent to anger management and is home with the kids. Birgitta hasn't seen her children in months and is being sent back to Germany.

The Englishwoman who, asked at the airport if she'd like to live in L.A., made the mistake of saying yes, just to be polite to the Angelenos.

She thinks, I would cross borders to be with my husband. My love for David isn't what—or only what—you think of as passion, but something now instinctual, in which he is so identified with me, with the home place, with destination and destiny, not so much in a fateful way, how can I say, it sounds almost as though I take him for granted, as living furniture, as breathing floor and ceiling and walls, he is home. And when I couldn't reach him, see, I don't take him for granted, everything crumbled. It started with a buzzing in my arms and then terror, it was like the Northridge quake, a hum and then instant sudden demolition in which everything falls around you and dissolves from the center, a loud noise, a swirling dust, a blindness. Our house stood. Then. Now, even now, I wonder if David will stand. My American husband, my American child. If I'm exiled, will they come with me? I will build. David will treat the eyes of Mexico's poor. My son will grow up in a foreign land.

They deprive us of human rights, she writes, *but I will not demand them. I want so much more than my rights, constitutional or otherwise. Mere rights are not enough. I want my life!*

David slips into Cliff's studio, turns on her computer and sends his mother cheery e-mails. His mother who, since his dad died, has moved from one retirement condo to another: Santa Barbara, Palm Springs, now Sedona, keeping herself busy with real estate agents and closings, betraying the fact that no place ever again will feel like home.

David tries to remember, when was it that Jews became white? To some people Jews still aren't, but when, he wonders, did he start to see himself as white? When did he stop feeling conscious, self-conscious, about the jobs you couldn't apply for, the people who wouldn't like you, the neighborhoods where you couldn't live. And what of the childhood terror, lying in bed, the fear of them coming for him, of the Knock on the Door? (This isn't the same.) Was this real fear or little different from any child's bogeyman? That childhood game he played in his head: what would you take if you had to flee suddenly at night? (This is different.) And if the fear still lives in him, imagine what it's like for his mother. Is that why he masquerades in cyberspace as his wife? He's protecting his mother. It will all be OK soon. (This isn't the same.) Why let Ida know? Why make her worry? This isn't, this isn't, this isn't.

He lurks around his own house in the dark, a night-dweller, a ghost, picking up Cliff's letters, trying to read them without rustling the pages. Cliff dwells behind walls and razor wire, he cannot see her, but she's the one events are happening to. It's David who's been disappeared.

Matt doesn't want to be like his father. He wants to save his mother, free her, but he hasn't done any better than his dad.

Matt used to think he was a good test-taker. Now he understands he was never before tested and now it's for real and he's failing.

When you've been done a great injustice, righteous indignation coexists with a deep and trembling sense of guilt. Everything you ever got away with. Everything about you, not only what you've done, that's bad.

He thinks, Elián González will grow up with great guilt. In the pictures, he's always smiling even though his mother is dead.

Matt thinks about his father. The guy just doesn't get it. His father thinks they still have a future here.

Click: On the 1300 block of Londonderry, a woman in a red Subaru gets into a tight parking space on her seventh try, then stands reading the restricted parking sign for a very long time.

Click. At Carmelita and Randolph on the line between Huntington Park and the City of Bell, police have a suspect spread-eagled on the hood of a car.

At the Site Where Vision Is Most Perfect

Click. Grant High School. Matt hasn't been to class for weeks, but now he's got a purpose. The security camera in the hall runs as he walks up to Billy Vakhizian who the week before Christmas taunted a new kid from Central America—*Hey, I'm gonna move up to a higher level*—and now Matt walks up to Billy and taps him on the shoulder. "Yeah," says Billy, without turning around. Matt takes a step back. "Turn around," he says, and Billy does, and Matt pulls his arm back and makes a fist and swings. He's never hit anyone before and it's not much of an impact. Billy's punch hits him in the stomach and he goes down. There's a fist in his face and he's bleeding, but it's all right, it feels good, it feels better than he's felt in weeks and there's a zero-tolerance policy at school. Matt is suspended—that's the whole point of this exercise, with just a little revenge thrown in.

Matt gets what he came for. Now maybe his father will make up his mind to leave.

Matthew,

I was building my adobe house when the tallest guard swept the pieces to the floor with one sweep of her hand. She told me to pick up that paper crap and throw it out. Why?

Now the only building I can do is in my head.

There is an exit door that opens onto a brick wall that opens to a tiny room just large enough to let you in and once inside the wall swings shut and an invisible door locks automatically behind you. Was this designed by intention? By mistake? Was I meant to enter? Will the door ever open again? At my command? Or is it set automatically to open in twenty-four hours, in twenty-four days, in twenty-four years? This locked room poses a question for which I have no answer.

I will build a swimming pool with a glass bottom and beneath it excavate a pit and in the pit I'll build my home and the only light that enters will be twice filtered, through the rippling water, through the crystal sheets of glass.

I will build an underground palace for the narcotraficantes.

There are cameras and screens everywhere but no one watching. So much worse than being watched is surveillance by the blind.

I will build a merciless demonstration, a building with mirrored surfaces, all tinted, so that everyone who sees himself will see himself with browner skin.

My pathological camouflage: I disguised myself as an American and so it was assumed that money would be enough, I didn't need a heart.

We used to build stores with lots of glass so you could always see what was happening inside and this prevented crime. Now we cover the glass with advertising and put up security cameras—not to stop crime, but to record it.

Sixty of us in here. When I build my house, I'll have a room to eat in, a room to shit in, a room to piss in, a room to dance in, a room to read in, a room to fuck in, a room to dress in, a room to wash in, and a floor that responds to your footsteps, that can tell from the way you step what sort of lights you wish turned on or off, what music you wish to hear.

Where is my existential space? The relation between enclosure and boundaries. Corridors and chambers, sew the edges of horizons, let columns radiate like fibers all white and brilliant to the depths.

A building is meant to be lived in—don't let anyone tell you otherwise—and that's why it's always haunted if no one's there.

Don't let your father hurt Desirée. I know he doesn't love her. I can see him: opening the door, tossing her out. You can spend your whole life in a place and then they decide to get rid of you.

(Cliff is right. No one pays attention to Desirée who languishes for weeks and then begins to pounce on mice that no one else can see. It is known that a bored cat will stalk prey that isn't there, but no one can say whether this is imagination or psychosis. One evening when David comes home from the work that isn't work, she's out the door past him and gone.)

Why hasn't your father sent a lawyer? Why hasn't anyone told me when I'll see the judge?

(David keeps phoning her deportation officer who never calls back. One day, he lucks out and Mr. Lebron himself answers. Before David can even say Cliff's name, the man hollers "How can I get anything done if you keep bothering me?" and hangs up.)

Everyone is talking about what Olga said at her hearing. "Who's going to take care of my children? If you don't let me out of here, are you going to support them?" We never saw Olga again. Some people say the judge let her go, some say she was deported, and some say he threw her into solitary for her fresh mouth. Just gossip. We get no facts here, no truth.

Cliff writes, *You have to strip and slice away till you see clearly.*

Matt's in his room, on-line, White Aryan Resistance, Militia of Montana. They're the only ones who believe in something enough to sacrifice for it, even die.

His father must be thinking of Mexico, too, these days. Matt emerges one night from his room when he smells something burning. David is seated at the kitchen table staring into space, surrounded by open cans and spattered sauce. There's a greasy frying pan on the stove and a block of cheese on the counter and enchiladas forgotten in the oven.

That night, for the first time in weeks, they talk but he finds out there's no point sharing any of your deepest thoughts with your father.

"You won't get far as a white supremacist," David tells him.

He is seething, but he's still Matt, sensible, studious Matt Pearlstein, whose father isn't an unemployed loser, but a scientist, whose mother isn't a criminal but the smartest—or at least most intellectual—person he's ever known. And so he knows his anger is both justified and a consequence of hormones, the surge in testosterone appropriate to his age. If he were fucking Courtney, he wouldn't feel quite so angry, but that's reason enough to stay away from her, he wants it channeled, all of it, into this raging capacity for some yet-to-be-discovered form of neo-guerrilla warfare, something bigger and more awful than he's ever dreamed.

Click. He finds himself again and again at the house on Hatteras where Courtney lives. He rides his bike back and forth. Sometimes at night, he slips through the bushes and stands beneath her window. Everything inside him hurts.

"What are you doing here?" she says. "You could call me. You could see me. But you lurk around like a stalker," and he does what's unthinkable, what he cannot imagine himself capable of doing: he hits her.

"I knew it would come to this," Courtney says, and he has fallen so low there's no way back from this place where he hates himself and is so ashamed, he can only go on living if it's guaranteed he'll never again chance to see Courtney or any of her friends or anyone who used to know him. Violence has a long, rich history. Why fight nature? His face burns. He's burned his bridges, sold his soul. He is no innocent victim. He has within himself all the destruction he needs.

Courtney doesn't scream, or flounce into the house. She doesn't hit him back. She stands there, standing her ground in front of him, looking at him curiously, waiting. He's aware of two things: his erection and his fear. He mounts his bike. Expecting the police in hot pursuit, he pedals furiously away.

Matt is hungry all the time. He eats constantly and yet he's never been this thin. He reads about canine health care—in Mexico what if they can't find a good vet for Ruby? He remembers how he pasted leaves on the dragon's claw the last normal day of his life, how skillful he was, they thought he was good at it and told him so, he did it so meticulously. Now he thinks that with craftsmanship just as careful he can make weapons, high explosives, firearms with silencers from ordinary house and garden products, from plumbing devices, oil filters, PVC pipe from Home Depot, he can make flamethrowers and grenade launchers and bring INS and the whole damn police state to its knees.

Does his father ever feel like this? The young must lead the old. He doesn't care if what he feels is or isn't normal. These aren't normal times. These are the end times. Hypocrisy has been revealed. Lies stripped away to naked truth, a truth so bare and ugly you must blow it up and cover it with rubble.

Cliff has slid to a private interior where nothing exists in built form. She surfaces long enough to write:

My dear husband and son,

I have been in here almost five months. There is still no hearing date scheduled. I can't fight this anymore. I have asked to be deported without further delay. I have signed the papers. This was not what I wanted, but if I stay here any longer I'll die. I cannot survive this place. I don't know what this will mean. I do not know what will become of us. I wanted to be stronger than this. Forgive me.

Her deportation order is signed but INS has lost her. The paperwork and the woman can't be found. "She's here," says the officer-in-charge, "but not here."

Days pass. Weeks. Somewhere a record is being kept. A reassurance and a threat.

David brings home books and language tapes. He says, "There's an American community in Cuernavaca, and one outside Guadalajara, and a lot of Americans in San Miguel."

"I don't want to live near Americans," says Matt.

Now he's neither here nor there, but he's far enough removed so bit by bit he can feel bitterness lifting.

God bless America, he thinks at last: the Armenians in Glendale, the Persian Jews in Westwood, the Vietnamese on Bolsa, and the San Gabriel Valley Chinese. The Ethiopians dancing at Rosalind's, the Pakistani spice merchant on Pico, and every Thai restaurant in East Hollywood that's open late. Bless the Irish voices at Molly Malone's and the teenagers beating the Korean drums, the mariachis in Boyle Heights, and everyone who ever blew a horn at 5th Street Dick's. Bless revolving sushi bars and German films, the Russians reading poetry in Plummer Park and the Filipinos throwing a party on Magnolia. Matt sees it all, golden, at the point where vision is most perfect: the dream of having a son like him—a healthy straight-A American boy.

He is floating, drifting. A millennium from now, who (or what) will recall him? Why didn't Courtney like to kiss him? Was it his breath? Was she ashamed of wearing braces? He can't imagine Courtney ashamed of anything.

He's seen Latino men in tears, they don't hide it, but Matthew has to guard his face. A boy like him! He hunches, clutches his knees and cries.

At the Site Where Vision Is Most Perfect

Cliff has vanished. There's a realtor's sign on the front lawn in Van Nuys. Inside, Matt and David study Spanish while somewhere in the Hills, a gringo stands naked in his window. He doesn't know what they know. He thinks that no one sees him.

The Atlas Mountains

The answering machine clicked on and it was Ralphie asking could I please please come in and get a fecal sample from the African pigs. No way. It was Christmas Eve and I had no intention of running over to the zoo and besides I was lying beside the tech guy and even though he kept talking about his wife, I didn't want to get up.

I'd found him in the Yellow Pages when my computer crashed. As soon as he walked in, he complained his back hurt. He pulled a cushion off my couch and rested his head on it when he lay down on my floor. Then he invited me to join him.

"She's American," he said, "and now I can't take her back to visit. They used to say they hated the American government but loved the American people. Now they hate all of you."

His voice vibrated up through his diaphragm and chest and through the cushion we shared and through the floor and through me and I have to say I liked it even though I was beginning to think that lying there with him was probably not very smart and it might not even be the best idea to let him touch my computer.

So I made a deal with myself: his wife could keep his hands, his legs, his lips, his tongue, and his penis. Surely she wouldn't begrudge me a little bit of voice.

"Where are you from?" I asked.

He didn't answer.

Iraq. Yemen. Lebanon. The accent, well, maybe. I couldn't tell by looking. We lay side by side, only the hairs on our arms touching. Like being tickled by a warm breeze, there was a slight charge, not quite static electricity.

"Tunisia?" I said.

I didn't think so, but I wanted him to say it. I wanted those syllables. *No, not Tunisia.*

I don't mess around with married men. I mean, I'll mess around, but I don't *mess around.*

He told me he married his wife for the green card. Why would he tell me that? Because it was a marriage in name only, as the romance novels say, or because he doesn't even realize he's a sleaze?

"Am I paying you by the hour?"

"Travel time and tech time, yes," he said. "And it's double time because of holiday."

"Then maybe you should get started."

"I'm not on the clock right now," he said. "Hunching over the computer, so bad for the back. And the eyes." He reached an arm, then cried out. "Ow! There's a little...package? In foil. In pocket of the jacket."

You gotta be kidding, I thought, but I rolled half on top of him and reached in.

"This?"

"Yes. Good. Artificial tears," he said. "The doctors said to me, 'Do you have dry eyes?' How could I? I was crying all the time, what is happening in my country. Tears, tears, tears, but my tears did nothing. They didn't help my country and they did not bring the oxygen into the eyes. The kind of tears that do nothing. So," he said. "You take out one vial. Twist off the top. Good. Don't touch the tip."

Right.

"Now please," he said, "a few drops in each eye."

His eyes were green. My weakness.

How can you hate or fear someone you're taking care of? I mean you can, you can resent him and sure he was being manipulative as hell, but still...

"Now," he said, and I lay back down. I stared at the ceiling and felt his voice. "What is wrong with your computer?"

"I got a virus," I said. "I went to Symantec.com. I tried to remove it according to the directions."

"You should never do that if you don't know what you're doing."

"I know that now. So when everything got screwed up, I tried what I thought was the Startup disk."

"What do you mean, you thought?"

"Well, it said Startup Disk, but it shut everything down. It didn't start anything."

"The Startup Disk doesn't."

"Then why is it called that?"

"You should leave these things to people who know."

"Now all I get is a black screen with some funny codes in white."

"Yes, yes, that's what happens. Well, we'll have to fix it."

"You can?"

"That's why I'm here."

It occurred to me: I don't know who this man is or where he comes from or who, really, he represents. And the thing is, not all that long ago, I sent three e-mails to the White House. Not obscene. Not threatening. Just critical. At which point, the White House blocked all mail coming from my address. They know my computer. Now my e-mails go only to those who already agree with me, and all their names and addresses are right there, on the disk, if what has crashed and been deleted can be restored, in which case this man would soon have access, if I let him, and he could report everything—*everything*—to his masters, his handlers, to anyone. Of course, under the Patriot Act, the bastards could probably get this info anyway. Maybe. But at least I shouldn't make it easy for them. And it occurred to me next I would have to have sex with him until it was time for him to go to his next call to keep him away from my hard drive and protect the identities of my friends and even as I'm thinking this, he's saying *No, not Tu-ni-si-a-a-a-a,* and I'm asking myself whether I am truly paranoid or just looking for an honorable excuse to behave dishonorably and fuck a married man here on my hardwood floor. No, I am not paranoid. I only lay down beside him as an act of trust, in this world where we see everyone as an enemy.

"Libya," I said. And I thought, My voice, my voice vibrates, too. I am reaching him.

"Not yet."

"Not yet?"

"I can't look at your screen. That was liqui-gel," he said. "My vision blurs, five minutes, maybe ten."

When I had a cat, I would put my head against her every morning, I'd lie across her, scratch her ears, and hear and feel her purr. Now I wanted to stroke this man. I wanted to hold him. Ten minutes, I thought. Ten, at most. A relief to be with a man and know in advance exactly when it will end. Instead, though, I was honorable. I thought, Just keep him talking.

"Tell me about your country," I said.

"Parts of my country are very beautiful. We have mountains, very rugged and beautiful mountains. My country has towns where people slaughter one another. A proud history. A sad history. I wish I'd never left my country. Now I hope I never have to go back."

"Afghanistan," I said.

"You Americans, you like to think there are always choices," he said. "What if your choice is kill or be killed? Your heart stops or your heart breaks. You lose either way. A bullet through your heart, or a piece of ice."

I thought of bullets and ice and all the places he could possibly be from and how I was probably connected to them all with my taxes fueling the bloodshed.

"I feel for you," I said. "As a matter of principle." For years, I explained, I refused to feel my own pain and that refusal gave rise to empathy. "A few years ago," I told him, "my whole body would have shuddered at the thought of your suffering country. I wallow in my own pain now, so I have no visceral response to yours. But it's still a matter of ethics, of right and wrong. I still question everything, all the time, and I would cry for you if could. I would like to, really, even knowing the tears would do nothing. This country's coming down, I said. "There will be nothing left, and maybe it's about time. Why should we have it better than everyone else? They've already restructured the economy to resemble the Third World. Now the government becomes the tool of repression." Even as I spoke, I realized I was enacting a ritual of entitlement. We had ten minutes and I could have learned so much from the man beside me and instead the only voice to be heard now was my own. I was American and loud, though not as stupid as some, being a person who could name lots of countries and even find them on the map. One was his. "Why should we go on having it better than you did back in wherever it is that you come from?"

He said, "But why do you think I come here?"

Ha! To take the jobs Americans refuse to do. To make money. To undermine us from within. Every stock response. To change our racial makeup. To drain our resources. To visit Disneyland. To bring over two dozen family members. To send remittance money home. To commit a terrorist act. To provide a better life for your children.

"Do you have children?" I asked.

He didn't answer. He seemed to be staring at the wall. I looked where he looked. His eyes were clear and mine were not. I'd removed my glasses when I lay down beside him, considerately, so in case he turned his head in my direction he wouldn't be clipped by a sharp plastic edge.

"What's that?" he asked.

"I don't know." I reached for my glasses. "Oh, that's a nail. I was trying to hang a picture." I'd driven the nail too far into the wall, flush against the surface, and the claw of my hammer couldn't pull it out.

He approached the wall as though he intended to walk right through it. He placed his lips against the small black spot. A long sucking sound, almost a whistle.

"All right," he said.

I could see the nail head protruding now, just a little. He kissed the wall. When he turned to face me, he held the nail in his teeth.

"Bravo," I said.

He spat it to the floor and I thought, That's that, that's as far as this goes.

"Let me write you a check," I said.

"I haven't even touched your computer."

"What do I need it for? More horoscopes and forwarded jokes, e-mails about how the election was stolen, and about larger harder penises in an overseas bank account that can be mine, trusted friend, if I..."

"If I don't work, you owe me nothing," he said.

"You shouldn't be working today."

"We need the money."

"How American," I said. "Hey, it's Christmas Eve. You should be home with your wife."

"It's not our holiday."

"It's not mine either. So why are you charging me double?"

"I'm not charging you anything," he said.

"Why not?" I said. And then I told him he'd better leave.

I got up and went to the door and unlocked it.

"Why?" he asked.

"It's my home. I call the shots."

He picked up his black case full of disks or wiretaps or bombs or condoms or whatever the hell was in there. He came close. Those green eyes.

"I would like very much please to kiss you," he said.

Why? I thought, and then *Why not?*

Algeria, I thought. *The Atlas Mountains.* I wanted to feel their geography on my tongue. If it ever came to that, I would tell his wife I was kissing Algeria, and not her husband.

"Merry Christmas anyway," I said.

I imagined the nail, sharp, metallic, passing from his mouth to mine. I imagined the explosion. I imagined all the countries on the map, and I was glad I didn't know which one was his.

Our lips touched lightly, very lightly.

Maybe it meant something and maybe it didn't. I imagined I was connected, gently now, to all of them.

Angle and Grip

It suddenly occurred to us that when famous people undergo surgery, someone must end up with the organ or bone that's removed. What becomes of all those celebrity body parts? In general, I believe the patient has first refusal rights. The doctor will pack the part of you up as take-home, except when it's a fetus.

During the pregnancy, I gained so much weight I'm still wearing maternity clothes, and well-intentioned people keep asking when the baby is due. When I tell them I lost the baby, the baby is dead, they are horrified and I feel a small but very satisfying twinge. Embarrassment is all I can inflict on people who haven't suffered as I have. It's only my mother-in-law, former mother-in-law now, who has no shame. You didn't lose the baby. You killed him, she says. Rodney's son, my grandchild. You killed him.

The horrible people are back in town. They take over the laundry room every morning. They throw in their clothes from the day before and wait outside in the patio, he barechested in his boxer shorts, she in bra and panties, and they argue. She's drunk (already), he's pissed off.

The horrible He shouts, "Good morning."

The horrible She says, "Oooh. When is the baby due?"

I tell her the baby is dead and she's horrified. She was horrified when I told her yesterday. She's a drunk and she never remembers.

They come every month to visit their son Jimmy who stays with a friend throughout their stay. I don't know what Jimmy really thinks of them or where the friend lives. I don't know when they wash their underwear.

When they aren't here, they live in their RV or else with Jimmy's sister.

Jimmy says, "My Dad's the friendliest guy you'll ever want to meet." He says, "Ma's a live wire."

When you live in this kind of building, around a shared courtyard, you know things, and Jimmy knew it wasn't great between me and Rodney.

What happened to my husband is, a tire came flying off a semi and through the windshield. As the saying goes, he never knew what hit him. Two freak deaths in a family may seem strange. My father used to say, Some families serve as lightning rods for everyone, but he thought he was referring to other families and not to us.

Just because Rodney's dead doesn't mean I can't criticize. Once when we were arguing, I said, "I married the only gay man in America with two left feet." Rodney wasn't gay. I said it for effect, though it had none. Rodney didn't dance. I do, or used to.

Jimmy's mother looks like someone who would know the cha-cha.

Morning and the horrible people are at it again. When they're in town, this becomes a shitty place to live.

I'd find a new place, but my cat hates change.

Such courage and loyalty to curl up or stretch out beside me each night. When she stretches, the sheet vibrates beneath us like a drumhead. I'm a dozen times her size. When I roll over, it must feel to her like earthquake, disaster. She's used to it. When we had a tremor last year, she just sat up, alert, and listened to the neighbors' dogs all crazed and howling.

I always tell people I have the world's most wonderful cat. Jezbelle is the perfect companion but last night, as I was folding laundry, I found myself shouting Goddamn it, Jezbelle, why do I do all the work around here?

The TV news:

Acting on a tip, police arrested a man when they found one shoulder, two severed heads, three hearts, one penis, and five skulls in his freezer. He was later released because, "It appears he had a license to trade in body parts and all the appropriate paperwork."

Jezbelle sighs and stretches, touches me through the sheet with one paw, then curls up to sleep. She lies across my hand and I feel two pulses beat unevenly. One must be mine. I'm not sure what I feel after a while, numbness or pain. It occurs to me to remove my hand but I can't bear to disturb Jezbelle's sleep. My fingers will die and be amputated. I'll lose them. What will I do without my hand? I know what I'll do with at least one finger, take it to a jeweler, a church jeweler who knows how to fill a vial with holy water and hang it from a chain, my finger in formaldehyde suspended inside glass.

Rodney's mother resented me all along because of all the jewelry he gave me. She believed these were the bribes a man gives a wife who withholds sex. The opposite was true. Rodney thought if he gave me gifts he didn't have to talk to me or touch me, but could have me stashed away while he went about living his dead man's life. It's no wonder my baby was conceived without liver or lungs and with only half a heart.

Rodney said, "You're not eating for the baby. You're not eating because you're hungry. You're fat," he said, so I ate to spite him.

When the horrible people leave, Jimmy moves back into his apartment and tells me he's starting his own business and I can come in as a partner because I've got the life insurance money and he needs investors, and my bitching is what gave him the idea.

Apparently I said something about men being dolls, all manufactured in the same fucked up factory and damaged beyond repair. Each one is damaged in a slightly different way which is how you can tell them apart. If you're desperate for a boyfriend, you can prop one up and carry it with you. You can use your imagination to make it talk and make it move, but aside from what you do in fantasy, there's not much fun in having it around.

"That's the difference between men and women," Jimmy said. "A man will pay good money to fuck a doll."

So anyway, that's his line of business. He's already got the warehouse space. Where else? Van Nuys.

Everybody has one famous cousin. Jimmy's is Baby Dill. Jimmy, who grew up with her, still calls her Susan, and he assures me, though I've never heard of her, that she's the ticket.

I trust him on that but I'm not sure he's right to call them *Love* Dolls.

Jimmy says, "Society was born as mutual self-defense, right? People gathering together to protect themselves. From what? From each other." He says the only reason to pair off or stick together is fear and hate. "If you believe in *love*, what do you need other people for?"

I think in every family there's someone with a bitter knowing heart. And someone, like Rodney's mother, who believes in miracles or transplants. "Damn you," she said to me. "There's always hope."

I tell Jimmy that being a silent partner is not my style and I want to be there when they do the cast of Susan's body.

The problem is getting out of bed. Lately, it takes me a long time. First I have to find sensation in my toes. This is like threading a needle in the dark. Trying to engage the muscles, the nerves, to find them. To feel them, as it were, slip into gear. I lie there, wondering if I'm just depressed or truly paralyzed. I count to a hundred before I even try to flex a toe. If the news is bad, that's how long till I'm willing to know it. So: test the toe. Try the foot. Wake up the ankle to be sure it will be my foundation.

I think about Rodney and about his mother and how now that he's dead I don't have to see her again. I hate her. I hate you, Sheila, I allow myself to think. Could this be a mood swing, some post-partum (or post-mortem) hormonal madness? No, it's just that Death trumps Courtesy. I hate her. Thinking it feels good, so I think it louder. Then I think about the baby. The baby was a boy. If they had packed up the fetus for me, then what? Even in the freezer, a thing like that won't last forever. It helps to think of it that way, a perishable object. A thing.

Some projects Baby Dill says she starred in:

Undressed for Suck-cess!

Pussy Kreme Kombo!

Faster, Harder, Yuppie Swine!

Jimmy ends up leaving for the warehouse without me.

. . .

When I get there, they've been working for hours. Baby Dill is leaning on armrests, neck-to-bellybutton in plaster and Jimmy's saying, "Suck in your stomach. Good and flat. Suck it in."

He's got a couple of art students—she's got blue hair; he's got pink—slathering on the plaster. Then the guy holds a can of Diet Coke up to Baby Dill's lips and lets her suck through the straw.

There's a how-to video playing continuous loop on the VCR.

"What's alginate?" I ask.

"Some kind of seaweed shit," Jimmy says. "But we're not using it. This is a production line, not a spa."

"This stuff weighs a ton," says Baby Dill.

The pink-haired boy says, "Actually, at this point, you're probably talking no more'n two, three hundred pounds."

"What about the plaster bandages?" I'm watching the video.

"Faster this way," Jimmy says.

He shows me his plans. Three workable orifices or, as he says, super-realistic entries. Custom sculpting of the nipples, labia, and clit. Extra silicone injections in the silicone breasts so they feel pliable and real. A doll, Jimmy says, with star quality. Multiracial, multiethnic. Choice of hair color and skin. And oh, those toes!

He says we'll get into Special Tastes. "We could cast you, too," he says. For pregnant? I wonder. Or fat?

I wonder about no ventilation and the fumes.

"You work in special effects," Jimmy says, "you get used to it."

That's when Baby Dill says, "Do you guys know what you're doing?"

The young artists don't answer.

She says, "You ever done this before?"

Jimmy says, "They're good kids."

She says, "They're not professionals."

"Business decision," Jimmy says.

Baby Dill says, "It hurts in here." She says, "Jimmy, I can't breathe."

Jimmy says no problem, but the young artists get it: the plaster's drying fast and she's getting crushed. Baby Dill is being pressed to death. She starts screaming and the young artists are screaming and knocking on the cast with the handles of their brushes.

Baby Dill starts begging for the Fire Department and Jimmy runs next door for help.

That's how we meet Reggie. He comes running in from the machine shop and they've got a hack saw, a power drill, a hammer, and chisel.

Baby Dill is moaning, doing the ooh and aah, and those staccato oh-oh-ohs.

The artists are screaming. When Reggie connects the drill, Baby Dill shrieks and I do too.

"All right, all right." He puts it down and tries the hack saw.

"Faster," says Baby Dill.

I'm probably not the only one to think this sex should have been safe, but no one says it.

Baby Dill's head whips back and forth like she's trying to rock her way out, and she's crying. Jimmy says "Susan, baby, hold still," and Reggie bangs against her with the hammer.

Jimmy says, "That's my cousin. You gonna hammer her, do the buttocks."

Reggie says, "Tip her forward." The young artists help. Then he whacks her.

When Baby Dill's mostly free and can breathe, and she's calling everyone an asshole, I can see her tits are fake, but those washboard abs you've got to work for. Her skin is slick where they prepared it with Vaseline, and red with trauma.

Reggie is a physical anthropologist, or at least that's what he got his degree in. What he does for a living is make bicycle gears at the shop next door.

Physical anthropology is the discipline that trains men to know people through their measurements, not their words and not their works and above all not their souls. Touching the bones of the dead. Touching the bodies of the living with a tape measure and a touch that is not supposed to feel like touch.

Physical anthropologists measure people. They take their blood, analyze it for blood type and DNA. Check the consistency and composition of earwax. Record the distribution of the Mongolian spot. These are the scientists who proved the American Indian male has a pendulous belly because he's prone to hysteria like a pregnant white woman. That the jutting jaw puts you lower on the chain of being with the Africans and Irish. These are the great cataloguers of craniums and cocks. Most of all, the cocks. That was the point, after all, all those white men in extra-large-cranium-size pith helmets checking all those dusky virile members. Bigger, they reported, yes, but not harder. This is common knowledge or, if not common, easily available. Go on-line. Read a book.

"You," I ask. "Why?"

"Fossils," Reggie says. "Bones." He feels my knee. "I'm interested in the way joints and bones articulate."

"We could use you," Jimmy says.

Reggie says, "I would welcome the chance to use my expertise."

A Scotsman, he would bring a certain dourness to the enterprise.

He says, "As long as it's off the record, off the books." Reggie doesn't have a green card. He says, "Why the devil else would I be working in a machine shop?"

It's not easy to make a lifelike life-size Love Doll satisfying enough so customers will shell out $6,000, which is what we're charging, options extra, and not even that great a profit margin.

Baby Dill is wary of another try. We tried making the parts separately, but you can't get a good seam with silicone. We've got shelves of arms and legs and breasts and torsos. Not to mention too many bubbles in the mix.

"The flesh doesn't feel real," I tell Jimmy, though it's possible I don't remember what real flesh feels like.

"Use her in the Jacuzzi," he says, "and she'll be soft and warm."

The prepaid orders are already coming in and we don't even have a prototype.

These are the challenges you face.

Reggie touches me beneath my muumuu while Jimmy watches. Jimmy votes no, but Reggie and I both vote yes, so pubic hair remains an option.

When we have our first doll, we'll do the promo video, romantic yet explicit, showing customers how to use her, or as our copy reads, enjoy her. I'm putting together the douche kits, with the recommendation to clean her after every use.

In the meantime, Jimmy wants to throw away the useless body parts. Reggie says to keep them. "Macabre? Well, yes," he says, "but maybe holy."

Sometimes I pick up a severed hand, and hold it.

. . .

Baby Dill brings her own special effects team. We pay them plenty, but we get the cast. It's hinged. They open the bivalve lips and she rolls out like Venus from an oyster, but not quite as graceful.

Reggie volunteers for the video. Jimmy says no, he's too good-looking. The ideal would be an ordinary guy, someone everybody can relate to.

If you're an ordinary woman, would you rather sleep next to A) a silent doll, B) a snoring man, or C) a purring cat? At home, I whisper the question to Jezbelle and need no answer.

Our doll isn't ordinary enough. Reggie saws her breasts off and sculpts them smaller. He plasters her stomach and adds some girth to her waist. We want her drop-dead gorgeous, but normal. It's a group grope as we swarm her, sanding her down till she's perfectly smooth. The frame is fiberglass with gelcoat. Reggie's doing the skeleton in aluminum. Plastic joints are for shit.

The head still has to be separate. It takes six pounds of silicone, and a change in the weather means it doesn't set. I come in and there's a naked headless body hanging from a hook, the head at its feet drying next to a heat lamp.

We put in teeth and tongue for the realistic look, but the tongue is detachable to facilitate entry. Her eyes have to be done over and done over again. The window to the soul isn't easy to get right but somewhere around the tenth try, we do.

The horrible people are back in town, and when they walk into the warehouse, there's our first Baby Dill doll, legs splayed open, on the table. The skin is soft and smooth and the breasts have jiggle and give like real ones. Jimmy has a finger in her vagina. I have my finger up the anus. We're checking for angle and grip.

The horrible She wears a tight leopard-skin print. The horrible He wears—and where did he get it? and why?—a dashiki.

The horrible She says "Hi, Jimmy. Hi, Susie," and to me, "When's the baby due?"

I say, "The baby's dead."

She's horrified. I take my finger out of the anus, and I take the horrible She's hand, and we go sit down in Jimmy's office. She reeks of what she drinks, and Tide, and Downy.

I tell her that at the clinic, I was treated differently, a pregnant woman who had just lost her husband and was carrying a doomed child. Everyone was kind to me, but not to the teenage girls in the waiting room with me, some crying, some sitting cowed beside dry-eyed mothers and aunts. I was the exception and the girls took the blame. The nurses looked at me, there's no other word for it, with awe. When someone started yelling at a pregnant little girl, I wanted to intervene, but held back. I felt radiant as a goddess and perhaps if the girl had thrown herself at my feet and embraced my knees I might have been able to enter into the course of human affairs, but the cruelty shown her was what made it clear to me that I and my role were different.

The baby I was carrying was all fucked up. Five different organs that wouldn't work, and for six months, no one knew it. For the six months he'd been inside me, he was nourished by my blood. My organs cleaned his toxins. The moment we were made separate, they told me, he would start to die. He would struggle for air but would have no lungs to find it. His kidneys would turn on him. Choking, poisoned, entering this world accompanied by brief but total and unimaginable pain, my baby would agonize and die. We—doctor, nurse, me—we would watch and we'd be helpless. So I had the late-term abortion where they crushed his little head and he never had to suffer and afterwards, the nurse cried and thanked me. She had seen a baby born like mine. The doctor had seen it happen twice. "I couldn't go through it again," she said. "I couldn't bear it." And I realized it wasn't awe they felt toward me, but gratitude.

This is often an ungrateful world. I had spared them, they were grateful and they showed it, and with such experience of gratitude, it's no wonder I felt the golden aura radiate around me and I walked out of the clinic thinking myself not Author of Death, but Creator. "Who did you do it for?" said Rodney's mother. "The doctor? The nurse?" Maybe I did it for that moment, when I was not the vengeful, but the merciful, the loving and beneficent God, the one whose fist is not raised to strike but whose fingers hold the contaminating pain and close it off isolated in their grip. A hot coal in my hand, and people still mistake it for the glow of pregnant and triumphant life.

"Big shot," said Rodney's mother. "You don't fool me."

Outside, there's a shout from Baby Dill when someone pops open the champagne.

"I wish I had a relic," I say. "I didn't even name him."

Jimmy's Ma says, "Jimmy's the only name for a baby boy."

Outside, they're shouting, "A toast! A toast!"

I'm afraid the horrible He will say, "To Jimmy!"

Jimmy says, "Suck-cess!"

The horrible She snuffles and pats my hand, and holds it as though it isn't burning.

California Transit

The sea lions stopped barking after the last feeding. It was quiet there at night except for the occasional sneeze and the constant sound of water moved by wind. I stood at the fence in the dark and sometimes a patrol car came by and I'd turn and wave as if I were one of the volunteers who belonged there.

The female I came to watch slept peacefully but sometimes there was a tremor through her light-colored fur and her flippers trembled against the pavement.

This is where I got to know Burton. Even when you're most alone, there's bound to be someone.

This is what happened in Los Angeles, the land of reinvention.

I didn't come West to reinvent myself. What I didn't expect: after I arrived, I had to reinvent my desire to go on living. I found myself in a bare room with a shared bathroom down the hall. Utilities were included so I got no mail. It sounds a defeat to say I found myself there. I chose it.

I turned down an apartment with a balcony overlooking the Pacific and the sandy beach beneath the bluff. From the living room window, the view was of the working harbor, the gantry cranes and offshore rigs, and in the distance the forty-foot containers piled on railbeds all along the flats. Even the kitchen had a view: the other side of the point, where the shore was rocky and wild. I could have had a place with carpets and ceiling fans, the second floor of a pretty little stucco house with ring-necked doves cooing on the flat roof, with rose bushes, with bougainvillea spilling over the stucco wall. Then I saw what I needed: the room to let over a line of boarded-up stores and scaffolding somewhere in-between the homeless Feeding Station and the spruced-up block that people called Yuppie Gulch.

The room reminded me of the past. In 1968, after the assassinations, when I was twenty-two years old, I'd run off and lived in San Andrés, an industrial port on Mexico's east coast. It was a new city, modern, open and so different from the other Mexican towns I'd seen with their adobe walls that gave the street a human scale and hugged you. San Andrés was not a city that could love. I rented an ugly room in someone's apartment. I knew no one, I never got enough to eat, I was very much alone and very happy.

When I arrived in L.A., I was two years past fifty. I'd left New York at the end of my rope and en route to California I lost everything.

Empty hands are unencumbered hands. That's what I believed when I lived in the port of San Andrés and I thought, I can be that woman again. I thought, Don't despair. Revel in your freedom.

It was only natural to take the bus down to San Pedro, the city L.A. annexed in order to have a harbor. I moved into my little room. Emptiness is conducive to the meditative state. There was no reason I couldn't be happy.

My room near the L.A. Harbor contained a sink and a two-burner hot plate. There was a mirror over the sink. There were no blinds or curtains, but the windows were so filthy, when I lowered them, no one could see in.

California Transit

I undressed. It was the middle of July and I was covered with sweat before I could get my clothes off.

There were two hangers in the closet. I had one change of underwear. I washed my bra and panties in the sink and hung them up to dry. Then I pulled the string to kill the light and opened the windows.

That first night, I slept on the floor and enjoyed the strong breeze off the ocean.

Once upon a time, I slept on the floor of a jail cell in Mississippi. There were fifteen of us. It was Freedom Summer. We were all beaten and arrested and beaten some more. Then whites in one cell and blacks in another. We wondered if they would come and lynch us. A lynching was not a mere hanging. There was usually pain involved, torture and mutilation.

In Mississippi, if you were white and from the North, salvation was having empty hands. After you've been in a sharecropper's shack, any regular house with carpet and indoor plumbing, a room with curtains made of something other than flour sacks, can make you hate yourself.

Do you remember? I asked Burton later. The way we used to feel? Until we could abolish poverty, the only honorable thing was to share it.

The cells were dirty, crowded, stinking with waste, but we sang freedom songs and when they unlocked the cell to shove us in, it felt as though the gates had swung open to Paradise.

A jail cell. A bedroom in San Andrés. I hadn't thought of those days for years. A motel room in the desert. A room to let by the harbor. The room hardly changes. I wonder if the woman has changed, or just the meaning she makes of it, of feeling beyond the reach of everyone she used to know, closed off inside four walls, with a change of underwear and a toothbrush.

Don't forget the room in Chelsea. A studio apartment up four flights of crooked stairs, a room so narrow I hung cheap mirrors for the illusion of depth.

Paul gave me a black eye. "Still want to look at yourself?" he said.

Who is this woman?

She was beaten in Mississippi and she wanted to adopt a little Mexican girl and she was beaten by her husband and she fell for lies when she really knew better and she hit bottom in L.A. and she did something terrible that could never be undone. If this is who I am, it must all add up. *And* plus *and* plus *and*. I will not stoop to a *because*.

Who she was then: No one.

She thought her life had value—this was her power—because she was willing to lose it.

She was a white girl from the North who'd never been around black people. They didn't live in her neighborhood, in those days there were none on TV, so in Mississippi her brain flashed a purely visual confusion as though she were walking around in a photographic negative. Then she got used to it and, in the segregated cell where everyone was white, only her wounds and the human stench proved she was not a ghost.

After Mississippi, what was she to do?

She could be a waitress or a secretary. She could enroll in school again to be a teacher or a nurse. She could marry Paul. She could take up arms and join the Revolution because, though she practiced nonviolence, she'd begun to suspect all power flowed from the barrel of a gun.

No, she didn't believe that. She was frightened to even entertain the thought.

She deferred her fate and ran away to San Andrés.

. . .

California Transit

I didn't expect to love Mexico. I went because it wasn't home and because I wouldn't have to care. Because I knew no one.

And it was cheap. People had told me that for forty dollars a month, I could expect room, board, and laundry. Yet I chose to live with Doña Vicky who provided only morning coffee. I did my own wash daily, proud to be independent with the further satisfaction of feeling cheated. I scrubbed my clothes in the wash trough on the roof and hung them up to dry. Sometimes I heard sloshing sounds and whirring from behind a locked door in Doña Vicky's part of the apartment and I tingled with resentment at the thought of the washer and drier she kept secret from her tenants.

I'd left behind the towns where people welcomed me. In Oaxaca, strangers were quick to invite me home and they took my *no* not as refusal but as courtesy. I didn't want to be friendly or courteous, and I kept moving.

In San Andrés, I didn't even have to smile.

Doña Vicky's other tenant was a journalist who worked nights. I had wanted to be a journalist once. As I knew that all journalists in Mexico were corrupt, I didn't wish to know him, besides which we shared a toilet and he didn't flush.

Forty dollars, but remember this was a long time ago.

And now, San Pedro. What a perfect name. A Mexican Saint Peter with the keys to Heaven, but the California gringos dropped the "San" and called it PEE-dro.

I had no idea where my new life was headed, that I would do something terrible. Not a crime of conscience, or civil disobedience, but of violence and blood.

. . .

California Transit

I came West because Maureen had phoned and offered a job. The job was too good to be true, and the offer came from Maureen, so I should have known better. I got off the Greyhound bus and stood on an unfamiliar street in a city where I'd never been before and within minutes knew I'd lost everything. Everything was wrong, except that the people around me were speaking Spanish—not just Spanish, but Mexican Spanish—and their voices took me back to a time when I was alone and glad to have nothing but one change of clothing in a backpack. I asked them please, where was the port, and how to get there.

Who says L.A. has no public transportation? In fifteen minutes I was aboard the 445 Express bus with its welcome painted on the side in small black letters, small enough to avoid offense to Anglos: Bienvenidos.

I sat beside a brown-skinned woman and it wasn't Mississippi and no one could beat me for it.

I wanted to believe myself back in Mexico, but this place both was and wasn't. San Andrés had been wide open, but these treeless boulevards were much too wide, the buildings too low. This was not open horizon, but a violent exposure. Cars hugged the side of the bus, seeking its shadow. At last a stretch with colorful little flags planted and flapping, something for an agoraphobic to hold onto.

Most Mexican towns smelled of charcoal fires and something oily that penetrated your clothing and skin and the aroma of roasting chiles, coffee, and corn. San Andrés smelled of tar and rotting seaweed and brine. Los Angeles smelled of bus exhaust and fast food and jasmine.

On the side streets, a riot of bright flowers in the dust. What are those trees that look like pineapples? Trees with frilled and ruffled bark? There's a rose of Sharon tree, there's a banana tree, there's something barren next to something lush. And magnolias. But this isn't Mississippi. It was Long

Island strip malls to eternity. It was Detroit with palm trees. It was billboards in Spanish and then Korean and then English.

On the freeway, a gigantic Felix the Cat looms over the horizon, advertising something about smog. A huge black garbage bag from nowhere covers the windshield and is entangled in the wipers, flying off again just before we crash and then the road climbs into an artificial isolated stretch where the bus stops seem like space stations. Occasionally, the tops of trees protrude over a sound wall, or a mural explodes in bright colors and larger-than-life figures. There were glass high-rises shooting straight up out of parking lots and then the renewed assault of billboards—a bimbo riding on a beeper and beer cans and Oprah with the topic of today's show (could it actually be painted fresh each day?)—and the car lots and the long industrial flats, and the reflectors on the exit signs so covered in grime they were unreadable and fire and steam and white-domed fuel depots, cylinders so great in circumference they looked short and squat until I realized those vines winding around them were stairs for people to climb and then the sense of scale gave me vertigo, and the peach-colored security lights began to come on, and the lights on the breakwater, and the port cranes looked like orange brontosaurus necks against the sky and I thought with surprise, It's all so ugly, and I thought, All over the world, this is the city people dream about.

I dreamed about my cat. Her name was Dinah. When I first brought her home, I thought I'd made a terrible mistake.

Suddenly I was living with a Creature. Things would be chewed on, moved, carried off by a living being that would not understand me. As a child, I was not allowed pets and I'd wished for a poltergeist, a ghost, something that would come unbidden beyond the reach of my parents' rules. Now this sudden evidence of life terrified me. She clung to me, climbed all over me, purring, lapping at my hand, my hair. She needed care, she needed love and I was afraid there was not enough inside of me to give her.

By the time I left her in the motel room in Blythe, she was just a little over a year old. She didn't purr much anymore and she didn't particularly like to be touched, but I always opened my eyes to find her eyes looking back into mine, and I couldn't imagine life without her.

I woke on the floor in Pedro and Dinah wasn't there and instead I was looking into the wide dark nothingness inside me.

* * *

Paul said, "If you leave me, by the time you're thirty, you'll be living alone in a shabby room." He didn't say *when you're forty or fifty*. By then, he said, I'd surely be a suicide.

I woke up in Pedro in that shabby empty room but he was wrong.

He didn't know that in the Mississippi jail cell, the freedom songs grated on my nerves. Even in the best of company I get claustrophobic, or it might have been due to the concussion.

My room at Doña Vicky's wasn't empty. There were four single beds, one at each wall. The west wall had a window: persianas—glass blinds with one slat missing. The north wall had room for both the bed and a small table on which I kept my soap and toothpaste and clock and the small jug of filtered water which Doña Vicky provided along with a glass. I also used the table as a desk. There were hooks in the wall for clothing and a low-watt bulb hanging from the ceiling. I couldn't reach the pull without standing on the chair. I had to ask for a chair. Until Doña Vicky agreed to lend me one, I wrote standing up or sitting on the bed. I stacked books on the floor. I was not allowed to have food in the room. There were no pictures on the walls. The sheets were yellowed and so worn that one night when I rolled over, the fabric tore. I always slept in the bed beneath the window, but when I masturbated during the day, I used the bed against the east wall on the other side of which was Doña Vicky's hallway. I liked to hear her footsteps. She knew I must not be disturbed; I was "studying."

I masturbated a lot, thinking of Paul. We would be married when I returned. I would work as a waitress and he would go to graduate school, and Paul wanted babies.

No one expected me to marry at all. I would show them—all those people who said, What a shame, too smart for her own good. I would marry right away and not the sort of man anyone would expect. What excited me most was when he pinned me down with his body and said *I know what you are*. It was true. No one else knew I was a girl who let herself be hit. I walked to class and into stores and through the streets smug with my secret.

In high school, Mrs. Leigh said I feel sorry for you.

Mr. Tunney said I feel sorry for you.

Mr. Cassil said I feel sorry for you.

Mrs. Schafer said I feel sorry for you.

My father said I feel sorry for you.

I don't feel sorry for you, young lady, said my mother.

When they beat us in Mississippi, we were together.

When Paul beat me, I was alone.

"I feel sorry for you, all alone," said Doña Chepi.

The building where I lived with Doña Vicky was home to many widows, or women who claimed to be. Doña Vicky, Doña Chepi, Doña Juanita, and Doña Susana—at one time or another, they all said: *May God forgive me, but I don't miss that man at all.* I heard it from each of them: Doña Rosario and Doña Maruja and Doña Eva.

It occurred to me that *Mrs.* was an ugly word. It wasn't pronounced as written. It looked like someone grumbling and it was followed by someone else's name and not your own. *Miss* was a pretty word. Before feminism, I used to like to write it before my name. *Miss Anita Martin* and I imagined a voice full of longing: *I miss you.*

And *recluse,* not pronounced as you'd expect, but close to *reckless.*

Doña Chepi had the apartment downstairs. She had no children of her own, but two little Indian girls to keep her company. "She gets them from Oaxaca," Doña Vicky said. "Simple, humble Oaxaca girls make the best servants."

Doña Vicky said, "All you have to do is feed them." She was angry Doña Chepi wouldn't find her one.

"How can you stand being far from your family?" Doña Chepi asked. "I'd be afraid. I'm afraid to be alone. That's why I have the girls. They don't do any work. I have them here for only one reason, so I don't have to sleep alone."

The girls slept on the floor by her bed like guardian dogs.

"You don't act like an American," they all told me. "You are very simple." Muy sencilla. If I couldn't change the world, I could at least refuse to be worldly.

When I did my laundry on the roof, I often met Rufi, rubbing sheets against the wash trough, wringing them out with her tiny hands.

Doña Chepi said, "She has to learn how to work, that one. Who will marry her with those ugly eyes?"

Rufi's eyelids were heavy, hooded. Sexy, I thought. Of course she was only nine years old, but her body gave off a kittenish warmth.

Why should she want to marry? In San Andrés, I came to understand I didn't have to either. I learned I didn't have to return to Paul, but then my money ran out and anyway, I told myself, *You are afraid of nothing,* and so I came home and did all the things normal women do and barely escaped with my life.

In the nonviolent movement, the point was not just to refrain from fighting back, it was to win the struggle within yourself and be free of the very impulse to hatred and anger. You accepted the pain and violence inflicted upon you and responded with love until the person who mistakenly believed himself to be your enemy would have no choice but to love you.

I'd found Doña Vicky by going to the Tourist Office and asking for a list of guest houses. In Pedro, I found a place to live by walking the streets and reading signs on lawns and in windows.

I had a backpack, a pocketbook, a cashier's check from my bank in New York, about $200 in cash, and another $200 in traveler's checks.

In San Andrés, I had a daily routine. Every day, I rode a different bus at random to the end of the line and then back. I startled whenever someone approached me and spoke. They were always asking for the time. I was a walking wristwatch, not a person, and that pleased me, and when I stopped wearing the watch, I was left alone.

In Mississippi you could be beaten for riding buses, but that was if you sat with black companions.

In San Andrés, almost everyone had brown skin except for me, and once I watched when the driver refused to stop for a barefoot woman with braids and called her a dirty Indian. In Mississippi, I was proud to be an outside agitator, but in Mexico, I was a foreigner and I kept my mouth shut.

California Transit

In California, I was an alien.

The Department of Motor Vehicles was at the other end of Gaffey Street. I kept mispronouncing it—Gaffer, Gaffney.

Have you studied for the written test?

No, I said, and lied. I don't drive. I just want a nondriver's ID.

The bank had sent me after refusing to open an account with my cashier's check. ID? the girl asked. Oh, no, Ma'am, the U.S. passport isn't valid in the State of California.

I waited on one line and then I waited on another. They took my photo and my money and my thumbprints. The sign said, If you have no thumbs, fingerprints will do, and I wondered how many people had chopped off their thumbs to keep from being recognized.

They took my fingerprints in Mississippi. That was all so long ago, I had forgotten.

When they beat you and used all those horrible words, you were supposed to look into their eyes and imagine them as they'd once been, babies, vulnerable, without language or hatred.

When they beat me, I did not fight back or resist, but I couldn't make myself love them. Instead, they fueled the silent hate inside me. Fuel needs to power something, it shouldn't just burn, but I took their blows to increase my hate. I incubated it though no one could tell just by looking. But I knew. I failed through an insufficiency of love.

I was afraid I might someday be dangerous.

In San Andrés, I was safe, in quarantine. Even if my hatred burned, harmless.

Evenings, I watched out the window while the temperature—always 20° C.—and the day's headlines flashed in Spanish across the electronic sign over the newspaper office. Then, in the early tropical dark, I'd go out to buy two rolls for dinner, fresh and hot from the bakery, the last batch of the day. I was always hungry and felt very much alive. I wrote letters to my parents and to Paul because it was expected and I feared if I didn't, Paul might show up, or my parents might send someone to get me. One day, I walked into the bakery and the calendar had changed to show the Prater in Vienna, an autumn scene. I wrote home that at the sight of the fall leaves, I'd burst into tears. This wasn't true. As a child, I had a diary with a lock. I filled it with lies, carefully crafting the sentiments I believed a young girl was supposed to feel and this was, perhaps, another reason for leaving home. It had always been necessary to act as if what other people valued mattered equally to me.

I miss you, I wrote. *I miss the autumn leaves.* In truth, I missed nothing.

* * *

If I hadn't met Burton, what I did would not have happened.

Even in San Andrés I met people. You may want to, but you can't stay isolated long.

The American wife of the wealthy Mexican husband.

The exiles from Franco's Spain who met the Spanish sailors on the docks for smuggled cheese and sausage and little Spanish finches carried in captivity across the ocean to remind someone of home.

Little Rufi with the funny eyelids who worked for Doña Chepi downstairs. We met on the roof.

"What's your name?" I said.

She straightened her shoulders and stared straight ahead. "Rufina Sánchez Sánchez, at your service." She shouted it out like a soldier.

I wanted to bring her home with me.

Now my home is PEE-dro where the Maersk line has a ship big enough to carry 6,000 railroad-car-size containers on a single trip. Auto carriers hold 4,500 cars and stevedores drive Hondas right off the ramps, or so Burton's told me. I see the trucks barreling away from Long Beach, but I've never seen any of the cranes move. One of the busiest ports in the world and all I see is this Monopoly game grid, frozen immobility.

I see advertising signs that line the streets like totem poles and the ad on the bench at the busstop—*Divorcio en 14 Días*, painted in the pretty colors of the Mexican flag.

Why on earth am I here?

In New York, the landlord replaced the boiler in the cellar with individual heaters and then claimed it was no longer an apartment building. We no longer had rent-stabilized leases. Even I, who had once practiced law, could find no recourse.

I went looking. For $1,200/month, I could have had a shabby little room small enough to touch both walls if I stretched my arms. I didn't have $1,200/month and I promised Dinah we weren't going anywhere unless there was space for her to run and leap and play.

Was there a moment, a specific moment when it happened? When money became the measure of a person's worth?

On my own, I needed very little. I lay on the floor in Pedro.

"You're like a secular nun," Maureen said once. "You're a saint."

"Hardly," I said.

For years, I refused to speak to her. Till she called from Los Angeles. When I arrived, the phone number she'd given me was disconnected. The consulting firm that was to hire me—if it had ever existed—wasn't there.

She would be self-righteous. It would be my fault: "How else could I get you to talk to me?"

Once upon a time, she said, "You're the one person who would never hurt anyone."

Even then, I wanted to wring her neck. I said, "You have no idea."

* * *

Maureen said friendship was the greatest gift a person could offer. Refusing someone's friendship or not valuing it at full worth was the ugliest demonstration of human cruelty, the small essential seed from which all greater cruelties could spring.

She loved me in some way and I did not love her and so I felt I owed her.

We met at law school, which is where I went after I got out of the hospital and left Paul. Queens College was committed to turning out lawyers for social justice. It was a school that accepted women, unlike everywhere else in those days when you were told, You'll just be taking a place that should go to a man. Why train you when you'll never practice law? You'll just stay home and have babies. And even if you don't, who will hire you?

I could see why Maureen thought we had to stick together.

Those were the days when classified ads came in two sections: *Help Wanted-Female* and *Help Wanted-Male*, when you had to wear makeup to get a job but not so much that the cops would roust you if you waited on the corner for a friend. You brought a brown-bag lunch or ate in the company cafeteria or in Woolworth's or else went on a diet. What decent woman would expect a decent place to serve her unescorted?

The days of men with their loud voices; women with their swinging hips. And then the new consciousness: women can only trust another woman. I tried, but couldn't.

Once I told Maureen I trusted no one.

She said, "What have I done?"

I said, "Oh, Maury. It's not that I *distrust* you."

I called her *Maury* when she seemed particularly vulnerable in a way that made me fear consequences if she didn't believe I was her friend.

In New York, I'd found her an apartment. I recommended her for a job. Two months in a row I lent her money for rent. She used it to get her ears pierced and to buy diamond studs, and when she was evicted, I let her move in. She ate my food and never contributed a dime. Weekends, Maureen always had parties to go to and though I was never invited along, she'd come home late and wake me to say I was her only true friend and because by then I truly disliked her, I felt too guilty to even think of asking her to leave.

When Maureen finally moved out, she said it was to save her reputation. She said, "Everyone thinks you're a lesbian."

"How flattering," I said. "A woman is generally taken to be a lesbian if she doesn't appear to be stupid."

Maureen lied about everything, so when she said, "I'm going to win your trust. I'm going to be worthy of it," I wasn't stupid enough to believe her.

* * *

The movers I contracted with in New York didn't show. Why should they? I had so very little to move.

California Transit

I should have left it all behind and gone to the airport with Dinah or at least sent her on ahead of me by air, but I couldn't bear to part from her. I rented a U-Haul and we set off.

Our first night on the road, I checked into the motel and Dinah was afraid to come out of her carrier. In the middle of the night I woke to find her under the covers and clinging, trembling, to my leg.

I'd brought her home when she was four weeks old, a tiger-striped tabby with turquoise eyes that would soon turn green and light eyebrows that gave her a sweet but oddly reproachful look. Of course she slept with me, on the pillow beside me. She'd wrap herself in my hair, tread on my scalp, and purr loud as a lawnmower, her little claws flexing.

It had not been my intention to adopt her. The ASPCA trailer was parked at Broadway and 72nd and everyone was going in to look. I only wanted to pet her, but she climbed up my arm and clung to me and when I tried to put her back she clung tighter and she cried and I didn't know what else to do, so I took her.

How attached she was, before I'd done anything to deserve it, and at first, I admit, I didn't trust her. She'd lie beside me and I'd be too afraid to sleep. She might claw my eyes out. After all, she was a beast, and capable of anything.

But Dinah trusted me. She loved me. She'd nap on my shoulder. She'd lick my hair and groom me clean.

Living with a cat is like walking into a room and finding a vase of fresh flowers. It's like spending every night within the sound of the sea.

Somewhere between Phoenix and the California line, the needle on the temperature gauge shot all to the way to HOT. I turned the air conditioning off. I turned the heater on. Just a little while, babydoll, I promised Dinah.

Just a little while, but when the needle hit the top of the gauge I pulled over. We waited on the shoulder, Dinah panting, till the needle began to drop. Then, key in the ignition, I couldn't get the truck to start.

We waited there, on a long empty stretch of highway in 120-degree heat hoping a car would pass and call for help, and I left the door open so Dinah could get some air. She seemed so miserable, I took her out and let her lie beneath the truck where at least there was some shade. The poor thing needed water. I'd come prepared. Of course I'd brought a plastic jug. Though, yes, I'd failed to put the cap on tight. I was dizzy and my hands trembled and I knocked it over and the water spilled, evaporating almost instantly on the ground, and I grabbed for the jug and saved an inch or so and poured it all in Dinah's dish. I gave it to her, not to me. I tried.

I lay down on the shoulder, my head under the truck, and talked to her. I blew my breath at her, hot, but at least it was a breeze.

It's going to be OK, I told Dinah. We're going to California. You'll like it there. You're going to be a California cat.

We've been through this before, I told her. When she had her first shots and she lay at home feverish and moaning. When she was spayed and I swore I'd never do such a thing to a little animal ever again. She shivered uncontrollably as the anaesthetic wore off and when I tried to cover her with a towel she screamed in pain and her little body was shaved so she looked like a skinned rabbit ready for the pot and strangely, frighteningly erotic. I thought she would never be well but a day later she was leaping to the top of the bookcase.

You're going to be all right, I told her.

But by the time someone called for help and by the time the tow truck came, I was delirious from the heat and Dinah had stopped panting beneath the truck and was hot and stiff and dead.

. . .

There was a shed. A mechanic. He said, You gotta learn how to drive in the desert. Worst thing is to turn off the engine if you overheat.

There was a hose and water running hot. There was a soda machine without refrigeration. I drank the water and three cans of not iced iced tea.

You might need a doctor, the mechanic said. How long were you out there?

All I knew was I had to take Dinah and go.

You shouldn't be driving, he said. Heat. Dehydration. You start seeing things.

They stopped us at the state line, looking for fruits and vegetables, and I held my breath, sure I had contraband I didn't even know of.

I checked into a motel. Dinah, we're here, in California.

I couldn't part with her. I couldn't look at her. She'd grown up to be drop-dead gorgeous. You never saw her slink around in that sneaky cat way. She always came bounding so forthrightly. Dinah would tear things to pieces with her claws and teeth, but when she played with me, wrestling, pouncing, she always kept her claws sheathed and never closed her sharp teeth all the way. I thought, human children have to be taught not to hurt and many of them never learn. Dinah? I never taught her a thing.

I placed her under the motel bed and the cold cramp in my stomach spread through my blood. I slept and woke. The air conditioner filled the room with a stale smell and I could smell it all over my body, coming out of me with clammy sweat. I trembled and the television glowed with malevolence and I saw a Japanese man.

He was forty-three years of age, victim of a hit-and-run in Desert Hot Springs. His son spoke on-camera: "Who could have done such a thing?"

He was inside my dream, he was inside my fever, and I was riding so high in the cab of the truck it was the top of his head I saw rather than his startled eyes when I hit him. It was a single thud, his body, my heart, the jolt as I jumped down to the street and looked at him wedged beneath the front tires.

From the screen, his son looked right at me. "How could anyone do this? To back up over my father's body."

I tried to remember. I got back behind the wheel and backed up over him only because I was so upset and confused. That's how it must have been. It wasn't.

The news reporter gave the number to call if you were a witness. The same number, I assumed, if you needed to confess. I picked up the phone. But it didn't make sense. I was just across the California line. I was sweating in places I didn't know a body could sweat. I was dry as a brown leaf. Shivering with chills. I could feel the thump of the body, a sense-memory, a thud that made me sick.

Where the hell was Desert Hot Springs? I grabbed for my maps. There was the town, west of Indio, and Indio was still ninety-six miles away. I was nowhere near where it happened.

I spilled out the contents of my backpack looking for gas receipts. I clutched the proof—I was still in Arizona when the man was hit. But the impact, the thud. And then I stood before the judge and he was asking for my plea. *You'll start seeing things.* Someone had told me that. Or did he warn me *hearing things*? This was terrible, terrible, and it didn't make sense. I was in a motel room in Blythe, CA, not in court, and there was no one I could ask to make sense of it and the judge called a recess for commercials.

My heart slammed inside me. I knew I hadn't done it. I believed I had.

Paper. I needed to write my confession. In the drawer, just the Yellow

Pages and a Bible. God, I thought. People who believe in God betray other people again and again. I put the Bible underneath the bed with Dinah.

What would I do without her?

When I failed in every other way, I'd come home at night and hold my breath and listen to the crunch crunch of Dinah eating her dry food and her healthy little sounds would put my heart at ease. Until I heard her panting in the desert, I never heard her breathe. She must have thought I was some huffing wheezing laboring machine. I heard her tongue clicking against her fur and I heard her footfalls. I woke sometimes at night in fear knowing someone was in the apartment with me, the floor creaking, the brush of a body against the fabric of a chair and, lying in bed, I could feel the presence of someone there looking at me, and I would listen for the sound of the intruder's breath and, hearing none, would know it was Dinah.

In Blythe, I woke expecting to see her eyes, huge and black with just a thin circling line of yellow, calm and alert. I woke shivering and clutching a credit card receipt from Arizona.

Outside the door, my truck looked lopsided and woozy. As though there'd been an accident.

I checked out. The sun was already merciless, the pavement burned through my shoes and turned soft beneath my feet.

A dozen pulses beat inside me as I walked to the front of the truck to check for blood. How could there be blood? The television had said it was a black SUV, and this was your standard white and orange U-Haul.

The right front tire was slashed.

I went into the office to use the phone.

The man behind the desk said, "You already checked out."

"Less than a minute ago."

He shrugged.

"My tire was slashed in your parking lot. I have to call U-Haul."

He shrugged.

It wasn't my truck, and anyway, how could I trust myself now behind the wheel? There was nothing in the back I really needed. Clean getaway, I thought.

"Where's the bus station?" I asked.

He shrugged.

Heat was turning the world wavy. I hoped I wouldn't have to walk far. When he found her beneath the bed, I hoped he would show respect for Dinah.

I could still see the Japanese man's eyes behind his wire-rimmed glasses, though in my fever dream I'd never seen his eyes, only the top of his glossy black head. When I knelt beside him on the street his glasses were shattered and his eyes were closed and a Dodgers' cap was lying beside him. But none of that had happened.

Later, I would look back, amazed. Later, I would know my guilt that night wasn't only for Dinah. It was practice, a rehearsal for the real thing.

* * *

I'm lying on the floor in Pedro:

The warmth of Dinah's little body. The time that little Mexican girl came up behind me on the roof and covered my eyes. Guess who? and I knew at once it was Rufi, not so much from her voice but the radiant heat of her tiny hands.

I'm remembering:

When we linked arms together;

When the whole nation watched;

California Transit

When the words "mass movement" made you think "mass" and though you weren't Catholic, it was holy;

When your body didn't have to be beautiful; you could still put it on the line and change the world.

Such grandiose humility!

And so I chose San Pedro, because a person like me in Hollywood? No way. I figured women my age with too many face lifts, too many dye jobs. Vaginal laser rejuvenation. Liposuction deaths. I never had cosmetic surgery per se, but after Paul, a certain amount of facial reconstruction was necessary.

In San Andrés, as you entered the town, there was a pool with flamingos, all spotlit at night, fooling you into thinking there was something splendid about the town, tropical and special.

In San Andrés the butchers had refrigerated cases for the meat, something that was extraordinary in Mexico during that era.

In San Andrés, one day I boarded a bus and—strange—I was the only female and no one collected a fare. I didn't realize it was the sugar refinery's bus till we arrived and one of the workers asked, Would you like to see? We'll have to be careful, he said. You're not allowed in here. Insurance. I should have been conspicuous, the only woman and a foreigner, but I had perfected the art of invisibility. I followed the man across a cement floor sticky with rivulets of syrup. We climbed catwalks over cauldrons of bubbling molasses. Everywhere a sweet hot fog, and burning, burning. You're stuck here, he said, until the shift ends and the bus returns to town. I'll have to hide you. I sat on a crate behind burlap sacks. Every now and then the man came by and gave me a pitcher of water which I was afraid to drink. I wondered what it was about this man that had made him capable of seeing me.

Rufi, wringing those heavy wet sheets; the little huffs of breath, her little mews of effort like a kitten.

In San Andrés, the cats were scrawny and kept outside to kill rats and the dogs weren't pets. They were mangy and vicious. But little boys held shiny black roosters close to their hearts and stroked the glossy feathers, and some ladies wore cockroaches attached to their lapels by golden chains, and one day at lunch the pretty waitress had a little yellow chick peeping away and peeking out of her blouse.

That was another place, another life.

In Mississippi, the dogs bit our bodies.

I ate what I wanted to in Mexico and never got sick. My system was used to being challenged. In Mississippi, the stink of a jail cell in summer. I could coexist with a certain level of microbes. But in Pedro I began to feel an anxious disgust for my neighbors. After the first morning I was unable to use the shared toilet down the hall. I peed in the sink in my room and for the other necessity sought out public restrooms around town.

The Y opened at 5:00 a.m., Monday through Friday. The public library was closer, though its hours less convenient, the soap supply was unreliable and it only had hot air hand-driers. At the Y, I liked the paper towels, but the hot and cold taps were separate and it was impossible to get the water temperature right. McDonald's, Jack In The Box. I had many choices.

In one of my other lives, I used McDonald's many times to brush my teeth and change clothes and wash from the waist up. I was much younger then and it was my job to talk to children who needed protection. I followed the stream of migrant workers up and down the East Coast. They raked the blueberries and picked the apples and potatoes and headed south for winter crops.

Oh! What an interesting life you've led!

Most of the time I couldn't get into the fields and waited for them in their camping places under the bridges in Boston. I was no different from the people I served: I owned only as much as I could carry, and I didn't hesitate to wash up in McDonald's without buying food. But in Pedro, one day I stood crying in front of the library because it was closed and I needed a bathroom and there was a Taco Bell, but I suddenly felt ashamed and couldn't make myself go in.

On the migrant trail, we slept on the riverbanks and under bridges, and here in Pedro there are overpasses and pedestrian walkways over freeways, all enclosed in wire so you can no longer throw rocks at the buses and cars below.

And in Mexico I rode a bus for three days until the circulation stopped in my feet and I had to go to a doctor to restart it. We drove through cold forests in the mountains where orchids took moisture directly from the clouds, and through tropical lowlands where the grasses were so wet and lush the cows looked like they were floating. And once, at the end of the bus line, a boy with a raft ferried us across the river to "La Cabaña del Tío Tom." Fat men without shirts drank beer. I was thirsty but reluctant to sit with them. I stood by the river's edge until enough passengers gathered for the boy to make a return trip.

In Mississippi, Uncle Tom was not a kind name and for black and white to sit together was an act of revolutionary defiance.

In Pedro, sometimes the hills are so steep it's impossible to get the back door of the bus to open. Shadows cast on the pavement look like a row of spikes. I brace myself in my seat. Nothing.

In Mississippi, we went on hunger strikes. In Mexico, I was always hungry and often dreamed of food. In California, I was hungry again, but dreamed instead of bathrooms. In the dreams, I always had my period, though in real life, thankfully, I was past all that. In my dreams, everywhere the stalls were locked or occupied or overflowing. When I did go in, someone always followed right behind to watch me.

Later, Burton would tell me to always inspect a public toilet carefully, looking for hidden video cameras. "There's people who like to steal your private moment," he said.

In jail, the only privacy was deep inside your head.

When you live inside your own head, the terrain becomes so familiar, the idea of insanity can be appealing, knocking down the walls of one more claustrophobic room.

When I lived in that room in San Andrés, I spent part of the day with my mind blank and part of it in thinking very deep thoughts. I made notes about regenerating American society, about changing language to save the world. Why did the English language capitalize the first person singular? Why was the singular form of the noun the root and the plural its extension? Did our language itself assert unity over multiplicity? Did it demean the collective? There were Indian languages that had no comparatives or superlatives. Was there any hope for our culture? Was it simply too violent, too hierarchical, too male, too white?

I carried a copy of Lévi-Strauss—*The Raw and the Cooked*—and I made lists of oppositions in American culture and drew up mathematical formulae and transformations that made no sense even as I wrote them but that looked like the diagrams in his book.

Last year, when they arrested the Unabomber, he reminded me of me.

Once you start on that path, you have to tell yourself, No, I don't live inside my head. I live in a place. And if you live in a place, you learn the lay of the land.

That's why I began to ride buses.

* * *

I took a different L.A. bus every day. I went to the beach and thought of San Andrés where there was white water and black sand; seafood cocktails sitting forever in the sun, looking like strawberry sundaes; the smell of limes cut open; the bottles of beer; the children shouting *Shark! Shark! Tiburón!* I invited Rufi once to go with me. It's impossible, she said, *no se puede.*

I rode past the Del Amo Waste Pit and I rode up the terraced hills and through the canyons. I went to the piers where the cruise liners docked and to the piers where tourists ate seafood and watched the sea lions at play. I visited a restored adobe where a tall blond man said he was a third-generation Californian out of Iowa. "We've tried to recreate a typical Spanish family's life back in the early 1800s. Father, mother, and son."

I said, "One child. Hardly typical."

"The early settlers weren't Mexican," he said. "They were Spanish. European, and civilized."

Around the public-housing blocks, every bungalow had a yard sale. Clothes spread out on the ground as if drying after being washed in the river. Carefully cleaned take-out containers made of aluminum foil or styrofoam. A hardcover book containing twenty-four short mysteries, each one with the final page torn out. Beneath an awning a woman sold hundreds of boxes of Fruit Loops. A stray rubbed against my leg and left a bit of cat hair that I rolled into a ball and saved in my pocket.

With a traveler's check I bought a pair of scissors and an air mattress. I hacked off my hair. I needed it short so I could wash it more easily in the sink. I had colored it before leaving New York, but the roots were already coming in gray.

I had something now to sleep on. We slept on air mattresses in Alabama when we stopped for the night during the march to Montgomery from Selma. There was rain and discomfort that time, but no violence.

At a yard sale, with dwindling cash, I bought a chair, a table, curtains, a lamp, tiger-striped sheets, and a big blue towel. I carried the furniture one piece at a time to my room and when I left the lamp momentarily in the entryway someone took it. I couldn't figure out how to hang the curtains. The table and chair didn't make the room look any better and the sheets didn't fit the air mattress. I kept the towel and, angry with myself for wasting money, left everything else in the alley for someone to claim.

On still another bus, I rode to where land ended. I walked by a lighthouse and climbed a hill where families picnicked near a memorial bell inside a pagoda and I walked past the old fort and across a parking lot toward what I thought must be the dog pound, there was so much barking.

There were concrete walkways and pools and pens, plastic awnings giving shade, there were dozens of children crowded at the fences, and dozens of little sea lions barking.

"Is this a zoo?" asked a woman in dark glasses.

"No," said the children. "Yes."

"No," she said. "This is not a zoo. It's a rehab center. Like a hospital. We take care of the animals, and when they're well, they go back home to the sea."

She stared at me.

She said, "Who knows what El Niño is? It's a warm ocean current that causes changes in the weather. And because of El Niño, we're going to see more than 2,500 pinniped victims stranded this year."

Behind her, a man with a ponytail came down the walkway with a carrier.

"Who knows what a pinniped is?"

Several children answered: "Seals and sea lions."

"And walruses, too. A pinniped is a carnivorous aquatic mammal with all four limbs modified into flippers. Why do we say carnivorous?"

A teenage girl unlocked a pen; the man opened the carrier, tipped it, and the sea lion pup bumped out onto the concrete floor.

"Because they eat fish. And why do we say aquatic?"

A little girl said, "They live in the water."

The man tossed a fish into the pen.

"That's right. But some of them spend as much as half their time on land. People see them on the beach or the rocks and think they're sick or stranded when really they're just resting."

The little pinniped ignored the fish, so the man held the pup down and the teenager forced its mouth open. In the pen next door, the sea lions began to fight, snapping and biting at each other, aroused with hunger.

"How does El Niño cause problems for pinnipeds?"

"The ocean is too warm."

The sound of a blender, a food processor, coming from the shed, and someone laughed. The wind rustled through plastic trash on the bluff and someone turned on a radio. Someone turned a hose on. The splashing.

"Not all of it," said the woman. "Just the top."

They had whiskers and a bit of white around their muzzles.

The woman said, "The coldwater fish go to the bottom or migrate to colder waters. The sea lions can't dive that deep and the pups are too small and weak to migrate. Look," she said. "Now they're giving it antibiotics."

The sky was California blue but it isn't true there are no clouds. All morning, the gray overcast they insist on calling the marine layer, and now a sweep and blur of white rolling across the sky like surf.

I walked around the enclosure.

"What other problems do they face?" Pause. "Oil spills."

The pups were diving and splashing, sleek and wet.

"If you see one on the beach, what should you do?"

"Tell my parents."

"That's right. Keep your distance. It's against the law to bother them, and besides, they can bite."

A big light-colored animal in a pen all by herself.

"How much do you think a father sea lion weighs? Six hundred fifty pounds! And a mother? Only two hundred!"

She had a ruby collar of scars around her neck. "What is that?" I asked.

The animal began to shake in spasms. I could hardly bear to look at her, head and flippers hitting and flapping against cement. "What's wrong with her?"

"When a baby elephant seal is born, it weighs seventy pounds at birth. That's more than you!"

In the parking lot, an RV pulled up with handicapped plates. I don't really remember that but as Burton showed up every day at just this time, I suppose I must have seen it.

"WHAT'S WRONG WITH THIS ONE?" I said.

The man with the ponytail looked at me. "The scar around her neck is from a gill net. And she has seizures. About sixty adult females came in with seizures from a toxic algae bloom. Some kind of dynoflagellate. Most of them died. That's what we thought was wrong with her, but it turns out to be epilepsy."

She lay on the dry concrete and her flippers beat weakly. The man and the teenager held her and forced a feeding tube down her throat. He said, "She'd choke on a fish."

The woman and the schoolchildren came around. "This one will live here the rest of her life," she said. "In her condition, if she went into the water, she'd drown."

I interrupted: "What's her name?"

"We never give them names," the woman said. "These animals aren't pets. They have to stay wild."

"But she's going to live here for the rest of her life."

The female shuddered. She was a sea lion and the sea could kill her.

* * *

The insides of my ears itched all the time and my ankles and so did the skin underneath my fingernails.

BAIT/LIQUOR. BAIT/LIQUOR/ICE CREAM. White-domed Navy fuel depots; bail bonds in a pink trailer; the Sons of Norway; church belltowers; the silly green trolleys carrying tourists from Ports o' Call to Yuppie Gulch.

A couple waved the bus driver down.

"We're not here to ride. We're here to do the Lord's work." They walked up and down the aisle handing out pamphlets and saying Jesus loves you, and then got off without paying a fare.

"How late does this bus run?" I asked.

The driver said, "I'm not late."

"I mean, when's the last bus back in the evening?"

"I don't know. I don't work that shift."

A fat woman in a flowered housedress said, "If it's a night route that's been discontinued, give 'em a call, and they'll pick you up at home."

"Really?"

She rolled her eyes toward the front. "Depends on the driver. Most of them are very nice. And whether you live on a hill. They can't always make the hills."

I was still standing in the stairwell. "How much is the fare?"

He said, "Depends where you're going."

"To the end of the line."

"It's a local fare to board, but if you stay on, it's a premium fare."

"How much?"

"Put seventy-five cents in the till, lady."

I did, and the fat woman patted the seat beside her.

"I know it says DASH," she said, "but it's an LADOT. The route used to be MetroBus but it was discontinued. You would have done better taking a MAX. Don't worry about the stops," she said. "The real ones mostly aren't marked and where the signs say discontinued it's usually still running and where the sign shows a stop it's mostly not. Ask me anything," she said. "I've got all the schedules in my head and I never even finished high school."

"Thank you," I said. Good thing I was riding at random.

What I saw: Routes changed overnight as roads became off-limits each time subdivisions declared their through streets private and put up gates. Or when people complained: No buses welcome on this block.

Kids sitting on skateboards and racing downhill. Houses with porthole windows in funny places as if the houses weren't designed that way but one year when the money was good everyone had to have one put in. Croatian Hall. Dalmatian Deli.

On the freeway, the white stripes became invisible in the sun but the old paint came shining through from lanes changed and paved over long ago. Who says L.A. has no history? Ghost lanes.

California Transit

I rode north through South Central. No signs of the riots/uprising/civil disorder/major street disturbances. What you choose to call it tells which side you're on.

"You call that an uprising?" Burton would say later. "In Watts, in '65, the city burned for days."

All the black people seemed to be gone. In South Central, everyone was brown. Everywhere, murals with the Virgin of Guadalupe, and tortillerías, and there were children in the rutted dirt alleyways, and Mexican music from the radios, and Mexican flags.

And here comes a scary-looking tall man leaving his seat in the back of the bus and headed this way. He stands in front of a young woman. His arms are covered with scabs and he points at her water bottle. "Please." She hesitates, then hands it to him. He pours some water on a tissue and gives the bottle back and I turn and watch him return to his seat where he lifts a tiny little girl onto his lap and wipes her dirty fingers so tenderly clean.

I climbed a metal staircase down to the rocky shore and picked my way over the seawrack and the rocks. Around a point, in the shadow of a cliff, a Mexican woman was diapering a baby and a man waved a bottle at me—Hello! Come drink with us! Join us! I shook my head and wondered why I walked away when I felt so lonely.

I went to the Pedro Heights Improvement Association, because of its name, like the Montgomery Improvement Association, when Rosa Parks refused to give up her seat.

A white woman spoke, blond hair coiffed, shimmering fingernails. "Today it's next door to me, but if it's not stopped, it will be your homes tomorrow. How would you feel to walk out your door and see zucchini? Vegetable gardens may be all well and good in low-income housing projects, but here in the Heights, we identify with the Peninsula lifestyle."

The coffee was bad but they served good chocolate chip muffins.

I eavesdropped, listening for the right person's voice.

"Do you have an organ donor card? Tear it up," a woman said. "Destroy it. My baby's heart is beating inside of a little Muslim."

A woman grabbed my arm. "Would you like to meet Jesus? He's my next-door neighbor and we're very good friends. Even though he's a Communist. Most people don't know that. They even think Jesus was born in Palestine," she said, "just like they think George Washington was the first president. In fact, he was the eighth, but he bought off the other seven."

I was trying to understand something, or trying to be something.

I was looking for a feeling in the air, something that said change.

What they did to us in Mississippi was nothing new and none of it had ever been secret. The change was not in what we did or what they did, but in something I can't explain, that for the first time, people were ashamed to see it.

A man pointed to my plastic sandals. "Do you boycott leather?"

I thought, well, I could.

I made coffee in the morning on my hot plate. Lunch was the meal I ate out—cheaper than dinner—and at night I ate bread or sometimes corn chips or something chocolate.

I ate lunch Mexican-style, between two and four in the afternoon, which meant I was usually the only patron and no one could object to my taking up a table. I became a vegetarian. Now I could make a nuisance of myself with waiters and make them talk to me. Is there lard in your beans? Is the rice cooked in chicken broth? Is there shrimp in your eggroll? In the Filipino restaurant, the menu was printed in neat red letters on the mirrored wall. Pilin Mo Isisigang Ko—Pancit—Sago Gulaman. I watched a teenaged girl write the specials on the glass in lipstick. I didn't understand the words and went up to the steam table and pointed. Those look good. Are those oyster mushrooms? No, they're deepfried chitlins. We ate chitlins in Mississippi and toxic red hot dogs and drank soda pop that tasted like bubblegum and learned that a blow above the eye bleeds so much it can look a lot worse than it is and that you can have broken ribs and not even know it. And that, what's that? Taro leaves in coconut milk. OK, that's what I'll have. It smelled so good. A heap of taro leaves on rice. I could taste the pork mixed in and ate it anyway.

Summer in Mississippi: prickly heat and bug bites. Gnats, mosquitoes, no see 'ums, and when you were lucky enough to land a bed, bedbugs. We were supposed to present a calm and dignified appearance, but I was always scratching.

"Are you the good one or the other one?" they used to ask me. There were two white girls from the North and they had trouble telling us apart. I hoped I was the good one but before I could find out, they had a nickname for me: Little Itch.

I thought, I've bled on your behalf. I am risking my life. My name is Anita. It wasn't important.

In front of the homeless feeding station, I watched a priest present several homeless men with shopping carts for their possessions. The carts were confiscated by the police as soon as the men rolled them away.

This should have made me take a stand, but it was all I could do to get on and off the bus.

It was all I could do to keep walking.

* * *

Who says middle-aged women are invisible? There were eyes on me everywhere. Cameras mounted on the traffic lights, security cameras in every store and in front of homes. I walked out of the supermarket when they wanted to fingerprint me for using a traveler's check.

ID. Thumbprints. No one else seemed to mind or those that did had already moved to Idaho or else Montana.

The pretty green bridge and the candy-striped cranes. The beach. The kelp flies in the seaweed. The tidepool where I saw a mollusk that looked like a great big clamshell with a soft black eye. "Touch it," said the boy, and I did, and he laughed at me. "That's its feces!"

You can laugh at me. I always wanted to make people laugh.

"You came down here to laugh at us. To feel superior."

No, I'd gone to Mississippi in search of someone to admire.

How I used to admire the high school boys who'd lean against the brick wall and go through their comic routines. I wanted them to notice me. But what if I got them to listen and I bored them? So I took pratfalls. I flung myself into the air. Down the bleachers or down the stairs without warning. I may be the smartest girl in school, but see, I don't take myself so seriously. I may love books, but see how I let my books go flying. I wasn't afraid of breaking my bones. The impact happened before I had time to think. I was fearless.

If they had undressed me, as Paul would later do, they would have seen the bruises. Walking was painful and I had to hide how much it hurt because if people had known, that would have really made them laugh, that I would do that to myself just for attention.

All my life I've had phobias—spiders, heights—but never any physical fear.

And I rode the buses late at night, anything to avoid my room.

Up at the sea lions, the winds blew up from the ocean and one night behind the pens above the bluffs I saw a mockingbird attack a hawk. It flew right at it, pecked at its head and teased at its tail again and again and again until the hawk flew off and then circled at a distance and then gave up and was gone.

It occurred to me that with Dinah gone, no one depended on me. It would be all right if I weren't alive anymore, but I didn't deserve to be at peace, so I came home late and tried to sleep and instead the horror settled over me and sometimes I cried to the point of exhaustion, ashamed to be so hopeful: a person doesn't cry out loud without the faith that someone might hear her.

When I lived with Doña Vicky, I was not a nice person, but then North Americans have always gone to the Third World to misbehave. What I did was practice living with a heart devoid of charity.

One night, Doña Vicky's relatives came and there were whispered conversations. Where would they all sleep? I knew they were hoping I would overhear and open my door and offer to share my room where there was a single bed along each wall. Because I paid rent, they were forbidden to intrude on my privacy by knocking or asking. I pretended not to hear. In the morning, I came out of my room as though nothing had happened and drank my coffee silently while the girls complained of sleeping three to a bed, their cousins' smelly feet in their faces.

Rufi said, "Señorita, please. Please take me with you."

And the room in Pedro closed in on me till I couldn't breathe and at the same time seemed boundless so that as I lay on the floor I felt in freefall. If the door opened, it meant someone would come in, and there was never a good reason for that to happen. I used to like listening to the sound of Doña Vicky, just outside. Now I dreaded footsteps.

Why was it so different this time? Was it just that I was twenty then and now past fifty? Was I merely playing then, never imagining it might be forever?

* * *

There's the door. Open it. Walk out.

Isn't that why I had come? The chance to care again and to be useful.

I thought of going up to L.A., finding Maureen and confronting her.

The job she'd offered didn't exist. That didn't mean there weren't others.

I was once what they called a poverty lawyer. Those were the days!—when the government paid you to represent the poor and on their behalf you usually sued the government that paid you.

I was admitted to the New York Bar. And I could type.

I learned how in Mississippi. Up till then I had refused to learn. No way was I going to end up in that female ghetto. I would hunt-and-peck with two fingers, like a man.

But in Mississippi, they asked me to teach the teenage girls. How could I admit that what for me looked like a trap looked to them—and was—a huge step forward?

There was one typewriter in the field office, so I copied the keyboard onto cardboard. Thirteen pieces of cardboard, and that's how we practiced our fingering. I chanted as our fingers moved: a-s-d-f-g-f-space; semi-l-k-j-h-j-space.

When you work on behalf of the poor, what you hear all day is *I need help.* No matter what you do, the next day is the same. Different faces, same need. Nothing you do makes it change. Day after day, month after month, year after year, and after Reagan, it got worse, consuming yourself, putting Band-Aids on wounds that won't—can't—heal.

It was a relief when we got defunded.

I became an office temp.

a-s-d-f-g-f-space.

I believed I was recovering from the nervous breakdown I hadn't quite had yet. I believed it was for the time being. Temporary.

semi-l-k-j-h-j-space.

The machines in the offices got newer: phone systems so complex I couldn't figure out how to answer when I heard the ring; word processors and computers. The years kept going by. The woman using the machines just got older.

* * *

Nice people have nice apartments and I don't, but I must have a nice face, because on the street and at the bus stops, people talked to me.

The man said, "I had to walk home last night. Took me five hours. I went up to get a friend out of jail and ended up walking home in pointy boots. These are the boots I had to walk twenty miles in. Get someone out of jail who takes your money and the car keys and is out the back door and gone. Some friend, right? Actually, it was my wife. I think it's divorce time, don't you? Though she's no worse than anyone else. That's just the way people treat each other."

"I hope not," I said.

A woman said, "We have to teach the children. Not to be afraid of the muertitos." The little dead people, little corpses. She said it with the diminutive, with affection. "I was at a wake last week," she said. "It broke my heart. You go to a wake to keep the poor muertito company, and the children stayed in the back and wouldn't go near."

I tried not to think about Dinah: bounding to the door to greet me or sticking her leg in the air like a yogi or a dancer. When she flopped back, her head hanging off the couch. When she licked herself with that pink tongue, stretching her toes wide open. Lapping at her fur, crunching her food, when I could hear her scratching, so diligent, in the litter box.

I tried to teach her to meow but up until the day she died she cooed like a dove and clucked like a hen and to get my attention she'd make a sound like a child's squeaky toy and she chirped and cheeped like a baby bird.

At night, I couldn't hear surf from my room in the harbor and sometimes I wondered why don't I hear foghorns?

I could hear honking and honking and never see the car. I heard sirens and couldn't tell from which direction. Dinah would have known exactly. I thought of how she used to scan the world for sound, of the wonderful little muscles that moved her ears.

During the day, I watched people. Ladies with colorful umbrellas held against the sun. A man so pale he seemed albino walking almost naked across the parking lot. A shirtless man on his knees in the alley looking into a piece of broken mirror as he shaved.

I was lonely, but not in a human way.

There were holes that opened in the floor that I fell through at night and sinkholes in the sidewalk that opened while I waited for the bus and holes in time, hours that disappeared and days. My life cracked open and I fell.

A house can swallow you whole. An apartment is safe. Who's ever heard of a haunted apartment? But a room-to-let isn't the same as an apartment, and the walls of this room could crush you.

I climbed the hill to the sea lions one night. There was a big orange moon. The volunteers were in the shed and the door was open and I could hear their voices and the sound of a blender and a hose running. There was one visitor by the pens, an old man leaning on braces under each arm, one hand curled in the fence and he was watching her. He had a Hemingway beard and under his T-shirt what looked like a hernia and his lips were moving. She was shuddering in spasm. He began to hum and I saw he wasn't wearing braces after all, but ski poles, with straps looped around his wrists. A volunteer stuck his head out of the shed and looked at us and went back inside and I moved away and heard the old man whisper.

"Angela," he whispered to her. He called her by name: "Angela."

Once upon a time, when people were hurting, I longed to hold them. And then something broke.

I still felt it up at the sea lions, looking at her. And because Burton watched her too, something inside me began to stir toward him.

* * *

Metal detectors in the grocery stores, men killing their girlfriends and their children, gang members shooting at each other and anyone in the way, discharged workers opening fire on other employees, police and armed robbers in Wild West shootouts, snipers on the freeway. How was it possible to live in such a place without wondering where the bullet meant for you was going to come from? How could I live here without starting to wonder what makes a person kill, what it would be like to do it?

One night late, I boarded an empty bus to go home. When he opened the door, the driver held his arm away from his side so I could see his gun. I wondered if it was legal for him to carry.

And I wondered why I would use the word *home* for a room like mine. What sort of person would live there? One who valued the intangibles, or one who wondered how her own neck would look with a circle of ruby scars, who didn't trust herself with a razor, who had noticed there was no fixture in the room from which she might hang herself and anyway she had no rope.

I could track Maureen down and invite her over. Maureen loved her creature comforts. She used to look at me, the sandals I wore, one strap torn. The sweater with a moth hole. In Mexico, there was always someone who needed it and could use it. In the U.S., you can't give torn clothing away, so you have to wear it and she would give me that look, of disappointment, maybe disgust. If I brought her here, she'd look around and say, "You really do live in a horrible place."

I wanted to slam her head into the toilet bowl and hold it underwater till she drowned. As though I could ever do such a thing. Me, nonviolent not only by choice but in the most visceral part of me, still waking at night sick with the memory of that thud. *How could you do it?* asked the Japanese man's son, *How could you back your car over his body?* I hadn't, and couldn't. Killing was not something I could ever do. It was not an act I could commit. The thought, of course, is not the deed. And in a bare room, in a town where you know no one, you are free to think about anything.

California Transit

* * *

Burton had gelled his sparse hair. It was windy and a clump blew up above his head and stuck there.

He said, "It's OK to feed the seals but not the homeless."

He didn't look directly at me. He was leaning on his ski poles, under the security light, watching Angela. His hernia protruded like something shoplifted beneath his shirt. "Meddlers," he said.

Poor Burton. I thought he, if anyone, could stop me.

I'd never seen anyone like him, the way he waddled so forcefully, his weight all in the lower thigh as though his pockets were always full.

It was past midnight, the middle of August. I'd been in California for a month. Most of the sea lion pups had put on weight and recovered from seal pox and they'd been returned to the sea. Where there had been perhaps a hundred, now half a dozen lay sleeping.

Burton said, "We've eliminated all their predators. El Niño's all we've got to keep 'em in check. Save 'em, send 'em out to make more. . . . Where's the logic?"

It didn't have to be logical, just an instinctive response at the sight of suffering. He fought against it, but still came to see her. A man of cynical, helpless compassion.

There was that moment of mutual recognition. There's that moment when you know you're being led into something that may become complicated. I'd known from the first that Burton and I had something to do with each other.

I said goodnight and turned in a hurry to leave.

He said, "You don't have a car."

It got me nervous to think he'd been watching me.

He said, "I'll drive you home."

I could have walked away, but didn't. Our relationship would last just under three weeks.

I'd never been in an RV before.

When he dropped me in front of the building, he said, "You really do live in a horrible place."

When he came back, I didn't invite him upstairs.

The first floor is boarded-up stores. There's a narrow entrance with a row of mailboxes, then a door for which you need a key, and then the narrow ill-lit stairs. The second floor: scaffolding and concertina wire on the outside and no one lives there. The third floor, there's me, an invalid woman (how does she climb the stairs? I've never seen her, just hear her wheeze), a tattooed boy who looks all of fifteen. He worries about everything: a baby bird in the street that his cat might get; the next-door suite, unoccupied, that was once a dentist's office, where the left-behind dentist chair and *People* magazines might draw a break-in. I worry week to week that we'll be put out so that the building can be torn down.

Burton says, "They don't do it that way in Los Angeles, with permits. The wrecking crew will come in the middle of the night. They'll bring the roof down on top of your head."

You don't need a key for the bathroom in the hall, but once you're inside, you can bolt it closed behind you.

In Mexico, some people had no locks while the rich were weighted down with keys: the front door, the back door, the car, the second car, the strong box, the country house, the son's home, the patio shed, every cabinet and every armoire and sometimes the bath in the master bedroom had a padlock to prevent the help from sitting on the bosses' toilet seat, the door unlocked only when it was time for the maid to clean.

"I feel like St. Peter with the keys." There was an American woman in San Andrés, married to a Mexican, and she always said that when she pulled out her key ring. Then she would laugh at the joke, pleased at how Mexican she—a Jewish girl from Brooklyn—had become.

I have a key for my door and sometimes I put it in the lock and wait in the hallway, reluctant to go in. I have a key for the mailbox where I find circulars for Current Resident. I try to remember when I became Current Resident instead of Occupant.

The sound of the incoming mail used to make my heart beat. The postman's whistle as he climbed the stairs in San Andrés, the lobby door opening, the clunk of the mail in the box in New York.

What on earth was I expecting?

Burton.

He wore thick glasses, the kind of lenses that turn dark in the sun, except his never got very dark outdoors and inside the RV they never got quite clear, giving his face and the whites of his eyes a yellow tinge. He was missing two fingers on his left hand, an accident.

We ate lunch in his RV. Fake wood paneling and carpeted in orange plush. A VCR. He mixed a pitcher of vodka and orange juice, opened a bag of chips.

"Reason I have this thing, I don't travel much. It's because I like to drink. If I have too much, I don't have to drive home. Just pull over, open up the bed and sleep." He said, "My third wife was killed by a drunk driver."

"I'm sorry," I said. It was hard to imagine him being married even once. "And now," I asked. "Are you married now?"

"Nope," he said. "I'm looking."

* * *

The notice came from DMV. They had lost my thumbprints. I had to return and start the process all over again if I wanted an ID.

I didn't want it, I thought. The bank did.

I told Burton because I was almost broke, with the cash advances on my credit cards maxed out. Though there was no way I could come right out and ask, I hoped he would offer me a loan.

"What are you going through DMV for? You can get a fake ID today up in Wilmas."

Wilmas was what the Mexicans called Wilmington. "Up-channel," said Burton. "That's the only place they let em live." He said, "In Pedro, spruce trees and palms grow side by side. But Anglos and Mexicans live together? Never!

"Let's go," he said. "Never work inside the system unless you have to."

In Wilmas, the boy behind the tamale factory took my photograph with a whitewashed alley wall for backdrop. The Virgin of Guadalupe presided, painted large on the wall just outside the frame. Tamales sold forty-five dollars for a hundred and I tried to imagine what it would be like to know so many people you bought tamales a hundred at a time.

Burton gave the boy a hundred dollars.

I said, "I'll pay you back."

He said, "My treat."

"What about my thumbprints?" I asked.

Burton and the boy both laughed. The boy said, "Ready in three hours."

Burton's left hand couldn't give a full set of prints.

He said, "Why would you want to use your real ones?"

We killed time at a car wash. Burton had the RV washed daily. And this, I pointed out, in a desert climate, where any responsible citizen would conserve water.

"Mankind's a long way from perfection," Burton said. "My handicap plates? They're useful, but you think they're kosher?"

He said, "Hell, you think I waste water. The damn city has the sprinklers on all night in the public parks so the homeless can't lie down and sleep."

He laughed at the Embassy bombing in Kenya. "Imperialist agents. Should have killed more of them."

"Mostly Africans died," I said.

"So what? How many Africans you think would cry for me?"

Burton was a terrible, terrible man.

The boy handed the ID over to Burton. He took it, tilted it, to check the holographic seal, he said.

I waited for him to accuse me, because there was my name as plain as day, Anita Martin, when I had lied and told him I was Angela.

"Identity cards," he said. "Harass the working class and create an underclass."

He said, "You think you're free. You're in the discard bin. In the grab bag. An irregular. Half price. A discard."

He didn't notice the name, or chose not to.

* * *

I am a citizen now.

The bank opened my account and put a hold on my check.

The man said, "Your monthly statement will be provided to you quarterly."

I have ID now so I can recycle. I carry my returnables over the top of the hill, around the bend.

The recycling center is a trailer with a tent in the parking lot of a supermarket. Outside, on the steaming pavement, big pails attached to hooks. Two scales. A long line of people waiting and a ragged man in charge. He talks to the person first in line who then spills what she's brought into one of the pails. He shakes his head and yells at her. He upends the pail and pours the contents into the other. He attaches the pail to the scale. Slowly, slowly, he fills out a paper. Pushes a clipboard at her. One by one, he takes the bottles out of the pail and throws them into the trailer where they smash. He removes a plastic bottle and scolds the woman and has her step on it until it's flat. He studies her signature. He hands the clipboard back and tells her to step on the bottle again. He fills out another form.

It's very hot and I'm dizzy. I leave my bags on the ground and turn to go.

"Wait one minute, just one minute here. You're not going anywhere. Just where do you think you're going?"

"Just take them," I say.

"They are your cans and bottles. You are responsible for them."

I say to the person in front of me, "You can have them. The refund."

"She cannot have them. I saw whose they were. Yours. You're not going anywhere."

. . .

California Transit

"Of course it makes no sense," said Burton. We cruised the hills in his RV. "Now here's where Upton Sinclair got busted. How come? For reading the Bill of Rights in public. Registered Historical Landmark Number 1201. The police chief said, 'The Constitution don't cut the mustard at the Harbor.'"

The cliff above the sea. The garden around the lighthouse. A mackerel sky, cumulus clouds, a shattered scattering of luminous white like what's left after the color fades from a burst of fireworks. Burton tapping his mutilated hand on the steering wheel, or walking with his ski poles, like a Spanish grandee, and the way the tips scraped on the pavement.

He knew it all: "Avoid any Mexican restaurant with sit-down tables, piñatas, printed menus. Look for a stand attached to an auto wrecking yard or car wash. You can open garage doors with a flashlight beam. Security gates? Roll a tin can across the sensor."

We cruised the docks and hills. There was Monterey cypress, pepper trees, fan palm, fig, bougainvillea, and jacaranda. The neighborhoods where they plant maples to show how Eastern they are and civilized. There was a monument on a dirt lot wedged between a steam-generating plant, a warehouse and stacks of iron beams.

He said, "This town is where Joe Hill joined the IWW. Where he wrote 'Casey Jones the Union Scab.' Can you smell the blood of Dickie Parker? A high school boy, just graduated, and gunned down at Berth 145. And here's where Hammond Lumber and the KKK raided the union men. It wasn't a meeting going on but a family dinner. They had these great big urns brewing coffee. The bastards rushed in and grabbed the little children and lowered them into those urns, dropped them in the way you'd boil a lobster."

"Now," Burton said, "who remembers?"

Why would anyone want to remember?

He said, "Me? I was an old-time dock walloper."

I had no idea what a dock walloper was. I said, "My ex-husband was a scab once on the docks."

Paul was in graduate school then. We went down to the Hudson River at midnight and a man jabbed his finger and chose him. I stood in the shadow of the West Side Highway, watching. A dozen of them unloaded crates of oranges and peaches and when a crate broke open burly men scrambled for the fruit, gathering up peaches and holding them gingerly against their bodies. Paul was paid in cash and bought us breakfast. Mafia joint, he said. Why else would a greasy spoon on the waterfront have chandeliers?

"A scab?" said Burton. "You should never have married him. Any children?"

"No," I said. Though once, years ago, there was Rufi, the little girl I wanted to take home with me. And when I took Dinah in my arms, I could feel our hearts beating at different rates and that had to be why she didn't like to be held close. It troubled me too, the different rhythms, her pulse versus mine, proof I could not be her mother. "No."

Burton said, "Wish I could say the same. I sent my son to boarding school in the DDR. A good school in East Berlin. Now he moves money in New York and won't eat a potato. Maybe the fancy ones—your Yukon gold, Peruvian blah blah. But your good ordinary wholesome white potato? Not a chance. Says he ate enough of em in boarding school. His kid, my grandson, makes TV commercials. He's the one tells the actor to go from despondency to hope in 2.3. That's seconds. Not 2 seconds, not 2.5. Despondency to hope in 2.3."

He said, "That was a tragedy in '89, when the Wall came down. Our last best hope knocked to rubble."

I said, "You were a Communist."

"Am," he said. "A Stalinist."

I burst out laughing. It all happened so long ago, mass murder was an embarrassment, not a horror.

"Burton, no one is still a Stalinist."

"I'll be a Stalinist until the day I die."

* * *

"Burton," I said. "How would you go about finding someone?"

He said, "I told you. I'm looking."

"No," I said. "I don't mean someone like a wife. I mean someone you've lost track of."

He said, "You call an agency. You hire a P.I."

I said, "Do you know one?

"I'm looking for Maureen," I told him.

* * *

I had Burton to talk to and Burton's RV to ride in. No more buses, no more sitting by the aisle blocking the window seat left empty so that someone would have to speak to me to get me to move.

It was like riding in a tank. An air-conditioned tank.

There were parked cars that talked when you got too close, like savage tropical flowers responding to touch. There was a bedspring mounted in a chain-link fence and used as a gate. There were thunderstorms but no lightning. I sat high up in the swivel chair, drank screwdrivers, and read the newspaper to him aloud.

The Elephant Alliance needs land for the growing numbers of abused and unwanted elephants in California.

Classified ads for boa constrictors and pit bulls, kittens that were "spaded and natured." Cemetery plots—a companion crypt, lot 149, $1500 obo.

"Who's your government bombing this week?" he asked.

"No more mine than yours," I said.

"Is anything left of Afghanistan? Sudan?" he said. "Not that I care."

I had stopped caring and suddenly it bothered me. It would be inaccurate to say it hurt.

I always knew that someday someone would hit me. Even before Paul, it was a picture in my mind, the sight and the sound of it, and all the variations of sound: the hand and the fist against face, against flesh, against bone.

In Mississippi, every hurt inflicted had a meaning, every act of cruelty—not hidden, but witnessed by the world—served our cause. Firehoses, baseball bats, crowbars, bullets. People left in comas, in wheelchairs, or alive and walking but ravaged, inadequate to the task through an insufficiency of love.

Then to return home and one day, there it is, just the simple matter-of-factness of it all: People hurt people. Once resigned to that, I still experienced pain but—there's a difference—no longer felt it. That is till Dinah came to live with me and, poor thing, dashed underfoot. I stepped on her. She yelped with pain and so did I, and then I spoke to her softly and she purred and I stroked her fur and she licked my hand, both of us passionate and frantic to prove our bond unbroken. I hurt her, and she still trusted me.

"Trust," Burton said, "A grown person who still needs to trust!"

How ugly my own thoughts sounded coming from him.

"See, about Maureen," I told him.

She went to work for the law professor who had been my mentor. And then she told me: "Bob gropes me in the office. He makes crude remarks. We went together to that conference? He spent the night banging on my door, trying to get into my room."

She couldn't stop crying. She made me promise not to tell. She didn't want to get him in trouble. She said, "He phones me at all hours of the night." She said, "I just needed to tell someone. But please, please, please. Don't tell him I told you."

I kept my word and never said a word to Bob, but of course he could no longer be my mentor and I could no longer be his friend.

It took a long time for me to realize Maureen lied about everything. You could never be sure, though, that it was not the truth. I had a boyfriend, a lover, at this point I'm not even sure what to call him. Maureen slept with him, or said she did.

"You have to understand. We're not having an affair. He's just helping me get pregnant." She said her life would be ruined if she couldn't have a baby. She said, "It's not like we enjoy it. When he goes down on me, it's no fun at all. He pushes his beard right into the most sensitive parts."

"Why does he go down on you?" I said. "That's not how you get pregnant."

Maureen said, "A woman's more likely to conceive if she's orgasmic."

I wasn't in love with the man and I'd had enough of Maureen. This was the excuse I'd been waiting for to get her out of my life.

She said,"If I had cancer, you wouldn't abandon me. Well, I *am* sick. I have a personality disorder. How can you—?"

I said, "I never want to speak to you again."

* * *

Burton said, "And you came to L.A. at *her* invitation?"

I never talked about it before because it shamed me, but somehow, it was all right to tell Burton.

I never understood why people hurt me. I asked for nothing.

Why would anyone want you? my mother would say. All it took was an invitation to a child's birthday party, and she'd look sincerely perplexed. I told myself she was wrong, but still, I held myself back, waited for others to approach, and when they did, when they urged their friendship on me so insistently, what could I do but believe they truly wanted to be friends?

"I lie," said Maureen. "I always have." And who was I to judge her?

Never never never say what you feel.

Back when our friendship ended, she told me for once what I think was the truth: "I walk around filled with resentment, with the feeling I'm being taken advantage of, and when I start feeling that way, I feel entitled to hurt people."

"Did you feel I took advantage—?"

"No," she said. "You've been good to me. That's why I feel so terrible now." She said, "When someone is good to me, I strike out at them before they can betray me." She said, "I don't want to lose you."

I thought, You never had me.

"Don't you understand?" she said. "You *glow*."

A person like me has no glow. Unless, what was it? that tenderness, that bruising. All that inward burning I could do nothing about and so I had learned to ignore it and I thought of Rufi, the little girl, a child born to be hungry, and of the heat rising off her silent, ever radiating pain.

Maureen said, "From the moment I met you, I wanted to get close. If I can't be where you are, I'll pull you down, here with me. But we'll get past this," she said. "I want to be a true friend."

And I said no.

There was a moment of clarity there, of revelation that should have, but didn't, change my life. My secret shame was still my secret pride. I was always hungry. I could always do without. I woke up some nights inside-out with emptiness, my skin peeled off me like a glove and I was falling and soaring, every secret inside part of me burning with the icy cold, then numb.

Over the years, Maureen phoned me like a stalker. She sent me letters, handmade Christmas cards, and quotations from Nelson Mandela. And I withheld not just forgiveness, but not even a word did I give her. Until the day I relented and picked up the phone.

She said, "I told you someday I would pay you back."

And I thought of Paul who said he wanted to take care of me, and later: I'm going to take care of you once and for all.

"Vice President for Legal Affairs," she told me, a public policy consulting firm. They had a contract for a complete audit and review of the juvenile justice system in L.A. "It's yours if you want it," she said.

I told Burton, "A lie, of course. But I came precisely because it was her invitation." And what a gift it was, or seemed to be: a chance to let go of my cynicism, and my fear. "I wanted to do that work and I wanted to be someone who could forgive." Someone different.

I don't know why the spirit changes or why I could say almost anything to Burton.

* * *

"Stalin loved slapstick and musical comedy," Burton said. "He pinned a medal on a filmmaker. He said, *You're the bravest man I've ever met. You dared to make me laugh.*"

He leans on his poles, his nose close to the fence. Angela's flippers beat on concrete. One sea lion does a jig, waiting to be fed while two weak little pups lie nestled together, one sucking away at the other's ear.

"It was a great great film," Burton said. "Stalin passed copies around at Yalta."

"How did it happen," I said, "to your hand?"

"What? Tell you, and have you tell Workmen's Comp?

"Which do you want?" he said. "Social justice or legal justice?"

What am I doing with this man?

Behind the tacky surfaces, the mini-malls, the potholed streets, Burton knew what was there. He reveled in the exposure. He didn't strip L.A. of its glamour, he took off its cheap clothes instead, its Fallas Paredes Discount torn-and-mended attempts at decency, he prodded with his dirty fingers *Look! Look!*

At night, he whispered to Angela. When we visited during the daytime, Burton liked to go inside the welcome center where he would fiddle with the brochures, making sure the stacks were straight.

We watched the volunteers feed Angela through a tube.

We heard Northern Elephant seals squawk like chickens. We learned: females may be injured or even killed during mating due to the size of the male. There are between twenty and 300 females in a harem and if one tries to get away, the male will stalk her and herd her back under his control.

Burton said, "Most of the real work of the world is done by people who don't get paid. I'm a union man," he said. "But still.

"I have rental properties," he said.

"A Communist and a landlord?"

"Why not? Under the capitalist system, it's my duty to bring contradictions to a head. As soon as your money clears, I'll rent you a place."

He showed me an automobile shredder and the apron conveyor for loading the scrap onto ships. He gave me a business card for Rolly Hanrahan, private investigator. He told me Southern California does too have rain, enough to disable the phone lines, the outdoor wires all uninsulated; enough to leak through flat roofs and make cars hydroplane on ungraded freeways and fill the dips in the street so that a woman stepping off the bus was swept away and under the wheels of a car.

He said, "That's not weather. That's climate."

And one night we pulled out both bunks and I slept in the RV, anything to avoid going to my room.

Burton snoring, Burton's rheumy eyes.

I lay there and ached and saw Dinah, the eyes that started out turquoise and then turned green except first thing in the morning when they were huge and black except for the thin outer circling of yellow, and the way she used to copy me, pulling herself up into the litter box every time I sat on the toilet, and I thought about Maureen and thought about hurting her and a memory from years past came suddenly to mind, a little boy sitting in the supermarket shopping cart: "Violence doesn't solve anything, right, Mom? Right?" A mother teaching her son well, or a little boy desperate for approval.

Rufi with her desperate affection, her arms around my shoulders: Señorita, take me with you!

"I'm putting her out in the street," said Doña Chepi. "She lies and she steals."

Rufi on the roof, crying.

"I caught her with a green lemon. Imagine! She cut it in half just to rub in her hair. And the other girl says she's taken lots more."

"The other girl makes up stories about me," said Rufi.

"Why?" I asked.

"Because there's food for one, and we are two."

I wanted to take her with me.

"See that bus?" said Burton. "That's the prison shuttle out to Rattlesnake Island."

There was no such place on the map.

A lot of places aren't marked. There was a map of Mississippi that people carried in their heads, that told you set off across this field and if you walk at my pace, in twenty minutes turn east and then keep going and then the round red Coca-Cola sign will guide you to a shack where the old men chew tobacco and you can buy some warm soda pop and sit and try to make the appropriate face—outrage, sympathy, delight—as the toothless men with slurred speech talk about their lives and you won't understand a word of what they're saying. Except this:

Get you a mule, they poison it.

Get you a horse, they shoot it.

Acquire a motor car, they blow your fool head off your body.

Burton said, "Life is not as you wish it to be. Life is as it is.

"If you don't believe me," he said, "look it up. Go to the library. Read Louis Adamic. Read the biography of Joe Hill. Read about the struggles of the IWW."

They were all in the card catalog, but none of the books were on the shelves. None had been checked out. They were just gone.

"Strange, isn't it?" Burton said. "About as strange as the fire that took Matson's container dock. It used to take eighteen men to move ten tons. Now you got gantry cranes moving thirty containers an hour. Five men on a team, you move four hundred fifty tons. They thought they could take our jobs."

"They did take them, didn't they?"

"They did," he said. "But that fire filled the sky."

* * *

"I'm an old man, I'm going to die soon, and I'll die bitter."

We drove over the pretty green bridge.

"Rattlesnake Island. Terminal Island to you," he says. "That's where tuna fish was invented."

How could tuna fish be invented?

"Aw, what do you know," he says. "You know what's there now? A prison. Full of refugees, asylum-seekers, brown-skinned people who thought this country meant it about democracy. There are women never committed a crime but for crossing the border and have been locked up there for years. One hour of exercise a week. They let them beg for a sanitary napkin."

"How do you know this?" I asked.

"How come nobody else knows? That's the question."

There's the Vincent Thomas Bridge, then the Gerald Desmond Bridge which mimics the curve of the earth and the drop off horizon's edge, and then before us, the Long Beach skyline.

"Southern California," he said. "People come out here because they have dreams. I was born here but I was a dreamer too. You want to be a star, they'll break your heart. You want to change the world? I had dreams all right."

I said, "You fought the good fight."

The window went down. He spat. "I fought the little fight."

"I fought the little fight, too," I told Burton. Keeping one kid out of jail. Getting one woman's medical bills paid. "I had the idea that if people just *knew*."

If they knew, they would be as unhappy as I was.

Dark heavy wooden doors with big brass doorpulls. A woman offered us earphones for simultaneous translation.

"Sí," I said, my heart light at the thought of Spanish words. "Gracias."

"No," Burton said, and made me return the headset. "César needs us here as Anglos." He led me. Scrape went his ski poles, scrape.

Rows of tiered seats upholstered in mauve and gray, turquoise and pink, and the long long fall of soft gray drapes, generous armrests, and the high curving ceiling with recessed lights, prettier than a planetarium. The city council members in leather swivel chairs, with their bottles of water, flanked by flags. The citizens speak:

"No one admired Caesar ShahVESS more than I did but put a Spanish name on our new park and you scare away investment. Instead of attracting business, all you're going to get are gangs."

"You're just looking for the wrong element with those basketball hoops."

"Hey, I *live* in the park," says the man. "I'm not homeless. I'm a person who's experiencing homelessness."

Burton at the microphone: "The meaning of the life of César Chávez is not about being Mexican or Mexican-American or American. César

Chávez was a *union* man. You disrespect the memory of César Chávez, it's an insult to labor, to every workingman in the nation. And an injury to one is an injury to all!"

The kid swaggers up, all baggy pants and tattoos: "You people talk a lot, but you don't know nothing about gangs. A gang wants to take a park, we take it. We don't care what you name it."

Burton said, "I think we're gonna win this one."

We drove back to Pedro and I couldn't keep from singing.

Burton, did you burn the pier?

Hal-le-LU-jah

Burton, did you burn the pier?

Hal-le-lu-u-jah.

* * *

We drove.

Burton said, "I'd like to take you with me to Mexico."

Tiny white bulbs climb up generator grids; flames from the refineries. A door adorned with what must have been an M, one leg sawn off to make a cockeyed N; new Current Resident, new last name.

Maureen said, You can't fool me. I know the kind of nurturing person you are. She said, You're guileless.

No, I knew how much I hid but she was right, I never tried to replace my absent self with anything pretend. I thought I could pass, safely, without notice. Maureen noticed me. She sought me out. It was maybe time for me to find her.

"Your friend the private eye," I said to Burton. "How much does he charge?"

Burton, what have I done?

"Mexico," he said. "I want to take you there. Or Vegas. I don't gamble, but I love the buffets. All you can eat."

"Mexico," I said.

"This weekend?" I said. "Don't you want to stick around for Labor Day? Won't there be a parade?"

He said, "They march up in Wilmas. But what for? Celebrate the labor movement's demise?"

He said, "I'll observe the date. South of the border. Gonna blow up a maquiladora."

The part of my mind that thought he meant it was very quiet, really very small.

* * *

I pushed the shopping cart. He chattered, giving orders. "Aisle 2A for the mayonnaise and mustard. No, I will not eat the house brand. It's on me. Don't worry about the money. I'll get it out of you later in rent. Bread. You want white or whole wheat? Tortilla chips, potato chips. Better pick up a jar of salsa. What kind of beer you drink? Get a case."

"Isn't that a lot for a weekend?"

"Orange juice. I want the fresh squeezed."

Why did his voice get so loud, almost shouting?

"Cold cuts. Get what you want. Bologna? Get the smoked turkey, it's better."

"I'm a vegetarian," I said.

"Liverwurst for me. But not this shit. Over at the service deli. A pound. Don't have 'em slice it. I like it thick and I'll do it myself. Napkins. Paper plates. Plastic forks. Paper cups. Get a roll of toilet paper, I think I'm out. Hell, get a second roll. We may need it at the Paraíso."

"I thought you said it was a luxury resort."

"It is. A bottle of tequila."

"Won't it be cheaper to buy it down there?"

"I told you. Stop worrying about money. Rum. Pick up that daiquiri mix. Not the can. The powdered. The Bloody Mary mix. Hurry up," he said. "Hurry up. I want to get an early start. I've got vodka. But get another in case we run out."

"What do you plan to do down there? Open a cantina?"

"I forgot the pickles. I don't like these. The ones back there in the refrigerated case. And celery for the Bloody Marys. And that styrofoam cooler. Plenty of bottled water. And ice."

At the checkout line, he pulled out a fat roll of fifties.

"Jesus, Burton."

"Always pay cash. You use a credit card, they accumulate all kinds of information about you."

He said, "I'm going to show you Mexico the way you've never seen before."

I was happy in Mexico.

He was drinking and driving. "Hey, pour me another."

"Burton, there'll be a checkpoint at the border. Burton, you have to be careful."

"Make me a sandwich. Let me have some chips. Pay attention," he said. "Orange County to Tijuana. From one nightmare to another."

Most of the food was on ice in the cooler because the little refrigerator was so small.

He was drinking and driving and talking. He wouldn't shut up.

"You went to Mississippi. What a fraud. People dying for civil rights in the South, and at the same time, no one bats an eye when California starts repealing fair housing laws. The gap between rich and poor," he said, "is greatest here and growing at the fastest rate. We're in a police state.

"You've got kids going to schools built on top of toxic waste. And take a look at this. Famous Orange County. What the rich have done to their own homes. And they won't pay property tax, hell, no, so what do they do? Sell their souls for car lots and retail stores, anything to bring in revenue. Look at it! Look at it! How could something so beautiful be made into something so ugly?"

He didn't seem drunk. He seemed to be in control. He asked for another. I said no, he asked again. I was a little frightened, and gave him what he wanted.

"Bosnia," he said. "Fuck the homeland."

He said, "You and I are alike. Not like these people who think the world is fine just as is, except for taxes. But no point in running," he said. "Where to? Your Nueva York? Where they're still patting themselves on the back, thumbs up their ass and their noses in the air.

"Here," he said, "you need a building permit for a cardboard shelter."

He said, "Modesta Avila served two and a half years in San Quentin for hanging laundry across the railroad tracks.

"Anything else you want to know about Orange County?

"Oh, I should mention," he said. "I put you on the insurance for the vehicle."

I said, "I can't drive."

"Then that's money flushed down the john. But my point is, at the Auto Club, they asked your name. So I say, *Angela*. They want your last name, too, but if I ever knew it, I forgot. The woman got weird on me. *You're taking this woman to Mexico and you don't even know her name?* So I said, *Davis, yeah, Angela Davis.* So you're Angela Davis this weekend. The name meant nothing to her. Isn't that a heartbreak?"

Before we got to the border, I put the booze under the kitchen sink and the empties in the trash. Burton laughed at me.

The American official waved us through. The Mexican asked us to open the door.

"Pásele usted," I said.

He was so pleased I spoke Spanish, he declined the offer to step inside and look.

I said, "Vamos a Rosarito. Dos días no más. A pasear."

"Diviértanse," he said and waved us on.

Until we crossed onto Mexican soil, I didn't realize I'd been holding onto the hope that someone would stop us.

* * *

He said, "Drunk driving's legal in Baja."

"I'm your hostage," I said.

"Look," he said. "What a pathetic country."

A multi-lane highway with vendors of baskets and blankets and sodas and beads and ceramic elephants and plastic Tweety-Birds at the windows of every car in gridlock pointed north.

He said, "It's a good thing we stole California."

Dryness and dust and shacks with sewage running down the hillsides and every street swarming with people, in rags, carrying things and walking.

"Where are they going?" he said. He began to laugh. "They come up thinking their life's gonna be better. And look at them. Hungry as dogs. And they think they're going someplace."

He kept laughing. I wanted to tell him to shut up, but he was drunk and it wasn't worth the bother.

"Let's get the hell out of TJ," Burton said.

"Here's where we're going," he said. A pretty little house of timbers and stucco, half-hidden by palm and banana trees. The dirt parking lot was full. Burton swerved and did a U-turn in the face of oncoming traffic. "Don't worry. We're bigger than they are." He parked on the dirt shoulder facing north.

"This is the Paraíso?"

"No. This is brunch," he said. "You don't get enough to eat."

They led us to a table on a patio looking out over the ocean. I had never been in a place so beautiful. I had never lived like this.

"Margaritas for me and the lady," said Burton.

Inside they led us to tables covered with food. Burton said, "Fill your plate." Mole de guajolote, enchiladas, enfrijoladas, chilaquiles, roasted quail, sopa de verduras, arroz, refritos, carne adobada, huevos rancheros, rib roast...

Why had I ever deprived myself of meat?

Burton said, "Round Two." He went back for more. He had salsa in his beard. I followed.

...fried chicken, gorditas, tortillas con asiento, chicharrón, pescado en mojo de ajo, coctél de camarón, bolillos, pan dulce, pozole, barbecued ribs...

"Eat," Burton said. "I want my money's worth."

...pineapple, jícama, watermelon, chocolate cake, strawberries, gelatines, mangoes...

"If I eat any more I'll be sick."

"Eat," Burton said. "I thought you were hungry.

* * *

"I could use a siesta," Burton said. He stretched out in the RV. He took his glasses off and they dropped from his hand. I reached to retrieve them from the floor.

"Don't fold them up," he shouted. "You'll fuck up the fucking frames."

He snored. He woke up and popped a cassette into the VCR.

"You see it? *Scream*? I think it got good reviews. Just a little break," he said. "You're no use and I don't feel like driving."

I couldn't concentrate on the film. People getting killed or else in danger of.

"You're gonna love this place," he said.

We rounded cliffside curves, weaving from lane to lane. Sometimes there were bluffs covered with garbage and pink plastic bags, flapping. Sometimes there'd be a view of the sea.

"The ocean's too cold to swim in, but they've got heated pools and spas. They have these pools where you float there with flowers, tropical flowers, and the bartenders come right in the water with your drinks. That's the life. With the mariachi band playing. And you won't believe how cheap even if you rent a room. But we just rent a hook-up and get to use all the facilities. You ever ride horses on the beach? You don't have anything like this back East."

He said, "You haven't lived till you've taken your American dollars to Baja."

I thought of how I'd kept my door closed, let Doña Vicky's relatives sleep three or four to a bed.

He said, "It's right around here somewhere."

Instead, there were soldiers.

Burton slammed on the brakes before we reached them, right in the middle of the road.

A man ran up to the door on my side and started pounding. He wore dark glasses so I didn't realize at first he wasn't Mexican, but Korean. Rather, Korean-American. His name was Tommy Kim.

"Let him in," said Burton.

"Maybe he's the one they're looking for."

"All the more reason."

I can't explain, that whole day, I did everything he said.

"At the roadblock," Tommy Kim said, "don't mention the Paraíso. Just say you're going into Rosarito. Into town." He told us it was a drug bust. "The federales came swarming in. It turns out the place is owned by some narcotraficante. The cartel's been using it to launder money."

Burton was delighted. "That's why it was so cheap."

I said to Tommy Kim, "Why are you running?"

Burton said, "Bad question."

Tommy Kim said, "I don't mind. They're gonna find ether and formaldehyde in my room. Bottles. Stoppers. My killing jars. All legit. I collect insects, but by the time they figure out what the stuff is, who knows what I'll have to pay in bribes or how many days in a Mexican jail. No thanks."

Burton asked him, "Would you like a sandwich? Would you like a drink?" He said, "Fix him something, Angela."

We parked on the street in Rosarito. The sun was going down.

They were selling necklaces. They were selling tiles. They were selling Chiclets and things to tie up your hair.

Tommy said, "The kids tore down my favorite place."

He walked us past a lot filled with rubble. "The kids got out of hand. Spring break."

They couldn't have done it with bare hands. The remains of a building of wood and brick.

We went to his second favorite place. They wouldn't let us in till we went back to the RV and left Burton's ski poles.

The DJ was spinning discs, in a cage protected by chicken wire. The kids were drinking.

Burton said, "Guess what her name is? You'll never guess."

The DJ was playing Donna Summer. I hadn't heard "Hot Stuff" for years.

"Her name is Angela Davis," Burton said.

He's so young, I thought. He won't know.

Tommy Kim said, "Funny, you don't look like an African-American Communist intellectual."

I said, "Funny, she and I even have the same birthdate." I had no idea when Angela Davis was born. "When I lived in the Bay Area, back in the Sixties, there were some unpleasant encounters with the police because of it."

Tommy Kim believed me. He had no reason not to.

I told him I was a marine biologist. "We're down here to look at the calving lagoons, the California gray whale."

"That's the State marine mammal," said Tommy Kim.

"And to party," said Burton.

Tommy Kim was young, maybe twenty-five. He wore designer braces. He said, "I'm from Riverside. I'm an Insect Technician II. That means I prepare meals for the bugs in the entomology lab."

"And what do bugs eat?" asked Burton.

"A hundred variations on nectar and rot."

"Look at her!" Burton said. "She thinks she's an outsider. Well, guess what, Angie-baby, one out of every eight Americans lives in California. You call that marching to your own drum? You call that being a noncomformist?

"Dance with him," Burton said, and so I did.

I danced and danced and danced, trying to sweat out the alcohol.

As we left, a flash as the photographer took our picture with a Polaroid.

Burton paid for it. He offered it to me.

"Oh, no," I said. "Let Tommy have it."

"Oh, no," he said. "After you, Alphonse."

Burton snatched it back. "Well fuck you two, both of you," he said. "It's mine."

Later, I ended up with the souvenir photograph, but I don't know what happened to that part they peel off and throw away. I don't know what sort of image stays on it. Evidence.

We went to Burton's favorite place.

Burton watched while Tommy and I danced, Tommy grinding against me, then pretending to be very drunk when I didn't respond. All that food inside me like something not quite dead.

"Not that the rooms at Playa Paraíso are infested," Tommy said. "But I never travel without my kit. You never know when you're going to see something you want."

Burton and I were the only people over twenty-five. Tommy was the only one who wasn't white.

Now that L.A. is mostly dark-skinned, this must be where you go to see them, all those boys and girls all careless and golden tanned and blond.

"I can't," I said. "I can't anymore."

We were sitting at a wooden table.

"She died in my arms," Burton said or, over the music, so I thought he said. "I'm the one who had to break it to her mother." He began to cry. It was so unfair, he said, how everyone blamed him. "Even my own mother blamed me." His face got very red and his hands balled into fists. "Am I telling you too much too fast?" he asked, like someone on a first date. He looked at me and then at Tommy Kim, pleading.

Whistles blew and a man grabbed me. I screamed, but Burton was laughing. The man pulled my head back and he forced my mouth open and poured in the rum.

I spat it out, and Burton was screaming. "I paid for that rum, dammit. I paid for that rum."

"They call that getting shaken," Burton said. "Specialty of the house."

"Bzzzz bzzzzz," said Tommy Kim. "Africanized killer bees are headed your way." He tickled my waist and my shoulders.

Whistles blew and a man grabbed a young woman by her ponytail.

I said, "Do they only do women?"

Burton smiled.

Whistles blew and they grabbed Tommy Kim.

We drank. We danced. Tommy Kim passed out.

"Let's go," said Burton.

"We can't just leave him."

"Why not?" Burton said.

* * *

The middle of the night.

"I could go for a fish taco," said Burton.

At the taco stand, he ate one after another. He ordered some for me.

"No," I said. "I feel sick."

He said, "I thought you were hungry."

Tap tap tap.

"Please," I said. "Stop, please."

Tap tap tap. Tap tap on my leg, the way Dinah used to tap-tap to get my attention. It was a little girl. Tap tap tap. I gave her my tacos. I gave her a dollar. You're a good girl. You're so beautiful. You're so sweet. Who's going to take care of you? I'll take care of you. I'll always love you and take care of you. But I couldn't say the words, the words I always said to Dinah.

"Jesus H. Christ," said Burton. "I brought you here to have a good time. Why the fuck are you crying?"

Take me with you, Rufi said, *Please.*

I can't, *no se puede*. Don't you have anywhere you can go?

All she did was take a green lemon and rub the juice on her glossy black hair.

She said, I have an uncle, but it would be very bad for me to go there. She said, The priest is my friend. Will you go with me to see the priest?

The priest said, The uncle will molest her. She'll go from bad to worse.

I said, I'll take her with me.

It's not allowed, he said. Besides, what's the point of saving Rufi when there are a thousand, a million other Rufis in the country? Why save her if you're going to leave the conditions that create her problem all unchanged?

Go back to your own country, he said. What about the children in your slums and the children in your fields?

I said, I love her.

He said, We don't need charity. We need a revolution.

He shook his head and laughed, and Burton was talking and eating and laughing.

Burton parked the RV in some dirt behind a bluff. There was a trash dump nearby. I could smell it.

He wasn't ready to call it a night. "Put *The Birdcage* in the VCR," he said. "It's a riot."

I made it to the door in time, and threw up.

"Good," he said. "You'll feel better."

The world wasn't spinning quite so much, but my throat burned and my mind was trapped inside my skull. I could feel him, chipping, piercing. He kept talking.

"Tomorrow I'm taking you for fried lobster. I get hungry just looking at these people. Make me a sandwich, will you? Liverwurst. That dirty little girl. They need to make abortion legal here—and retroactive. Stop crying," he said. "Use the good knife. And cut it thick."

I picked up the good knife. I was so tired. I focused on my feet, on connecting feet to floor. The floor shifted and I came up behind him. I put one arm around him and held the blade to his throat. He laughed. I was thinking of Dinah, the way she'd close her mouth around my ankle if I pissed her off. She never used her teeth or broke the skin. She just meant to let me *know*, not to hurt. And I thought of Angela's scars from the gill net, and those movies where the guy slices just a bit into someone's neck as a warning.

Burton said, "Where's my sandwich?"

I pressed the blade in just a little. What I was doing wasn't real yet. I hadn't yet felt anything and neither had he.

My legs wouldn't hold me up, so I held onto Burton. The pressure in my head eased a little. And I cut him.

Heat surged through my fingers. Just as suddenly, it was gone. There was no release, no relief. Just sadness, an immense sadness at everything in the world that was wrong, and that's what I was part of now—all wrong.

Burton jerked and made a little sound. He turned and grabbed with his mutilated hand. When he lost those fingers, there must have been blood, and there was blood now, running. We both looked at his blood.

Burton babbled like an idiot, just stuttering out sound.

Pictures flashed: me hurting Maureen. Why was it only hurt I could imagine?

Please let me see, I thought. Not *this*. But let me see.

Burton pushed against me, then fell. I fell with him. He was suffering and making awful sounds. He was terrible in his way, but he didn't deserve this. If I had stopped then, maybe it wasn't too late to stop. Maybe he would have been all right. The sounds didn't stop. All I could think was, *Make it stop*.

What I was doing made no sense, there was no sense and no answer but I cut and it got worse and I kept doing what I was doing, to get it done.

The knife fell. Burton kept making sounds.

In the end, it took a vodka bottle. Smash to his head, striking bone, shocking me sober. Then sick. Then grateful, because Burton was at peace.

There was no more pain. There was so much blood. I stripped. I toweled his blood from my body. I was too far outside my own body then to cry. It was just one foot in front of another. It was just focus on task. It was over and my fingerprints were over everything, and I tried to remember if that mattered and I wondered if the Mexican police knew how to handle blood to preserve the DNA and I wondered what they would do to me if they caught me and whether I hoped they would.

The glove compartment was where he'd stashed his roll of bills. I wasn't after Burton's money, but I took a fifty to pay my way home, then thought, why not take another? Then I thought, why not take it all?

I was a monster. I was a horror. I tossed my backpack out the door and climbed out naked. I climbed back in to get the Polaroid and a plastic bag. I put my bloody clothes inside and tucked the bag into the pack.

I put on clean clothes and started walking.

All I had to do was get back to Rosarito without anyone seeing. It felt good to walk. I needed air. Whenever a car or truck passed, I lay flat. Sometimes I doubled over with cramp.

There was just the one highway. All I had to do was follow it, and get to town and catch the bus. I always feel safe riding buses. I had a terrible headache. I could hear trucks. I could hear dogs.

* * *

The Border Patrol stopped the Greyhound somewhere north of San Diego. I thought they could smell me, the blood, the stale alcohol rising from my pores but maybe that's what Anglos always smell like coming up from TJ. They hassled the passengers with brown skin and that was all.

I awoke in my room in San Pedro.

I opened my eyes and Dinah wasn't there, and I thought, my God, what have I done?

* * *

I needed a shower. A hundred showers. A long bath. All I had was a sink and a towel. I stripped and soaked the towel and rubbed myself down, and did it again, and again till my skin was rubbed raw.

Who is this woman?

In the motel room in Blythe, I'd wanted to confess. Now, I was guilty and thought only of how to get away with it.

California didn't have my prints. Mississippi did, but that was a long time ago. Tommy Kim, when he came to, if he remembered anything, thought I was Angela Davis. I hadn't planned this, never in a million years.

In the closet I had a container of organic stain remover. I'd bought it for the drive to California in case Dinah peed on the carpet or the bed in some motel. I put the bloody clothes in the sink and poured the solution all over.

I had $1,650 in Burton's money. I counted it carefully, without meaning to, when I went through the bills checking for bloodstains.

I hadn't planned to get a false ID or to travel under an assumed name. None of it was planned.

I washed the clothes again at the laundromat and thought how much Dinah loved laundry still hot from the dryer.

I left the clothes in a Salvation Army drop.

I looked at the souvenir photograph. Me and Burton and Tommy Kim.

I went into a bar and had a beer just so I could pick up a book of matches. I burned the picture in my sink.

In the mirror, there was a face I didn't recognize. I had become someone else, but she was not the me I wanted.

. . .

California Transit

Now what? It was Labor Day. What does a murderer do on a holiday? With Burton gone, who would care? I could go to the parade upchannel in Wilmas. No, that would be an insult to the dead. He had mocked it.

Rattlesnake Island, Burton had said. The prison.

I took the bus, past the green and orange containers, and huge concrete beehives and exhaust hoses stretched out in the air above like futuristic tunnels, so big you could fly a small plane through. There was a guard tower dwarfed by the harbor cranes, and then the gate.

The prison on the left, coils and coils of razor wire.

On the right, the compound Burton had told me about, where they keep the foreigners who try to get in.

When I was unhappy, I fled to Mexico. No one stopped me. I came back across the border with blood on my hands. No one stopped me.

I walked toward the building. A stanchion in front of a bench said *Butt Stop*. How crude, I thought, then realized it was a receptacle for cigarettes.

At the gate, hundreds of people waiting.

Who are you visiting?

I said, I don't know.

But you have to tell them the name and the ID number and the pod.

The woman in front of me said, You're not going to get in anyway. I've been here since seven and it looks to me I'm not going to get in. It's just certain hours, Saturday, Sunday, holidays. You get fifteen minutes. There's five hundred women in there and only five visitors at a time.

There were people from Algeria and Sri Lanka. There were people from El Salvador. There were people on line who talked about torture and jailings and killings.

The woman said, They keep my mother in there five month. I'm coming here every weekend. All the way from Apple Valley. In five month, I have seen my mother one hour and forty-five minutes.

Why is your mother in there? I asked.

That's what I am asking. She go to see my sister in St. Kitts. When she come back, they snatch her at LAX. This is five month ago. They say they find her name in a computer. My mother has papers. Her papers are good. Why are you here? the woman asked.

I really didn't know.

I left the line and threw up and kept walking. Then I saw something on a whitewashed wall. A woman put her hand right there and let it climb on her. There was another one already on her arm.

"I wonder if they'll like each other," she said. "September, October, that's when you see them. That's when they come out looking for love."

Tommy Kim had said, "I could tell you a lot about spiders, but people never want to know."

"Tarantulas are very nice spiders," she said. "They tend to be very calm. It's true they can jump. To the height of say, your knee. But they don't do it to attack. Only to escape. A pretty little tarantula isn't going to hurt you."

She said, "Would you like her to climb on you? Don't be afraid. It feels nice. Just try it." She said, "Doesn't it look just like a plush toy? Know what it feels like? It feels like when a cat comes close enough to barely brush against you with its little face, with a nose just barely against your skin."

"Yes," I said. "Please." I held out my arm.

She looked into my face.

"Go away," she said. "You look nervous. It just isn't fair to the spider."

* * *

In the mailbox, an envelope addressed to Angela Davis. A note from Rolly Hanrahan, Investigations, asking me to phone him.

I thought of running. Instead I went to the pay phone at Burger King.

He said, "Burton tells me you're looking for someone."

I wanted to say, *Burton is dead.*

He said, "I found her."

* * *

For obvious reasons, I wasn't up to it. Maureen would have to wait.

In appliance stores, I stood in front of TV sets tuned to the news. I learned about the President's sex life. I learned that women driving white Hondas were being targeted by snipers.

"Good news!" said the anchor. "Postal service is about to improve." He added, "The price of stamps will go up in January."

"And now for some balance." An idiotic woman who sounded like a kindergarten teacher. "Most people drive the freeways every day without being shot."

No one said a word about Burton.

It wasn't fair. Why was a woman in a white Honda more important than he was? How was it possible he had disappeared, murdered, and no one noticed and no one cared?

I had Burton's money. I didn't have to haunt appliance stores.

I read the *L.A. Times* at a marble-topped table at the coffeehouse. Nothing.

And I used to think everyone else was cared about.

I checked into the Marriott and turned on the TV.

I took a shower and then I took a bath, and then another shower and then I went out and bought some bath oils and lay down in the tub again.

I looked in the mirror at the face of a killer, and went out and bought hair color and I bought a blue dress and came back and did my hair and in the mirror, I saw a human being.

But when I lay down in the big Marriott bed, I couldn't sleep. I was a person I couldn't bear to sleep with.

* * *

It wasn't right. Nothing was right. I went looking for a police station, but couldn't find one.

I stopped a cop on the street. "I want to report a missing person."

"Yeah, and who would this be?" he said.

"His name is Burton."

"Yeah?"

"I used to see him every day up at the sea lions. He visited every day. Always at the same time. It's days now since I've seen him."

The cop laughed.

"Please don't," I said. "He's an old man. He never looked in good health. Someone should find him and see if he's OK."

"Hey, you mean Burton Dadich?" said the cop. "The old guy with the ski poles? Missing person! That guy's been missing in action for years."

Someone told me the station's up Pacific where it turns into Gibson before it turns into Harry Bridges.

I went back into town and then I couldn't find a bus and so I walked.

The officer said, "Do you know an Angela Davis?"

I said, "Isn't that his wife?"

He said, "Burton Dadich wasn't married."

I said, "Well, I certainly thought. The way he talks about her. Angela this, Angela that." I said, "Burton's an eccentric man. Strange in his appearance but he's always clean. I figured someone that eccentric, unless he's got a wife keeping after him, he wouldn't be that neat."

I said, "Why did you say *wasn't?*"

AMERICAN TOURIST KILLED IN MEXICO.

The cop said, "People go down there, they don't realize it's dangerous. One more dead gringo." He said, "The Mexican police won't do a thing."

I sat there crying. I said, "He didn't deserve to die that way."

I wanted to confess but I was afraid. They would ask my motive and I didn't have one. They would ask my motivation.

I would feel too stupid when they asked me why.

The cop said, "Does something show?"

He said, "I just had the laser surgery. Best thing I ever did, though it cost a bundle. Threw my glasses away for good."

I didn't realize I was looking in his eyes so searchingly.

I gave him my address. I said, "It's just temporary and I don't have a phone. But I'm moving up to L.A. Should I keep in touch? Should I let you know where to find me?" I said, "He was eccentric, he could be mean, I think life had hurt him, but he loved animals." I said, "One day, the workmen were trimming the baby palms. He had tears in his eyes. Can you imagine? A man who felt tenderness for shorn palm trees."

I said, "I didn't know him well. But it's not right." I said, "I'll miss him."

The cop said, "Keep in touch. Though it's OK if you don't. If we need you, we'll find you."

* * *

I phoned Rolly Hanrahan. I said, "Something terrible has happened."

He said, "You've heard. I meant to let you know, but you know how it is. You don't have a phone, and no e-mail—"

I said, "Isn't anyone doing anything? How could this happen? Is there a funeral? A service?"

He said, "His son flew out. I'm sorry we didn't contact you. It's already over."

I went to see him in his office near the airport. He wasn't at all what I expected. For one thing, he was black. For another, he was very young.

I said, "And I thought you were one of Burton's cronies."

"No," he said. "I met him through his grandson. I used to be an actor and I worked with Brent and that's how I met Burton. And Burton and I were in some stuff together. He had a pretty distinctive look. It got him work now and then as an extra."

He said, "And I thought your name was Angela."

"That was his joke," I said. "Everyone was Angela. He started calling everyone—even this sea lion at the rehab center—Angela."

"So," he said, "do you have any idea which Angela Davis he went to Mexico with?"

I thought, He knows.

I said, "I didn't know him very well." I started to cry. "I moved out here just two months ago. From the East Coast. Everything went wrong, and Burton was kind to me. He was a bit of a monster, wasn't he? but he's the only one who was kind."

Rolly put a hand over mine. "Hey," he said.

I thought, He believes me.

We were quiet a little bit.

He said, "So what'll you do now? Stay or go back?" He said, "There's good stuff in L.A. and good people. In the margins. In the corners, kind of hidden."

I said, "I think there's two ways to be happy here. The way the rich do, ignoring everything around them. Or else, to pay very close attention."

He liked the way I said that.

I said, "That's what Burton taught me."

So we talked some more. He said his work probably wasn't what I thought it was, it was mostly done these days on-line, and I told him a bit about the work I used to do. The sleeping-under-bridges part I guess I laid on kind of thick.

He said, "Aren't you afraid of anything?"

I said, "I have phobias, but no fears."

"You gonna get admitted to the California Bar?" he said.

The thought hadn't occurred to me. "I could do immigration law," I said. "Burton told me what INS is doing out on Terminal Island. I went there to see but I didn't get inside."

"No one wants to help those people," he said. "No lawyer wants to tangle with INS. It's just one big runaround and headache."

I thought, someone has to do something.

He said, "You'll need to do something till you're admitted to the Bar."

He said, "When I talked to you on the phone last week, I figured you for one of Burton's strays. You sounded, forgive me, like a bit of a mess. Burton wasn't kind to you."

"Yes, he was," I said.

"You're kind to people you condescend to," he said. "You're *good* to an equal. Burton was *good* to you."

Then he offered me a job.

* * *

The rest was easy.

I went to DMV and let them take my prints and turned in my New York license and got a license to drive in California.

I bought a white Honda, cheap, from a woman who was frightened. Once I had wheels, I went to work for Rolly.

I found a one-bedroom apartment in Hollywood. It has hardwood floors and glass brick windows in the kitchen that split and burst the lights of passing cars like a kaleidoscope.

As soon as I saw the place, I was amazed that something so modest could be so beautiful, the flowers and lemon trees and the view of the mountains, and the cats draped on the balconies and stairs. The day the landlord showed me the place, we entered the courtyard and a calico cat rubbed against my legs. She had no idea what I'd done to Dinah.

My new neighbor asked if I'd feed her kitties when she's out-of-town, assuming just like that I can be trusted.

Working for Rolly, I get into every corner of the county. It's not all computers, though I'm learning that, too. And this time when I say "temporary," I mean it. I'll be opening my law office soon.

Most of the people locked up on Terminal Island won't be able to pay, but I don't need very much to get by.

I like the way asylum-seekers in the INS prison define "opportunity"—not the chance to get rich, but the possibility of staying alive. They've been brutalized and tortured. People they loved were arrested or abducted and killed. They fled to L.A. because in spite of everything, they still think their lives are worth preserving. That life is worth living.

Perhaps my life is, too, in spite of what I've done.

Every time I go into the office, I ask him, "Any news?" by which of course I mean any news about the murder of Burton.

I still believe in justice, though I am willing to evade it. I still believe in the commitment I made long ago to resistance in the nonviolent spirit, the greatness of heart at which I fell far short and failed.

I'm making new friends, but it's Burton I see everywhere and I hear his voice. I wish I could talk to him again, though what could I possibly say? I would just tell him that I like it here, in a city that runs—to the extent it runs at all—not really on money, but on love and hope.

* * *

The Rev. James Lawson is here.

It must mean something that both he and I ended up in L.A.

It was James Lawson who taught us the practice of nonviolence and the power of unearned suffering. It was James Lawson who taught Martin Luther King.

Now one of them is dead thirty years. The other has a church in Los Angeles. He was so young then. His hair must be white now. We were all so young. We believed in something together. We were not alone.

His church is on West Adams Boulevard. I looked it up in the phone book and found the street on the map and in my Thomas Guide. Each grid in the Thomas Guide is half a mile. I live five miles and a quarter away. I could walk it, but when I go, I will not walk.

I'll wake early on Sunday and set off on my knees, past the cemetery where Rudolph Valentino lies in his grave and past the studios at Paramount and the Mexican women on the early morning streets scolding, *Párate! Get up! We don't do that anymore!*

The world will look different at pavement level and the absence of wheelchair cutouts will mean worse pain each time I go off a curb. There is no redemption through this pain. There is no purity in this suffering because I deserve it and have earned it.

I'll ask James Lawson if he remembers me. I'll ask him please to look into my eyes and see the innocence I was born with. I wonder if he'll see it.

I wonder how I'll make myself do this.

* * *

I didn't.

Instead of crawling on my knees, it suddenly occurred to me how impossible it seemed that I could have killed someone. If *that* could happen, then anything could happen, and I suddenly felt alive and aroused and the world around me filled with possibility.

* * *

I never bothered to contact Maureen.

I do think about Angela in her pen and I keep meaning to drive down to see her. I'm the only one left who knows her name and I feel that I owe it to Burton. But life is full and there's never time. I've always got something else to do.

The Prosperity of Cities and Desert Places

It was strictly a business decision so we couldn't complain and there was no one to complain to. Those of us who had cars got into them, those who didn't found an empty seat or prepared to walk. We thought about North Dakota where, we were told, you could buy a whole town for $10,000. But there's nothing there, we said. Of course, once we arrived, *we* would be there. Nevertheless, we voted against North Dakota. A business decision. Being able to say that made some of us feel better.

We can start this story with the caravan. Or with a fifty-year-old woman in the desert trying to explain to two cops that the reason she walked around the body and looked at it but didn't scream or fulfill her duties as a citizen was that she thought the murdered person was a work of art. But let's begin with the collective.

We didn't really mind leaving town. Our city had changed. Those of us who lived in a house found ourselves living two families to the house, and then three, and then four. And then they said we couldn't because of zoning. The people who clean the houses and tend the gardens live ten or a dozen in an unventilated garage, but since they don't have papers, zoning doesn't count.

California Transit

The situation became impossible. For a while that was all right. Impossible, said some of us, that could be a condition under which I'd be interested in working.

First we tried a protest. In the end, we voted with our feet. And tires.

The architect Friedrick Kiesler said the environment is not constructed by objects, but by movement. Easy for him as I assume he had a house, but it sounded good to us when we set off in motion.

We. How do you constitute a *we*? A shared enemy makes it easy, and our enemy was surely shared though none of us could name him, her, it. Affinity groups occurred, that is, a multiplicity of little *we*'s sprang up, and one of these little *we*'s consisted of all the women who'd slept with Ramiro.

Ramiro! We loved that man. He was the only person we knew who said RevolYOUtion and he was furious with the working class for not starting it.

Ramiro was not his real name but his nom de guerre. Some of us believe (because he told us) he was born David Weinstein in Iowa City; some of us always called him Tony and believe he's from New York.

His bedroom was dark and square. Lots of books, *The Chicago School of Economics, Transitions from Authoritarian Rule, Perception of Threat,* just to name a few, but mostly books about baseball. Atop the TV, the plastic figure of Malcolm X with a cheeseburger hovering above his head like a halo. We all have sweet and vivid memories of his bedroom.

Which raises the question: How much do we seven owe one another just because Ramiro at some point in time briefly but memorably fucked us? And first of all, let's make that six, as Sheila doesn't want anything to do with the rest of us. Her loss, as she'll have no one to reminisce with. And second of all, the remaining six of us are not really friends, and I can't presume to speak for them, so "we" really means just Eileen and me and she lets me do the talking though I've invited her to chime in if it gets to where I misrepresent her point of view.

Eileen says I should mention the poster in his kitchen: *BEAN CRYING IN POT! We boil bean and bean husk together. Stop America's Disruption! Go Church Street Market Go!*, in my view, unnecessary to this story, but in a collective enterprise I understand there will always be compromise.

More important: Whoever Ramiro really was, if he were still alive and here, I would owe him an apology. He used to say his country—he pretended at times to be from Guatemala, at times from Peru—was all fucked up by Yanqui capitalists. I didn't understand how a few white moneymen could destroy a nation, leave millions homeless, make the lights go out, but now that they've done it here, I know Ramiro was right.

"In Argentina," he told us, "in Brazil, when men and women were tortured, the implements were American, and so was the audience." He told us advisors sent by Washington watched quietly in those terrible rooms.

"If you're a salon liberal, you are my enemy," he said to each of us, sooner or later, at one time or another.

I should never have told him about my dream. It was many years ago and I was going to assassinate Nixon. I made my way through the crowd and looked into his eyes full of pain. He stuck out his hand. Instead of shooting him, I shook it.

Come on, said someone. Let's go to El Monte and find the Nazis.

The moment has come when even I feel the visceral imperative to fight. We want to inflict hurt. Understand, we've become quite comfortable in distinguishing, for example, between S/M practices that liberate and those we feel free to label as pathology. But mainly what we were looking for now was a release from pent-up frustration. We were in the mood to trash something and in general these days you don't get in much trouble for bashing Nazis.

Some people said the Nazis lived in Idaho and some said in eastern Washington State, but we're Californians so it's hard to get us to leave California, thus: El Monte, just outside L.A.

Our caravan moved south.

We understand that people can't really care about a collective, a more-or-less anonymous though suffering group. If we are going to provoke sympathy or understanding on your part, it will be for each of us individually, or at least some of us. We should tell you personal stories, ones that will make you angry, make you shake your heads in disbelief—like how about Michiko and Mr. and Mrs. Ruthenberg. She lived upstairs, they lived downstairs. Since her accident, she uses a wheelchair. The Ruthenbergs swapped apartments with her and the landlord evicted them all for violations of tenancy. They're traveling together now, Michiko in the backseat, her chair folded up in the trunk. It's a bond like an unhappy marriage. We've seen the Ruthenbergs leave her in the hot car when they get out to stretch their legs or get a Coke. But that's just a thumbnail sketch. To make you care, we should include dialogue and interaction. Maybe we will, but frankly, at this point we have been scorned, dismissed, betrayed. There was a time when your opinion mattered. At this point? Maybe we don't really care if you care or understand.

Eileen thinks you care.

OK. There's a woman who brags about her cousin who used to be on *Bowling for Dollars.*

Someone else says, My cousin Bonnie reads *The Atlantic*. Not only that, she has a subscription.

We don't laugh at them. We understand everyone desires respect. Besides which we know if you begin to realize you're better than someone else, you're on the road to ruin. First, because you've been trained to know it's wrong to think you are, and so you're already guilty and in a precarious position. If you maintain your own standards of intelligence, morals, ethics, you're acting superior, and if you're a woman, that's a capital offense. If you really love the one you love, you will not set yourself apart, and slowly, inexorably, you will betray everything you hold dear. So when we want to laugh, we don't, which may be why some people say we are humorless.

Kathy's Olympic athlete of a cousin, faced with an out-of-control car coming right at him, vaulted over the hood and landed on his feet, unhurt. This does not make Kathy herself special and, we feel, she may be lying (or at least exaggerating), but still, this is a story we all like.

Among us, there are those who still believe in recycling, and those who've lost all semblance of civilized behavior.

There's Rosemary who says, An alcoholic will break your heart. A pothead's just a pain in the ass.

And Virginia. She was a good enough mother when the children were infants, but Sally grew up to have cancer and Eddie just went through a triple-bypass so, really, what kind of mother could she have been?

An Apache Indian with a guitar. Oh, Exotic Romance! Ah, the miscegenistic thrill! And Jake's not just an Indian, he plays the guitar! We don't admit it, but we're a puddle of slush at his feet.

There's Ronald, who wasn't a political prisoner but is now a political free man, one of the hundreds let loose so that the prison can be renovated as luxury housing. He has organizational leadership skills, being used to regimentation.

You may note the preponderance of women and the color of the men. It's not that no white men have been dispossessed, but they take failure harder than we do and for the most part tend to lie low. Or, like the homeless twins—I'll get to them in a bit—they aren't joiners.

Me? I have always been overlooked because of my uncanny resemblance to ordinary everyday people.

Do you need to know more?

There were those who didn't come along.

Thanks to her wealthy lover, Esmenia was able to stay behind in the city, on top of which he bought her weekly time on public access cable. The night before we left, she was seen seated at a grand piano, candelabrum burning, with closeups on her exalted face and then on her untrained fingers striking again and again the wrong keys.

And the homeless twins. You don't think of homeless people as having a twin, or at least not a twin who is also homeless. We had seen them for years, one on the east side of town and one on the west, and always thought they were one person who walked a lot. We didn't realize till they showed up together when we were getting ready to leave. Their story is no doubt a very interesting one, but we never got to hear it. They decided they didn't need to travel with us. Their situation, after all, hadn't changed. For a moment, we didn't want to go. Only now at the moment of leaving did we realize how much about our hometown we had misinterpreted and misunderstood and, if we stayed, might learn. We had misgivings.

We think you know enough.

I'll tell it my way. Our "we" is defined by what we don't have. Which means, who would want to be one of us? Who would join this rapid descent of downward mobility, this reversal of manifest destiny? Unless,

unless we can demonstrate the joys of solidarity, constitute ourselves not through our shared oppression but through an enviable bond of love.

How?

Songs were floated, and silenced, different musical tastes giving rise too quickly to contention.

We agree on only a few things, chief among these being that when stopped by hostile local authorities, we explain ourselves this way: we're caravanning for breast cancer.

I was the one dissenting voice: To raise money for breast cancer *research*, I insisted. Eileen points out I did not so much insist as mutter my disapproval to her privately and she's right, but why make a public issue about sentence construction for what is, after all, a lie?

The lie worked. When we got off the freeway we were met by friendly waving crowds offering bottled water and Gatorade.

While the others mingled with the natives, I was selected as scout, sent over to a cybercafe to check the Web for Nazis.

I believe I was chosen because I've always lacked leadership qualities and success has become something suspect. Now, Eileen says a little bit of power has made me pedantic. I think it's made me see how hungry I've been for it all along.

In town, I couldn't resist checking my e-mail. Amazing how people can reach you even when you yourself have no idea where you're going or even where you are. It's less and less necessary to have a home. I found several forwarded messages with the hoax about tampons containing asbestos. Three virus warnings. Two opportunities to win fifty dollars. Good news from amazon about free shipping.

Then I downloaded pictures of Hitler. You can get anything ugly off the Web except the damn address itself though once we get to El Monte, the place should be easy enough to recognize. Swastika flags and armed Nazis in brown shirts parading back and forth. We haven't quite figured out how we're going to bash them considering they are armed and we aren't. Besides which, we are having a disagreement over what we mean by bashing. Whether we are simply going to call them names or whether we will bash them quite literally with baseball bats or big sticks and whether we are all salon liberals if we decline the latter option.

We decide we can decide all that when we get there. We understand there's a Mexican deli on one side where you can get great homemade tamales. There's a muffler shop on the other side. The neighborhood is definitely changing but the Nazis, bless their evil little hearts, are hanging on.

That first night, when we circled the wagons there was no singing around the campfire. No marshmallows. No ghost stories, which for some raised religious objections and for others the fear of vicarious traumatization of the children.

Those of us who are older tried to instruct those of us who are younger about the way things used to be. The younger ones can hardly believe what we used to hear in school. Such as:

Hurricanes are named for women because a woman is destructive and can always change her mind.

America's difference from other countries and greatness lies in its strong and dominant middle class.

Teachers used to say, *Hang up your wraps in the cloakroom.*

The second night, we followed the signs to Camp Beavertail. We traveled miles past a security gate left—we later learned—inadvertently open, through the rolling hills to the compound, huge improved-on quonset huts dropped down on the earth like something the space program would land on Mars, each bearing a name: AT&T, IBM, Microsoft.

The armed guards asked if we had cancer. "Breast cancer," we answered promptly.

"The children," said a guard. "This is a camp for children with cancer."

We pushed some of ours forward, but they looked healthy.

Sheila went prowling and said pornographic movies were being filmed in the quonset huts.

"Not movies," the guard said. "Cable."

"With children?" we asked.

"No, no. There are no children," he said.

"But this is a camp for children with cancer."

"That's what it's *for*," he said. "But what it *is* is a tax deduction. And a hobby for a certain media personality. Now get the hell out of here."

We made camp that night in a gravel pit half a mile off the freeway, heavy of heart.

Choose a partner, someone you don't know, said someone as the sun was going down. *Hold hands.*

I was holding hands with a woman with a pierced nose and tongue. Near us, a young couple, wrapped in each other's arms, counted themselves as one, and his hand linked with Eileen's.

My partner was shorter than I am, and, as you might guess, younger. I liked her smile.

Close your eyes and take ten steps away from one another.

With your eyes still closed, take ten steps back and find each other's hand.

Hands outstretched, we touched, and with touch, safety, home, as much home as anyone would need.

Step apart.

Step back into each other's arms.

Somewhere out there the coyotes called to each other and to our dogs.

My partner was crying.

"Everything's gonna be all right," I said. "It will all be all right."

"No it won't. Don't lie to me."

"Why do you have to call it a lie? Think of it as the eight hours of sleep you need before you face the world again."

"It won't be all right," she said.

"Sleep is good," I said. "Nothing wrong with dreaming, as long as you can still wake up."

One of you must make a sound. Let your partner hear your sound.

Hoo, she said. *Hoo.*

She stepped away. My eyes were closed. All around, fellow travelers were whistling and hooting and chirping. I was in a rain forest. My head expanded and contracted like a heart, the air beating with life and sound, and in it a fabulous joy and the sheer happiness of locating the *hoo hoo* in it, the safety of her sound, my partner's sound, in the breathing night, *hoo* and the coyotes and frogs and crickets that might have been people. It was the whole world humming and chirping and her sound *hoo* and I followed that *hoo,* it drew me as though it were the water of life. Water, and what a flood of memories: the slanted hiss of the leaves with a thunderstorm brewing and the daytime clouds so dark you can trick yourself into sleeping, the tickle and stampede of distant running drops, the wipe of a swath of water across roof tiles, the curl and flap and fall of a window shade, doors slamming shut, each one like a single shot and the crash of thunder or something falling. Something. Drops that are silver and drops that are white and the drops that are colorless motion, and a vibration, a rattle, coming from what or where how could you know, like an earthquake, the kind where the world vibrates and purrs, the kind that's the crack of a rifle as the house jumps up in the air, then falls, the kind that sets everything clattering, or a gourd filled with pebbles or beans or seeds, and breaking through it all the *hoo,* the way it rose above the singing earth and over every other sound that swirled in the night *hoo hoo* and when I couldn't hear it anymore I stood still entranced by the rain forest around me.

Do you know when I left what had been my home, I expected I would look around at everything, the empty apartment, the street, the trees, the storefronts I would never see again. I thought I would want to memorize it all, but when I turned off the lights for the last time, it was all already dead. There was nothing to look at. Something inside of me failed to ignite, in this room where I had at times laughed myself sick, felt as hurt or scared or deeply loved as I could ever be, this place I thought was mine. It was gone, I was gone, though I could remember there were times the very furniture glowed when Ramiro (and certain others) sat there. I thought the light was gone for me and from the world until I heard the *hoo hoo* and the chirps and cries and with my eyes closed the world was still alive and therefore I was. I couldn't find her but it was all right to break down and dissolve into everything. Somewhere there's a *hoo,* somewhere there's an I, somewhere in this spill of life. The world grew quiet. I could hear her. I walked toward her. Our hands met.

Open your eyes.

All the other partners were together. Some were crying, saying, *I thought I'd lost you.* Some were scared.

My partner held my hand and said to the women near us, "Everything is going to be all right."

* * *

While we're on the subject of lies, Ramiro didn't leave us. We each at some point dumped him, sick of the lies and deception and his flamboyantly hidden double life. That's what brought us together at first, comparing notes, sharing anger and sense of betrayal, seeking to understand how we'd let ourselves be fooled.

Eventually we (except for Sheila) acknowledged that we sought each other's company because we like to talk about him. We miss him, and we've agreed to say he's dead to remove the possibility of future competition among us.

If it's agreed upon, is it a lie? More like a treaty, though we know how much an American treaty is worth, I say loudly, hoping for Jake the Apache's favorable regard.

Our agreement is more a matter of setting boundaries, though we know that borders violate nature.

Morning. We consider what has so far gone wrong. Like the hassle of keeping order during stops for bathrooms and gas, the dogs barking and the children howling. We reach an agreement, separate camps for people with kids and noisy animal companions. Renee stays with our group at first as her Burmese python is silent but it makes too many of us nervous. Separate campground, we declare, for snakes.

That's the micro scale. On the macro: Capital run amok. The unfettered market. What if it were easier to know who to blame? What if it were all because of that woman talking to her husband while their two teenaged boys set up their tent?

Last night she whispered in my ear. "I used to be a high achiever. It seemed so shameful I wished I were black so I could be great not for myself but for my race." Not only that, but I've seen her use a cell phone. I've seen the way her thin lips gesture their distaste. She smiled at me, a thin-lipped smile, and tried to start a conversation this morning. She's the kind of person who worms her way into your life if you're too polite to stop her.

Somewhere in a group this size there's bound to be a spy, an agent provocateur, a closet Republican. Just because we're all on the move doesn't mean you can take solidarity for granted. Doesn't mean we haven't got our differences and needs, in the scramble for survival surely some of us will be quicker to betray the rest than others.

What I really want to tell you is how much I want to be alone, to have a door I can close, and four walls to enclose me like skin. What would we be without skin?

Sometimes there's a person and the nearness of him, the sight of him, even the thought, makes your skin feel alive. Sometimes your skin is your protector and I will keep it between me and her, whoever she is. Now that I've started looking at her, I find I'm really afraid of her. I've chosen this unsuspecting woman. I've made up my mind she can hurt me, and the idea grows till I find I'm in a mounting panic. I try to find my partner, all the safety and comfort of a woman whose name I don't even know, and I can't find her, and it occurs to me that just as I, without reason, have a mounting fear and distrust of the thin-lipped enemy, what if my partner has suddenly, irrationally, become afraid of me?

We are on the road! Isn't that the most American way to be? There are other caravans: fleeing brush fires (or so they say), holding family reunions, publicizing the plight of women in Afghanistan, a cause no one at the time could guess would not remain marginal for long. I expected we'd mingle, that there would be classic exogamous exchange, but no, our groups remained intact and unchanged and we moved on.

We are seeing a land we, in our city, never knew was there. We move across inhospitable environments: inland through smog, over salt flats, through oil fields and toxic waste dumps. We walk gingerly. Oh, the surfaces of things. Over gas lines that might explode. Beneath cosmic violence in the star-spangled peaceful night sky. Wreckage.

Yet, we are lucky. Nothing likely to rain down on us but rain.

Near the truck stop, in front of the strip joint, a woman calls out. She's holding a child's embroidery hoop and stitching.

Sulfurtown comes by its name honestly eight miles off the freeway and down a dirt road where chickens scratched in the dust around the gas pumps and we entered a dark bunker to see barechested men lounging around a pool table. We thought we were on the right track.

I casually produced the photo of Hitler. "Friend of yours?" I asked.

"Never seen him before," said the men.

We paid the dentureless woman behind the counter for the gas, Slim Jims and Cokes.

"You get that hate literature out of here," she said, and we were on our way.

Across the county line we found a farmer who asked us to call him Daddy. He had a camp of his own in the old elementary school. The windows were broken out, crisscrossed with lumber and through each gap, a pig's head protruded in welcome or warning. Pigs rooted in the classrooms under and over the tumbled down chairs. Pigs sat attentively at desks, watching the door with intelligent, measuring eyes.

"Town closed the school down," Daddy said. "It's cheaper to pay tuition and buses and send the kids out-of-town every morning. They weren't making no use of this facility at all, at all, and now they're coming after me for trying to make a living." He said, "You're welcome to stay as long as you'd like. I could use some witnesses here when the sheriff come to put me out. Just watch out for them boar hogs. They could hurt you."

Pigs rooted for bits of undigested food in feces. Pigs rolled in mud and boar hogs snapped at our legs.

"They make good pets," Daddy said. "As a race, that is. Not these ones."

I made a foray into the nearest town to go on-line. It was the village of the damned, everyone wide-eyed, speechless. They looked at me as though we shared a deep unspoken understanding. What's with these people? I wondered. I reeked, I knew, of pigsty, and yet they treated me with delicacy. Why?

I booted up. Something flashed on the screen, ominous in a subliminal way. I clicked past. When you pay by the minute, you hurry. Click. Nazis. Click. I tried every search engine, every key word I could think of. Then my e-mail: a fourth-generation forwarded invitation–none of the addresses familiar—*Violate Nature! An artist's conceptual intervention in the desert environment.* It sounded interesting. If anyone wanted to lure me out into the desert alone for unknown purposes, this invitation might do it. I downloaded and printed the map. How had I been targeted and why? What made them so sure I would go? They didn't know I wasn't traveling alone, but with an army.

I didn't really plan to go. I didn't know I'd end up not a victim but a suspect, the interrogator asking me the same sorts of questions Ramiro used to.

Isn't it true that during the recent economic boom, the richest one percent in California saw their incomes nearly double?

Yes, I say.

In 1980, the income of the average CEO was how many times greater than the average factory worker? Forty-two times greater, I say.

By 1998? Four hundred nineteen times greater, I answer, certain I'm not spiking the polygraph line.

Real wages for workers? Declined for everyone, most severely for those at the bottom who saw their hourly earnings decline twenty percent in twenty years.

Doesn't that make you angry? (from both Ramiro and the cop—one seeking to motivate, one seeking a motive).

But that's later.

In the cybercafe, people were crying, moaning, keening, making animal sounds, whimpers, and howls. The report on the screen. I read it. NO. Clicked past it. Clicked back. My mind blinking on and off. NO. Outside, there were two crows on a wire. My people back at the campsite knew as little of what had happened as those two birds. How could I tell them? I wished I could be a cat or a squirrel. I wanted to be alive but unknowing.

Hadn't they made me a leader only because I was unsuited to lead?

I told them nothing and led them to the spa: derelict, bankrupt, the wind blowing dust through the rooms. No water in the tubs. Massage tables laid out like slabs in a morgue.

All the lights had been removed. The sunlight slipping in showed us beds, dry Jacuzzis, closets. We opened closet doors and found, in one, a lifelike woman's head. In others, women's clothing: nurse, Catholic schoolgirl. Hanging on the doorknob, instructions: *Each doll is professionally cleaned and sanitized for your use. Douche bags in the closet are for recreational use only.*

The dolls themselves were gone. Had there been male dolls? Anatomically correct men of silicone rubber. If I could find a brown shirt and boots, I could have dressed my Nazi. Nazi, I would have said, I have come to give myself to you and love you.

That is the fantasy I try to talk myself into having. That sort of fantasy is sick but normal, not like my real fantasy. Blowing up the Pentagon. Hadn't I imagined that many many times? And seeing the center of world capitalism vaporized. Hadn't I thought it? The thought is not the deed. Or so I tell myself.

And so I try to imagine evil redeemed by love, how I would hoist myself onto the Nazi's prick. How there would be not one doll, but a second, and I'd take a towel to wrap it like a turban round his head. My terrorist, I would coo. My darling. It would be the most difficult thing I'd ever done but what is love if it cannot transcend, well, everything?

Sick, sick, and wrong. That's why it's a fantasy.

Where was I?

"Something's happened," I said, "I've got to tell you."

The spa was bankrupt, the dolls were gone, I was sitting on the concrete surface of a cracked parking lot crying.

Only Eileen was listening. Children were playing monkey-in-the-middle with the head. Our people were scattered into the private rooms and I would have to go after them.

This was in the flat empty spaces where there's a golden light through the marsh grasses as the sun goes down. The world smells of cow manure and wherever you are you can hear the trucks whooshing by on the freeways, going fast trying to reach a place where the radio signals crackle and fade and the news can't reach you.

In the Rooms

I found Renee behind the door marked *Voodoo Queen*. She had her Burmese python draped around her neck and she'd costumed herself: a billowing robe and so much silver mesh it looked like chain mail. Her hands dripped blood.

"Sacrifice," she said. "Sacrifice means to be made sacred, and so something must be killed."

"What did you kill?" I asked.

"A chicken," she said. Her snake stirred. "It doesn't have to be a chicken, but that's what we say. Killing chickens is legal."

"I don't want to kill," I said. "I want to be healed."

She led me inside. "Then you need a doll."

The dolls were gone.

"You don't understand," she said. "When you have a doll, when you name it with your enemy's name and put the pins in, you do this because this person has attributes that offend you. And you hate these attributes because they mirror your own. When you put in the pins, you are healing yourself. But . . ." She leaned toward me. Her silver mesh whispered with her. "When you rid yourself of what you hate about yourself, maybe your enemy sickens or dies. Not because you hexed this person. But there must be balance. Your enemy called it down on himself. It's all right if this person dies."

"No," I said.

"What may happen, will happen," she said. "Stop it!" she said, and grabbed me by the wrist. Golden bubbles rose from my fingers, chiming. "Stop it," she said. "Stop it now, this bleeding-heart wringing of hands!"

There was the tolling of something cracked and bronze and then it subsided low enough that I could hear her voice: "Your idea of good and evil is... childlike."

There was the low deep vibration echoing in my head fainter and fainter till I couldn't tell when it died. There were holes in my head and the fabric of everything.

I remember waking up from the Nixon dream and stumbling to the bathroom before I knew why I was there, and even then couldn't make up my mind, whether to stare at my face in the mirror or scrub my tingling hand clean. There's a certain sameness to the many ways people demonstrate their pain or choose to hide it.

At *Arabian Nights*, s/he wears a burkah. S/he could be anyone. S/he could be Eileen, or Ramiro, or my partner.

"Come, come. Come in," s/he said. "I am so sorry. We, too, are in mourning."

We held hands and cried. S/he stroked my face. "People hate me now," she said. Tears spilled down, disappeared into the veil. "I fled my country and took refuge here," s/he said, "and now you hate me—"

"I don't hate you. It's not your fault."

"—and I've done nothing."

I said, "I know you've suffered."

"Someday Americans will understand," s/he said. "The action was not against your people, but your government."

S/he might as well have fired a gun. Inside the roar, I felt intensely without knowing whether I had or had not lived through it.

"Yes, yes," s/he said. "Propaganda of the deed. What every movement learns it must do, paint icons, create images of the saints. This was someone's Sistine Chapel. This is how to make mystery visible to those not ready to understand words."

I ran from the room screaming before I could hurt her.

The thin-lipped woman stopped me. "Are you proud to be an American?"

No, I thought. I was born here. How can I be proud of what I did nothing to earn?

She pointed. *The Death Row Suite.*

The man was naked except for restraints at wrists and ankles, leather straps across his bare chest. He writhed with what might have been pleasure.

"What does it feel like to kill?" I asked.

"How do you know I did it?" he said. "How do you know I won't be exonerated?"

"But just supposing," I said. "Hypothetically."

"In that case. When it was happening," he said, "what I recall is confusion and terror, being so torn apart by guilt it was easier to act than to refrain, as though I weren't killing people, but uncertainty."

"What we need is revolYOUtion." A voice from behind the one-way mirror.

Ramiro, my hero. A hero is what he does. We can subtract the human. To be a hero in this day and age, to get as far from the ego-driven ego-driveling modern postmodern individual condition as you can go, and when you fail, you bring everything down with you.

"Admit you have bloody hands," Ramiro said. "We all have bloody hands."

He asks me what things have been done in my name.

"I don't know."

"Why not?" he said, the son of a bitch.

The gong was silent. The sound had died, yet I followed it through the maze of rooms.

I said, "Teach me the way of peace."

The man in the kimono turned to face me. Ronald.

"Peace," he said.

"What are you doing here?" I asked. "Why aren't you on Death Row?"

"I'm where I belong," he said, "but *you*—you've come to the wrong place if you're looking for peace."

"Can't we just meditate?" I said. "Learn to see the universe in the petal of a bruised camellia. The grace inherent in a menial act..."

"Yeah, yeah, yeah. Zen sanitized for your convenience. Sister, Zen was born in war, in murder. Kill—and forget it. Kill—and forget it. All is transient. Life is a process of dying. The system was formulated to take peaceful little peasants and turn them into killing machines. Bypass the conscience. They went and killed for their masters but the conscience could not be rooted out for good. The sound of one bloody hand dripping clap clap clap on stone. Zen, as you think you know it, evolved from century after century of remorse."

I said, "Teach me, then, how to live after enormity."

"Now you're talking. We will welcome you. None of this Baby Jesus weeps when you masturbate fucked-up Western notions about sin and all that shit. We do the real stuff. We'll send you up a mountain and have you scrub a single floor tile till eternity. That will keep your bloody hands busy."

"I wanted to hurt her," I said. "Or him. The person in the burkah. I lost it. I almost went mad."

"Ah," he said, "aum," and crossed his legs. "The blinding flash you can't even imagine. Skin peeling off a body like a glove, people on fire, people crying help me, help me, please, help me help me help me help me help me help me help me."

Our action was against the Japanese military, not against the Japanese people.

I don't know whether Ronald spoke the words or I did.

Then I'm on the cracked parking lot talking, telling, and everyone is listening.

There must be a theory of speech acts. Statements of fact, lies, commands, questions. The speech act of pleasure. The act of exploration, putting it into words to discover what you think. The act of madness, the dam breaking to let language free, the river-babble that some of us channel into something akin to rational speech, it has grammar and syntax and vocabulary but its function is mere release from the terrible pressure, enough to blow holes in the brain. If I talked more maybe my mind wouldn't be shutting down and lighting up again with these gaps. There are holes in my head and in the fabric of... everything.

Then everyone is talking at once. No one knows anything for sure. Everyone suddenly has wisdom.

Eileen says everything has changed and so everything from here on in has to be Part Two.

Part Two

I'm not sure I agree. What's happening now may or may not be different. I can name at least a dozen times in my life when I said aloud *I have lost my innocence now for good. I will never never never be the same.*

But I cooperate. I bend, because I recognize that in myself I'm lacking, compared even to the musk ox. If I were going to draw the Great Chain of

Being, that's who'd be on top. They were around in prehistoric days and they're still here. Every other species had to adapt or die. But the musk ox, driven out of California, driven from the South of France, it was equally suited to the arctic North. Ready for anything, perfect, the musk ox didn't have to change.

See what happens through a simple shift in perspective? Here's a simultaneous and contradictory truth: Our caravan grew larger. Our caravan grew smaller. Hundreds of immigrants from the Middle East joined us, afraid to stay home, seeking safety in numbers, but we also divided pretty neatly in three, some of us still anxious to find the Nazis—one group to bash them, one to join them because my enemy's enemy is my friend. Others set off in the opposite direction to trash a mosque.

"No, that's wrong," I said, but I could also put it this way: being Americans, we didn't know why we weren't beautiful, young, successful and famous. We didn't know why we didn't have homes, fast cars, rich lovers, functional parents. Now we know: it's because of Islam.

We even have to reassess Ramiro. We remember how people used to tell him to go back where he came from. (New York? Iowa?) "If America's so bad, why does everyone want to be here?" (His answer: "When you're here, you're less likely to be a victim of American foreign policy.")

Now some of us say it was just sex.

Some say "Ramiro who?" as though we never knew him.

Some of us say it was associating with the likes of him that made us homeless.

It's not in my nature to be unfaithful. I miss him and the next thing I know some cop is saying, "This is your chance to explain yourself."

"Ramiro did it."

. . .

Not so fast.

As I said, my mind kept shutting down, then booting up again with a stutter.

I found myself alone, but due to the gaps I don't know if I left them or they left me. One foot in front of the other, one step, one day at a time, I set out hoping that art can redeem. *Violate Nature, an artist's intervention in the desert.*

I wandered hours or days without thought. I can't say whether my mind was empty or full. So full there was no space for it to stand and comprehend itself. So full that I translated it as blank. But a blank empty *pressure,* the welling and growing and swelling of feeling or of thought. Ramifying, burgeoning, self-completing. A ballooning that might in the end turn out to be empty and false, like a hysterical pregnancy of cognition.

So: The wind tooting in my open water bottle, the creosote bushes creaking, my footsteps with their brittle crunch over crusts of salt and sand.

The only sound my footsteps and the wind.

The only sound my footsteps and the wind.

What do you think you are, a folk song?

An airplane overhead, but no bombs fall. They're not so lucky *over there*. Then a helicopter, looking for me or someone bad.

* * *

The simplest things are more complicated now.

I'm not saying it's cause and effect. I'm not placing blame. It's more a questioning of difference, of claiming to be the splendid exception.

I'm out of my element here, but I'm not afraid.

There are rattlesnakes in the desert but I'm not afraid of snakes. They were not put on this earth to be my enemy.

The Prosperity of Cities and Desert Places

A rattlesnake could enter you and be your lover. Very exciting, that vibration, but you would have to hold the head tightly to keep from being bitten, though for some I suppose the threat would make it more intense. Not for me. How can you let go and surrender when you've got to keep your presence of mind and a firm grip? You'd need a friend, or nonjudgmental acquaintance, someone to hold the head for you, a masturbation assistant, as it were, and you would need to trust that person implicitly, not that s/he would intentionally let go and expose both of you to the poisoned fangs, but most people are simply not that competent.

Everything human is alien to me.

My consciousness twinkles like Christmas lights. Like stars, everything coming from a great distance. Or like one of these terrible faulty fluorescents, and the dead man has been identified as Milton Friedman.

Yes, yes, I wanted to kill him!

No, not *that* Milton Friedman. The check of his dental records has confirmed he is *not* the University of Chicago economist. It seems to be an unambiguous case of mistaken identity, somebody's tragic mistake.

Mistakes were made in taking Chicago economics seriously, all that concentrating wealth for growth, all that trickle-down sleight-of-hand.

The station house was air-conditioned and there was a television that never stopped its assault of terrible pictures.

I flush. I sweat.

"Feeling guilty?" asks the bad cop.

"Hot flash?" says the good one.

Outside, there's a click of branches or leaves. There's wind.

There's the interrogation.

"I wasn't myself," I tell them. "This is not an excuse, just an attempt to find common ground, to find my way into the sickness that we share. I was wandering in the desert, hoping art could redeem. With my mind blinking, it's hard to say how I got from one place to another. Then I saw it."

"And it was...?"

"A body."

"You saw the body."

"What looked like a body. What I took for the clever representation of a body. A conceptual intervention, but I was wrong. It was a set-up. I've been framed. Seize my hard drive. You'll see. They invited me to the desert. I thought it was a mannequin, an anatomically correct silicone rubber doll. I thought they were videotaping my response and I didn't want to let the artist down. I'll admit I didn't act naturally. I'm self-conscious in front of a camera. I just wanted to give them footage they could use.

"I thought it was art," I said.

"And he is...?"

"Art with a small a, not a capital. OK, maybe a capital, but not short for Arthur. Art, you know, Art."

"How do you define art?"

"The eternal question. You know the answer: I know it when I see it. Well, OK, not this time."

The cop says, "Thanks to Milton Friedman—the other one, trade unionists are assassinated in Colombia."

The other cop says, "Thanks to that Milton Friedman, this dead man died for a theory."

"That's sad," I say. "A theory not even his own."

"How do you create an inviting economic environment?" asks the bad cop and doesn't wait for me to answer. "Reduce wages, suppress unions, cut taxes and services."

"You need air conditioning," says the good cop.

When I thought it was art, it was troubling but in an interesting way. A tingle that ran from toes to the brain. In a real death, curiosity in the casual onlooker, the bystander, the random passerby is unseemly. Leave anger, grief, vengeance to the next of kin. The only correct response is to shut down. To avoid using the sorrow for your own selfish ends. But I circled that body. I knelt beside it for another perspective because I figured the artist had done the same. The blood looked real but I know there are artists who use real blood. There's a charnel house out there.

I say, "I was with these people. A group of people..."

"Conspiracy?"

"Not exactly. Good people, but they're going to hurt someone. You've got to stop them before they act. Before they scrub tiles on hands and knees for eternity."

"We want to know your whereabouts," says the cop.

"I've been everywhere," I say, "but there are gaps."

Where am "I" between the blinks? If I am two, I am myself a *we*. I look into the good cop's eyes for an answer.

"So many people died," I say.

The bad cop says, "And we're asking you about a death right here, under your nose."

"Yes, and it's the difference between a child's drawing and the Sistine Chapel. Let me ask you, then," I say. "What would you have done?"

I ask them to consider: "Is murder a natural act or a violation of nature? If that's the question the whole event is premised on, as a participant-viewer, I was faced with a bifurcation: to act spontaneously, or to calculate the response that would best serve the artist's intent. Do we have an experience here, or an agenda? And is it up to me to privilege one over the other? I am, after all, not the creator, not the artist here, but an invited guest. I try to be a good guest. Walk softly. Appreciate. Leave no trace, whether the landscape is weirdly attractive or somewhat less than appealing. Who am I to criticize the creosote, the ocotillo, or call the red rock more aesthetically pleasing than the gray?

"Is the spontaneous response the most natural? Or does its very spontaneity prove the training is so deeply ingrained we no longer realize we have forcibly learned it? Is the imperative to strike back born into us or is it the artifact of that great early rupture from a greedy, devouring, selfish, oceanic yet profoundly peaceful self?"

The bad cop shook his head. "I still don't think it's art, but it sure gives you something to think about."

I said, "I think about loving my enemy."

He laughed. "Loving thy enemy is not an act of love. The enemy doesn't wish to be touched. But the enemy's desires don't matter. Not to you. You will love him whether he wants it or not. You will force your love on him. We know your type. You will violate him. You will shame him until he cannot raise his head or make a fist. Your unwanted love will reduce him to a whimpering post-traumatic ectoplasmic puddle. You will love like a narcissistic parent. You will engulf him and absorb him. His hate becomes impotent. He becomes impotent. You will love him until he disappears."

The good cop took off the cuffs. "We're going to let you go now. We've got immigrants to round up."

The bad cop said, "Stay in touch."

The Prosperity of Cities and Desert Places

* * *

There are places that aren't places anymore. Holes. Gaps. Tunnels and tubes through the brain, bit and pieces of mind, blown out, carried away on rumbling flatbeds draped in black. Or in red, white, and blue bunting. But no light enters, there are no colors here.

Can you be in two places at once? I will always be alone in the desert. I will always be with you, a fly in the web, a cog in the machine, as much a part of everything as ever.

Hoo goes the water bottle *hoo hoo*. It gives me the sound to hold onto as I pretend everything will be all right.

I am walking to Los Angeles. I am speaking only for myself.

I am singing:

These hands are your hands,
these hands are my hands…

I sing and there is no one here to stop me.

Marina Rice Bader

The Author

DIANE LEFER is the author of two previous collections, *The Circles I Move In* and *Very Much Like Desire*, and the novel, *Radiant Hunger*. She lives in Los Angeles where she is an artistic associate of Playwrights' Arena, volunteers with the Program for Torture Victims, and serves on the animal behavior observation team of the research department at the L.A. Zoo. Her ongoing collaboration with exiled Colombian theatre artist Hector Aristizábal encompasses works for the stage, nonfiction projects, and social action workshops. She teaches in the MFA in Writing Program at Vermont College.